Honey Melon Fudge

To Jill –
With love & thanks!
Happy trails,
Heather

honey

melon

fudge

a novel by
heather rolland

MILL CITY PRESS
MINNEAPOLIS

Mill City Press, Inc.
212 3ʳᵈ Avenue North, Suite 290
Minneapolis, MN 55401
612.455.2294
WWW.MILLCITYPUBLISHING.COM

This is a work of fiction. Names, characters, places,
and incidents are either the product of the author's
imagination, or are used fictitiously. Any resemblance to
actual persons, living or dead, is purely coincidental. Unless,
of course, you recognize yourself, in which case, you are
right: it is you.

ISBN - 978-1-936107-79-7
ISBN - 1-936107-79-1
LCCN - 2010925185

Edited by Jill Dearman
Cover Design by Kurt Boyer
Author Photo by Thomas Moeller
Back Cover Photo by Paul Swieton
Typeset by Nate Meyers
Interior Photos: Lone Tree on Bearpen by Joanne Hihn;
Blackberries on Bearpen by Mark Schaefer

Printed in the United States of America

Acknowledgements

All the people who took that chance, bought a copy, and actually read Finders, Seekers, Losers, Keepers deserve mention and thanks. Your kind words were just the encouragement I needed to persevere (yes, this means it is your fault).

The Catskill hiking community, both online and on the trails, are an amazing, diverse, and delightful crew. Huge thanks to Peakbagr, Hermit, Snickers, Mudhook, the Swede, MattC, JayH, Rockysummit, Pirate Maiden, Edelweiss, Dick, Tom and Laurie, and all the Hundred Highest Hikers. I also wish to acknowledge Mark Schaefer whose knowledge is unparalleled and whose generosity with such knowledge is a true gift to all seekers. The warm welcome extended by this community to Flammeus and Halia was instrumental in getting them through their first thirty-five. Their experience, of course, paved the way for Asha's adventures in this volume.

Thanks is too small a word for all Jill Dearman has done to transform me into a writer. Jill is the hub of the writer's wheel, the center from which radiates out support, guidance, admonitions, and exhortations. She witnessed and named me, and I became empowered to write. I can offer neither higher praise nor deeper thanks.

To Michael Lally and Lydia Diaz go huge thanks for the editing and proofreading work. Kurt Boyer receives my undying gratitude for his outstanding design work and superlative crab cakes. Todd Essig and Catherine DiNardo: thank you for the recipes, consistent presence at events, the songs, and the community. Big thanks to the Lizard for doing a read-through at hyperspeed. Another big thanks to Eric Koppel for his webmastering talents and penchant for creative route design.

Thanks to Marta Szabo and Fred Poole for their encouragement via the Authentic Writing Workshops. The workshops were key in getting me over the hump.

Through all the burnt dinners, PMS-fueled writing marathons, and forgotten promises, my girls were there: thank you, Maya and Caitlin, for not killing me, Tom, or each other. Your sacrifices have not gone unnoticed.

Of course, there is Iske, with her graying muzzle and eyebrows now, ever in step with me. She knows me, sees right through me, and loves me unconditionally. You can love a dog no holds barred. You can pour every ounce of hope and dashed hope, of broken love and betrayed love, and desperate, hopeless, human love into the love you offer a dog. They can take it. What Iske gives back is beyond words.

Dedication

To Tom, with all my love, most of my wit, some of my sadness, and the remains of my ire. Please accept this dedication in lieu of a new pair of sunglasses, this year's flashlight upgrade, and a full complement of kitchen gadgets.

Lone Tree on Bearpen by Joanne Hihn

Honey's Sting, or the Near Death Experience of Hope

"Peach is the color of betrayal," Grace announced, the late afternoon sun warming her pale skin to a suspiciously apricot hue. Her audience was rather limited: her best friend, Halia, and the English sparrows hopping about hopefully underneath the outdoor tables at The Blue Eft. "That's what my feng shui consultant told me."

Halia concealed an indulgent smile of disbelief and refrained from rolling her eyes. Her efforts at expressionlessness left her olive-skinned face without telltale creases, but the corners of her eyes and lips tilted upwards ever so slightly. "Your what?" She wasn't entirely successful in her efforts to scrub the judgmental tone from her voice.

"My feng shui consultant," Grace repeated. She hesitated, then shrugged, long blond hair sliding off her narrow shoulders. "I have no idea why. Explanations were not part of the color consult."

"Color consult?" Now Halia was openly teasing, baiting Grace to defend her latest fascination.

"Yes, color consult," Grace took the bait and ran with it. "Red, green, and purple in the kitchen, to support the finances, and pink and white in the bathroom, for romance." Her short fingers ticked off room-color combinations in her house as she explained which areas of her life would be affected by adding or subtracting these colors.

"What do you think your consultant would have to say about my exterior paint colors?" The corners of Halia's lips now twitched with mirth. Her house was locally famous (or infamous, as the case may be) for its amazingly green trim and dingy-white, deep stucco swirls.

Their cast aluminum table outside the café was artfully decorated with watery circles, giving evidence to the heat that evening and the number of cold drinks consumed. Halia sipped her ginger-lime slushy and appraised Grace critically. Last month, Grace had gotten her Tarot cards read, and sometime last spring she had actually paid good money to attend a workshop on "The Secret." Reminds me of est, Halia thought when Grace tried to entice her to come along. To think that Halia might join her in any of this soul searching or interior decorating indicated that Grace had taken temporary leave of her senses, but that happened from time to time. Maybe it was Grace's way of escaping from the world of her small animal veterinary practice, and its scientific, medical-model constraints. So it's feng shui this month, Halia realized. So be it.

"Wasn't Asha supposed to meet us here tonight?" Grace broke in to Halia's thoughts.

"I tried to call her but her phone isn't working. Again." This time Halia did roll her eyes in an editorial comment on the telephone service provided by the local telecommunications company in their small town. "I left a note on her door. She'll swing by on her run." Halia checked her watch, and added, "Actually, she'll be running past us any minute." No sooner had Halia made this prediction, Asha appeared out from under the railway overpass, and slowed to a walk.

"Hey," she panted. "I'll be back in a few minutes." She picked up her pace again and the soft footfalls of expensive running shoes on asphalt faded rapidly.

Grace turned to Halia, the look on her face – a mixture of admiration, wonderment, and irritation – said it all. This time Halia deigned to explain. "When I put the note on her door, Brulee barked and Asha's car was there. Since Asha didn't come to the door, I figured that she was already out running. If she was already out, and nowhere in sight, at 5:15 p.m. on a Friday evening, she must be on a fairly long run. If she is on a long run, but left Brulee at home, she must be on roads with traffic. Her car is at home, she's on a long run, and she left from home. And we talked about meeting here when I saw her earlier this week. So," Halia paused to take a deep inhale and to enhance the dramatic build-up to her denouement. "The Five Mile Square is a natural choice, and to do it so that she swings by here at 5:47 p.m., to see if we're here yet, as tentatively planned, is pretty much Asha's style." Halia shrugged. "No mind reading: just putting all the facts together in a way that makes sense."

"Asha could have been on the phone or in the shower when you left that note. Or otherwise indisposed." Grace attempted to mount a challenge, albeit a little half-heartedly.

"Not on the phone. Remember?"

"Oh yeah." Grace grinned sheepishly. "But in the shower?"

"Mmm." Halia politely acknowledged Grace's contention before dismantling it. "It's late June. It's hot. Asha doesn't have air conditioning. All the windows that can open are open at her house. If Asha were in the shower, I would've been able to hear it. Her bathroom window isn't far from the street."

"How could you hear it, with Brulee barking?" Grace looked moderately hopeful, knowing that Brulee made a total racket whenever anyone came near Asha's house: leaping against the door, barking and snarling and doing her best Cujo imitation.

"I said 'chicken' to Brulee."

"What?" Grace was laughing. This was going to be good.

"I said 'chicken' to Brulee. I've noticed that when I cook chicken, Bezef gets really excited. I usually give her a little skin or fat or whatever, and I usually say something about it, like 'here's some chicken for you.' I've noticed that if she hears the word 'chicken' in conversation, she gets all attentive and hopeful. I figured that chances are good that since Asha and Pearl are not vegetarians, and neither is Rob for that matter, that Brulee has heard the word 'chicken' before. And Brulee being as smart as she is, I thought she might recognize it and maybe also recognize my voice, and that if I said 'chicken' she'd stop barking long enough for me to hear if Asha was in the shower."

Grace was shaking her head in pleased disbelief. "You said 'chicken' and Brulee stopped barking?"

Halia nodded.

Grace shrugged again. "Amazing." She squinted up the street in the direction of Asha's house. "Y'know, Asha should probably do something about the roses in front of her house. It's bad to have dying plants lining your front walkway."

"Especially now that she's got her house on the market. It's time to make it all spiffy and appealing to the masses." Halia agreed, a bit more bitterness showing through than she typically preferred to expose. Halia held an opinion about Asha and the sale of her house, and she was having trouble getting behind the idea that Asha was selling at all. The house was just beginning to come alive under Asha's loving, albeit quirky, touch. Sure, the roses died, but at least she was trying. She had cut down all the trees that were turning the front of the house into the spitting image of that Magritte painting where it's night at the front door and daytime above the roof. She was learning about the house, loving the house, connecting with the house, and taking care of the house. And perhaps on some level, the house was also taking care of Asha and her willowy, precocious daughter, Pearl, giving them something to focus upon and learn from during these tough, post-divorce pre-teen years. To leave now felt wrong to Halia, despite the fact that Asha had few and lousy choices.

"Yeah, that too." Halia gave Grace a slightly quizzical look and Grace admitted, "I was thinking in terms of feng shui. Bad energy and all that." Halia didn't respond.

Moments later, Asha arrived freshly showered. Levi's and an orange sherbet colored lacy tank top replaced her running attire. She looked as if she had been plucked straight out of an Athleta or Title 9 catalog; she just needed the caption saying something like

"Despite her busy lifestyle, Asha still makes time to relax with her friends." Her half-British, half-Sephardic-Jew ethnicity gave her a perpetual tan, and her athletic hobbies made for an eye-catching physique. The fact that she was actually quite tiny went unnoticed most of the time; her huge smile and big personality created the illusion of a full-size adult. It wasn't until you stood next to her or saw a part out of context – her wrist, for example, poking out of her sleeve – that you realized that she was at best the size of a fifth grader.

"Thanks for the note, Hali," she said. "My freakin' phone has been driving me absolutely crazy lately. When it does work, which is about 30% of the time, it makes this horrible noise like bacon frying. It is so annoying!" As she spoke she tossed her shoulder-length, espresso-colored curls around for emphasis until both Grace and Halia were freckled with water droplets.

"Now I can't stop smelling bacon," Grace teased Asha, as she got up and reached across the table to give her a hug. Halia did the same, stiffly.

"How are you guys?"

"Fine," Halia answered first. "Things are fine. As always."

Asha grinned the fleeting but quizzical grin Halia's enigmatic humor invited and turned to Grace.

"Things are fine," Grace echoed Halia's response without the layers of sarcasm and strangeness. "I've been doing some redecorating at home. Y'know, moving furniture around and thinking about painting. Nothing major, and not much else going on."

"You had a feng shui consult?"

"Is it that obvious?"

"Moving furniture and changing colors? Yep, it's that obvious. And I know you." Asha looked surprisingly relaxed and happy for someone living in the midst of the chaos of changing everything in her life simultaneously. "I had a consultant come in a couple of years ago – she was great – but most of the suggestions had to do with moving furniture around and adding or getting rid of specific colors in specific places around the house. And mirrors. There were lots of places where I was supposed to put mirrors. Did your person tell you to put mirrors everywhere?"

"Mirrors, crystals and plants." Grace teetered between looking crestfallen at having her latest treasure revealed as commonplace and a certain amount of relief in the permission granted by Asha's irreverent attitude to also adopt such a stance.

"I hope you guys don't mind that Rob is meeting us here in a little while." Asha beamed the self-conscious and sweet energy of a woman in love awaiting her beloved. She toyed with the flea market ring, a gift from Rob, spinning the purple glass bead. Grace smiled, knowing that nervous joy intimately. Halia looked tolerant. "He was finishing up at a big job on Quaker Hill. I talked to him a little while ago. He's been so busy at work lately; it's been really hard to do all the house hunting stuff we need to do." Asha shook her head, shaggy wet curls bouncing around like loose springs. "Moving is a royal pain in the ass."

Halia and Grace made sympathetic noises, and returned to their earlier conversation. Asha was distracted by her litany of woes: selling her home, the hassles of moving, her nonfunctional telephone, her impending unemployed status due to the elimination of her position at the local elementary school, and the impact of all this upon her thirteen year old daughter. She fidgeted and struggled to at least appear to be paying attention to her friends, instead of looking like she was on a stakeout for Rob.

Grace regaled her friends with tales of her husband's latest series of plumbing mishaps. It might have been standard "men are so dumb" fare, but eventually even Asha was laughing.

Rob arrived. He was landscaper dirty: covered in real dirt, fingernails to eyelids, from an honest day's work. He carefully kissed Asha hello, holding his black ponytail away from his face as he leaned over, making sure she didn't get a face full of dust and twigs. He pulled up a chair.

"Hey," he greeted Halia and Grace. Both nodded pleasantly in return.

As the conversation continued, Grace picked up on a strange energy, an undercurrent. Although no one said anything and Grace couldn't exactly explain to herself what it was that she sensed, she felt it clearly and watched Halia notice it too. Soon they excused themselves, chased away by the tension in the air.

Asha waited for Rob to return to their table, his business call interrupting their half-teasing argument about the relative intelligence versus trainability of different dog breeds. She admired Rob's tact: he wasn't one of those uncouth cell phone users who would conduct business anywhere at any volume. She smiled a tired, easy smile; it had been another long day, and she was mellow, appreciating her lover, and eager to get home.

They walked back to her place together. They held hands in the dark, her shoulder and hip brushing against his, seeking the closeness, not caring about the organic matter and organic scent he emitted. Asha chose not to speak. She felt the warmth and comfort of his hand in hers, and tried to disappear into that sensation, letting it blot out the various stress-related knots in her shoulders and kinks in her gut. Rob seemed grateful for the silence, grateful that she was refraining from worrying aloud, as had become so common of late. She was aware that she was officially Anxious, and that she was beginning to grate upon his nerves. She knew that she was not the person who had started dating him; the loss of her job and the impending move had replaced that carefree soul. Pretending to be unchanged by all that occurred, and worrying that it was impossible not to be, made her that much more anxious. In response to all she had begun to worry about, she worried that she was becoming intolerable.

They arrived at her front door and the sound of her key scraping in the lock seemed attenuated in the darkness and silence. Brulee barked once; Asha spoke to her and she whined softly.

"The night is still young. Do you feel like watching a movie?"

"Well," Rob's tone made Asha's stomach muscles involuntarily tighten. "I'm sorry, honey, but I need to go. I have to help at the estate tomorrow. They're hosting a big wedding, and I need to be there really early to help with preparing the grounds."

"How early?" She sounded angry, panicked, and plaintive all at once. "You could stay here and leave early from here. It's closer to Quaker Hill than your place."

"I need stuff from home. I'd have to drive from here to my place and then to the estate. It just doesn't make sense." Asha didn't ask what stuff he needed. Weed whackers, gas cans. Whatever. She was already hardening, becoming remote, her head spinning from trying not to feel all she felt. The kiss goodbye took place on the front step; Rob didn't choose to come in for a cup of tea or just one Wallace and Gromit episode.

She entered the house alone. She looked around, dry-eyed and dry-mouthed. First the fight not to cry. She marshaled all of Rob's reasons: it made sense, it would waste gas, they'd have to get up so early, they could see each other tomorrow night… Wait. Asha realized they hadn't discussed the rest of the weekend at all. She knew that he knew it was a Pearl-free weekend. But they hadn't actually made plans.

Well, of course they hadn't made plans, Asha heard herself thinking in Rob's voice. He was working all day tomorrow at the estate. And, she felt her breath catch as she realized, maybe Sunday too. He didn't say when the wedding was actually taking place. Maybe the grounds crew had been called in for the whole weekend. That thought brought with it an onslaught of tears and she caved under the pressure. Brulee, the prescient dog, slid her head under Asha's hand and leaned against her.

Asha found her way to the couch. Breaking all the household rules, she made room, squashing herself backwards into the cushions, and patted the couch next to her. Brulee understood and hopped up. After thanking her overzealously and almost getting ousted, she settled down warm and close, stretched out like a lover in her arms. Asha stroked her, feeling the texture of her fur, feeling her heartbeat, feeling her weight, tracing her muscles and bones.

She sought to numb out in pure contact. Brulee accepted the attention and relaxed.

It didn't take long for the demons in her mind to begin to torture her anew. Why, she began to harangue herself, why was Rob working this weekend? This was their weekend without Pearl: their private sacred adult time together. Why would he work? The voice of Rob inside her head had faded. All the reasons and logic were drowned out by hurt and anger. Why quickly became how: How could he do this to me? Asha struggled vainly to argue with herself. It's not personal. He didn't choose to work; he got called in. It will be good to have the extra money. We'll be living together soon. It won't matter because we'll be together every day. Beginning and ending every day in each other's arms, that's what Asha had said she was looking forward to most about moving to Warwick. She wasn't sure if she remembered what Rob had said he was looking forward to most. She didn't want to try too hard to remember.

Brulee wriggled uncomfortably and then slid down off the couch. She walked to the front door, toenails clicking solidly on the worn oak floor. She clicked back to Asha on the couch, licked her hand once, and click-click-click back to the front door. Asha got the message and hoisted herself to her feet. She glanced at the clock on the VCR. No, it's not too late to visit Halia, she decided. Maybe Bezef will need her last walk of the evening too.

Asha hadn't removed shoes or outerwear when she came in. She hesitated at the door, wondering if she was going to be cold outside. She realized that lying on the couch in late June, fully dressed with a jacket on and a large dog pressed against her, and not getting overheated was a bad sign. "My thermostat must be broken," she mumbled, remembering.

During the last few months of her marriage to Pearl's father, Asha had been cold. Pathologically, inexplicably, and demonstrably cold. She remembered October evenings around the house, Pearl and Carl playing in t-shirts and bare feet while she lay on the couch, wrapped in layers of wool and polar fleece. She hadn't felt cold like that in a few years, not until now. She recognized the sensation, acknowledged it, and felt the knowledge chill her even more, like an icy hand laid upon her vulnerable stomach. She clenched her teeth in response, exchanged her light jacket for a more substantial one, and tried hard to reason away the truth.

Halia was awake. Bezef acted puppyish when Brulee was around, and she bathed Brulee's stoic muzzle with loud smacking licks. The women ignored them, each thoughtful and distracted by the unpleasant direction the evening had ended up taking.

Halia didn't know about tact; she didn't know how to protect Asha. She didn't inhabit the realm of emotions, and when they forced entry into her world, her response was often swift and visceral. Tonight, Halia was quiet in the face of strong feelings, hoping that perhaps if she waited them out, they'd get bored and move on.

Night, darkness, and the graveyard were not intimidating to the women, as Brulee, for all her sweetness, was much more intimidating to strangers than anyone or anything could ever be to them. Short of a mountain lion or a loaded gun, Brulee was more than adequate protection.

Asha began to speak before they hit the pool of streetlight at the corner. "Y'know, two weekends ago things were a little off between us. I just discounted it, chalked it up to mood, weird day, biorhythms, whatever. Rob made plans to hang out with his friend, and that guy's daughter all day both days. It was really weird, now that I think about it. It was a weekend that I didn't have Pearl, and Rob arranged to be around someone else's kid all weekend." Asha paused but Halia did not fill the pause with comment, so she continued. "On Saturday, we hiked up Overlook to the fire tower. Rob's buddy and the kid were really not up to it. They had trouble just walking up the hill. We kept waiting for them, and they kept falling behind and arguing with each other." She shook her head slowly, remembering, realizing, reacting. "Strange," she continued, talking more to herself than Halia at this point. "That little kid probably didn't want to come with us. She definitely didn't want to go on a hike. What the hell was going on?"

This monolog carried the women from the street in front of Halia's house to the stone pillars at the gates to the cemetery. Asha hesitated imperceptibly. Tonight the graveyard held just a touch more symbolic meaning than she cared to acknowledge. Halia and the dogs strode in; Asha followed.

"Then that Saturday night things were just not right between us. Rob didn't want to make love. I was hurt and tried not to show it. I tried to give him space. But there was clearly something in the room between us. I just don't know what." Asha started to tear up. "I just ache when things feel like that. That coldness and distance and all the unspoken shit that someone, or both of us, are carrying. It brings back all the pain of leaving Carl, all the uncertainty and self-doubt. I end up feeling responsible for something I don't even understand."

At this Halia smiled a tiny bitter smile of familiarity and said nothing.

"The next day we went to this cool museum in Pittsfield. Again with Bruce and his daughter. Things kind of felt better for a while. Melinda was in a better mood at least, and we had a great time checking out this exhibit of insect-related art. But underneath it just still felt so tense between Rob and me. When we got home, after Bruce and his kid took off, Rob had to go too. It was like he didn't want to be alone with me." Asha heard herself say these words, and her core temperature dropped a degree or two. She felt it, and prickles of anxiety broke out as tiny beads of perspiration in her hairline and gooseflesh on her arms.

She stopped speaking, and for several minutes they heard nothing more than the dogs, sniffing, scratching, panting, all intensified by the darkness and the pall cast over both of them. The dogs instinctively moved away as the train rails began to sing in anticipation of the 8:02 out of Grand Central. A moment or two later, three lonely cars roared by; Asha waved out of pure habit.

"Come to think of it, the Pearl-free weekend before that," she remembered, "Rob had to work Sunday. He canceled Sunday with me, I got upset, and then he was able to get off from work after all…" Asha trailed off, trying to remember the entire sequence of events. "And that happened Thursday night too. We often have Thursday nights together because Pearl goes to her dad's at dinner time. Last week Rob had made plans to go to the movies with Bruce and some other guy, and I asked if they could go a different night so that we could still hang out when Pearl was with her dad. Rob got all weird, lecturing me about needing to be there for his friends. I just let it go. I figured if he wants to hang out with his friends, he should go ahead. I get time with you and Grace when I want it; it's not usually a big deal." Halia showed no visible reaction to these words, but both she and Asha knew they were bullshit. Asha ignored this and continued, grateful for the lack of interruption and Halia's tolerance. "Anyway, he changed plans at the last minute and sort of acted like a hero for making himself available again. I was really confused, but whatever..."

The only words Halia could find were utterly inappropriate and thoroughly unhelpful. She pressed her lips together to prevent their escape, glad that Asha couldn't see her tense frown. Asha, having finally aired all the recent events that troubled her, fell silent. They walked back to Halia's house side by side, each quite alone.

There was no goodbye party. No breakfast with a card and a cake, no afterschool surprise with a gift card to OfficeMax (for resume paper and toner cartridges). No publically-voiced well wishes. No hugs, no tears (crocodile or otherwise). The final chapter of seven years of service to the Dover Union Free School District came to a close on the last day of school with Asha picking up her last paycheck. It was hard for her to feel anything other than terror, looking at that check and knowing that there would be no more money coming in after this: that check in her hand represented the last of her income. She forced herself to acknowledge it, to look at it, to feel the fear; and she let herself cry a little behind the closed door of her office.

She had already cleaned up and removed everything of hers (and, well, yeah, a few things that weren't; crayons and construction paper might come in handy for a school project for Pearl). She wanted to make the last day easy, to leave quickly, unencumbered by boxes. Just get out, she repeated silently, as she made her way down the hallway, past a knot of fourth grade teachers deep in heated conversation. She headed down the stairs and out the door. Outside, the sun was bright, and everything looked pale, bleached, to Asha. She smiled weakly at the teaching assistants congregating on the front steps, and they had the compassion to catch her eye but not speak.

She walked home in the stunned, ringing silence of defeat. It was over.

It was also Pearl's last day of eighth grade, and it was also a beautiful, hot summer day.

"Let's go to Fudgy's for ice cream!" Pearl greeted her mother with a celebratory hug. Asha felt that moment's twinge of fear about money and then, with minimal effort, threw caution to the wind. Ice cream would sweeten the blow.

"Okay," Asha agreed. "Have you done your chores yet?"

Pearl sped off, and the clattering of breakfast dishes being tossed a little too enthusiastically into the dishwasher provided the answer to Asha's question. Asha ignored it. If something broke, so be it. Everything had come from a thrift shop, tag sale, or a dumpster diving expedition anyway. Besides, the more that breaks the less to pack.

And there was the spectre of Rob again, dominating her thoughts. What the hell is going on with him? Asha wondered as she and Brulee climbed up the stairs to the bedroom. It was hot and stuffy upstairs. She opened windows as she made her way to her bedroom, and turned a fan on. Work clothes removed, she stood in front of the fan, cooling off. Brulee flopped down at her feet, in the way as usual.

Asha surveyed her body in the mirror. She saw a thin and muscular, short and compact woman with dark curls grazing her shoulders. The past six months of stress and worry had taken their toll: she saw the fallout of exhaustion and anxiety written on her face. Even when she smiled, the vertical creases between her eyes remained deeply furrowed, and her skin had that dull flat look of someone who either needed antidepressants or whose dose was too high. She looked away.

She chose clothes to go to Fudgy's, her criteria no longer needing to include looking "decent" in case any of her clients were there. Fuck that, Asha thought. I can wear anything I want: go bra-less if I feel like it, wear gardening clothes to the supermarket, and booty shorts to go get pizza. The thought made her chuckle, but she still had Pearl to avoid embarrassing, if possible. She chose a simple tank top, shorts, and flip-flops. She ker-slapped her way back downstairs.

"Is ice cream going to ruin your dinner?" she asked Pearl, who was just finishing up watering the plants in the whisky barrels out front.

"Ice cream is my dinner," Pearl replied.

"Mmmm." Asha made no formal comment. Brulee danced around underfoot, annoying both Asha and Pearl, as Asha got her car keys from the hook and grabbed herself a fleece jacket. Pearl watched and raised an eyebrow. "You know I'll be freezing after eating my ice cream," she explained. Pearl rolled her eyes expertly. "Let's take Brulee," Asha suggested.

"Can we buy her an ice cream cone?"

"I guess so," Asha answered, thinking about that caution and wind stuff.

After ice cream, it was still fairly early and still quite hot. Asha took Pearl and Brulee to the swimming spot at the end of the River Road in Kent. As predicted, Asha wore the fleece jacket and stayed out of the water. Pearl and Brulee played for some time, splashing, screaming, and concocting insane games before Asha corralled them both back into the car for the ride home.

They arrived home to find a message on the answering machine: Pearl had been invited to a drive-in movie and sleepover with a friend on Saturday night. Her delight was expressed by relentless chattering, but Asha didn't mind. It was nice to see her happy.

Asha's heart was pounding as she dialed Rob's number. That was normal: she hadn't shifted out of that early relationship excitement, the nervous, giddy, insecure longing that came with each contact. "Hey."

"What's up?" Rob answered.

"Umm, Pearl got invited out tomorrow night," Asha explained, "so I though I'd invite you over to keep me company. Are you busy?"

"Oh honey," Rob sounded apologetic and exasperated. "I can't. Y'know, I really do spend every single bit of free time I have with you, but with trying to pack up and sell this place and get ready to move and the hours I need to work this time of year, it's just impossible."

"Okay," she strained to keep any emotion out of her voice. "Are you working tomorrow?"

"Yes," Rob sounded like he was about to launch into the list of what he needed to get done, and how long it would take, when Asha cut him off.

"Well, I'll probably catch up with Halia and Grace at The Eft. Stop by after work if you can."

"Okay," Rob acquiesced. "I think I can at least swing by and say hi. What are you and Pearl doing tomorrow?"

Asha described the day she and Pearl had concocted for themselves: sleeping late, pancakes for breakfast, and the afternoon at the park with roller blades, Frisbee, the playground, and a picnic. Asha suspected a boy from school might have to be there for a baseball game or perhaps babysitting a little brother. Not much else would have Pearl planning a day at the park.

"Sounds like a great day," Rob sounded a little wistful. Something about his tone made her feel like enjoying being Pearl's mom and longing for her lover were in conflict.

"Yeah, we'll have fun," she said, her low voice no longer dripping and flowing like warm honey. "And it'll be nice to see you tomorrow evening. I'll look forward to it." There was no lightness in her voice, no playful lilt left in her. She hung up feeling her neediness ruin everything.

It was a Saturday evening, not a Friday, and that meant that rustling up Halia and Grace required phone calls. Asha picked up the phone. She pressed the "talk" and "end" buttons several times to convince the appliance she meant business. After several thwarted attempts, the three button responded to Asha's muscle by connecting, beeping madly, and three-ing repeatedly. Asha hit "end" and "talk" one last time: no dial tone. With a sigh barely escaping between gritted teeth, she found another phone to plug into her one and only working jack. Still no dial tone. She looked at her pathetic phone jack, hanging upside down, the duct tape that had held it in place in years past long since losing its stickiness. "Well, fuck you," she muttered, addressing her comment to the phone whose numbers wouldn't work, the lack of a dial tone, the piss-poor arrangement of answering machine, telephone and electric cords tangled behind the telephone table, the ugly scar the duct tape left on the wall, and the pathetic emotional reaction threatening to erupt from the core of her being at One More Thing being wrong. "Fine," she snapped. "I still have my cell phone. So there."

The call to Verizon's repair dispatch ended with an appointment three days later. One good thing about being jobless, Asha thought bitterly, is that I won't have to leave work to deal with whoever they send out to fix this.

Grace, as it turned out, was not available. Her husband was out of town and Grace wanted to stay home with her son. Halia was not home when Asha called, so she left a "meet me at The Eft" message and hoped for the best. The Eft wouldn't be bad even if Halia weren't around. Asha knew Larry, the bartender, well enough to chat over a drink, and Anne Marie and Lukey Jane were often there in the evening to catch up on local gossip and unwind before heading home.

Halia was there, at The Eft, when Asha walked in. "I got your message," Halia greeted her with a smile. She explained, "I was up at Joanne and Henry's most of the day, but I got home in time to come over here, for a while anyway. Is everything okay? Don't you have Pearl this weekend?"

Asha explained about Pearl's social schedule and her own situation with Rob. Halia's face registered something; Asha didn't know what. She felt strangely angry and guilty. They dropped the subject.

Rob arrived on cue, looking like someone who'd spent the day working out of doors. His clothes bore traces of all the different tasks he'd accomplished and some of the tools he'd used too. He smelled of grass and dirt and gasoline, and he had more than a few twigs in his hair. Asha looked downright thrilled to see him. Halia made excuses and departed quickly enough to attract attention, but Rob didn't notice and Asha had anticipated it.

Tonight Rob was attentive and tender, and Asha melted under his touch. He walked her home, Asha dreading the goodbye, desiring him, missing him. She prolonged the kiss, drawing it out teenager style.

Rob disengaged himself. "You can't kiss me like that. It's not fair. You know I have to go home. That's teasing." He didn't sound all the way irritated, but he also didn't lean in for round two.

"I like kissing you," she said, smiling a wide open smile, arching her back to press her lower half against his. She looked up at him through half-closed eyes. "Making out can be fabulous all by itself." She may as well have crossed her fingers behind her back.

Rob shrugged. "If it isn't going to lead to something more, I find it kind of frustrating. It's a tease." This time it was clear: teasing is a Bad Thing. Asha took note.

She kissed him once more – a patented Rob-and-Asha-goodnight-kiss, no tongue, no teasing. A kiss that said "Not tonight, honey. I have a headache." A kiss that she found all too familiar.

Rob walked back down Nellie Hill Road alone, to collect his car at The Eft and drive home. She decided not to watch him go.

Although the town's Fourth of July fireworks were visible from Asha's back porch roof, since Asha didn't have Pearl for the Fourth, she decided to check out the fireworks elsewhere. West Point, she'd heard, put on a great show, but the distance, the hassle, and the huge crowds put her off. Checking her map, she realized that she could cut the driving distance in half and see the show from the river, just north of Cold Spring. A little park Rob had introduced her to offered a decent spot to park and hang out and get a great view of West Point.

Rob would not be around for the Fourth. He had gone to visit his parents on Long Island and wouldn't be back for a few days. She understood and forgave him in advance; it was tough to be the only son of aging parents. She tried to get an invitation to go along with him, but none came. She let it go without causing a fight; it didn't seem worth it. At this point, for reasons unexplained, Rob seemed to prefer to keep his family and Asha quite separate. Oh well, she thought, we're going to be living together soon. Things will change. They'll have to.

No one else was available either. Halia and Grace both declined to go with her, and Asha realized, sitting there in her kitchen, cell phone in hand, that there wasn't really anyone else she felt comfortable asking. Her relationship with Rob absorbed what little free time she had left after work, Pearl, and taking care of necessities. As a single woman only a stone's throw away from forty, she admitted she maintained a pretty limited social circle. I should do something about that once we move, she thought.

She parked, nose in, one of three cars in the pull-off on Route 9D. The sign threatened that the park closed at dusk. She hesitated, sitting in the driver's seat, looking around. She saw neither gates nor fences around the parking area and decided that the sign couldn't pertain to her and this evening's plan. Besides, she'd been here after dark before, not all that long ago, with Rob, on the beach, in the moonlight; she smiled at the memory. Rob was ready to make love almost anywhere. At the proverbial drop of a hat, she grinned. Well, we weren't interrupted by the cops last summer and I don't think I will be tonight. She wrestled the huge canvas bag stuffed full of supplies across the front seat instead of walking around the car to use the passenger door.

She found her way to an excellent viewing spot atop a small cliff as the gloaming deepened into nightfall. It was cold, breezy and damp, a typical summer night on the banks of the Hudson. Asha was prepared; she had dressed for winter in a fleece pullover and wool socks and brought a blanket to wrap herself in. She hated sitting still in the cold.

She waited. Alone, quiet, and anticipating, she let her mind wander down the well worn trails she frequented these days. Finding a job, selling her house, finding a house to buy over in Orange County, switching Pearl's school: she had plenty to think about, plenty to wish for, plenty to plan. She sat, nestled in an old aluminum frame beach chair with green and white webbing, alone on a dark chilly hilltop in Cold Spring, visualizing angle after angle of Happily Ever After. She fervently believed in being positive and going after what she wanted, so she sat there willing it into existence, waiting for the fireworks to start.

Sometimes things just have to be experienced in order to understand that they aren't a good idea. They sound better on paper or as ideas batted about among a crowd in a barroom. Fireworks alone from a distance are in that category. By the time the show was over, Asha felt disappointed and depressed. She couldn't lay a finger on precisely what it was, but somehow the distance, the "smallness," left her feeling wistful. They were pretty, but Asha realized that fireworks are a community event. The crowds and the plastic glowlight vendors and the amount of time it is bound to take to get out to the parking area: these are key components. Without them, she felt a little unmoored and unpleasantly tossed about. Fireworks alone, she summarized for herself, are not an uplifting experience.

The trail back to the parking area was treacherous. Rocks, tree roots, and pitch blackness challenged Asha and her unwieldy load. Competitive, even with the darkness itself, she pushed herself to move swiftly and confidently back to her car.

Rob's car. Her mind froze, but her feet kept moving. There, in the small circle of light provided by the streetlamp, she saw Rob's car parked a couple of cars down from hers. It hadn't been there before; it wasn't there when she pulled in. Of that she was completely certain. She began trembling, her fingers strangely numb, her heart crashing against her sternum. She dropped all the junk she had been carrying next to her car door and forced herself to look to be sure: she examined the green Jeep Wrangler and knew it was his. No one else had a homemade, poorly rigged, thoroughly rusted bicycle rack like Rob's. It was one of a kind. From where she stood, she couldn't see the woman's cardigan on the passenger's seat.

Almost before she formed the thought, she was moving. She turned around; she ran over the railway bridge, back toward the banks of the Hudson. He must be there since he wasn't up on the cliff. Maybe he was hanging out with Bruce. He must have watched the fireworks from the beach. Great minds think alike; Asha smiled a nervous, dry smile. Why didn't he call me? When did he leave his parents' place? Oh, Rob, so typical, she thought. He is such a man. Unable to communicate what women find important.

She jogged along the trail to the river, this trail flatter and wider than the one up to the hilltop. Rob is here, she breathed, excited and happy. That wistful gnawing will melt in his embrace. The memory of being here with him a month or so ago flashed through her body as she ran, and she stumbled for a step or two, a shudder of delight, half remembering, half longing, catching in her throat.

He wasn't at the beach. She moved fast, eyes now accustomed to the dark and the river reflecting what little light cars and stars offered. He wasn't there.

Somehow I must have passed him, Asha decided. She ran back, sprinting, panting, desperate to see him, to hold him, to understand what was going on, to hear him explain why he was here without her, why he hadn't called, why it really was all okay.

She had to nearly skid to a halt upon reaching the parking area. A Putnam County Sherriff's car, red and white lights flashing, mesmerized her, flooded her eyes, their visual drama matching all she felt. She walked towards her car. A baby-faced police officer walked toward her, and as she turned to face him, she saw them.

Rob was getting out his wallet, speaking to another officer. She was standing next to him. She caught Asha's glance and shrank away guiltily. Asha felt knowledge come crashing down upon her, and all she could sense was the blood pounding in her ears. She couldn't see or hear or think, and as her hands and feet went numb she noticed, as if from very far away, that the police officer was speaking to her. The ground beneath her developed a strange, marshmallowy sponginess, and everything went into slow motion. She was dimly aware of reaching out toward the officer; she wasn't sure if she cried out or not.

She came to in the back of the police car. The officer squatted next to the open back door of the police car, his elbows resting on his knees. Asha looked down into his face.

"What happened?" she asked.

"You passed out," the officer told her. "How do you feel?"

Asha looked at him, then remembered everything. She looked at Rob and the woman, and her head started to swim. She struggled for a few moments to find words, but didn't trust herself to speak. The officer followed her gaze.

"Your husband?" he asked as gently as one could ask such a question under the circumstances.

Asha shrugged. I thought so, one day, I wished, I pretended… there was no answer that made any sense. She looked at the cop, willing the ground to open up and swallow her. Or them.

"Excuse me," the officer stood up and motioned for his partner to step aside and speak with him. They stood out of earshot, and several short muttered sentences were exchanged. The rookie cop returned to Asha; his partner sauntered back toward Rob and the other woman.

"Are you okay to drive?"

She was startled by the question. She hadn't thought that far ahead. She did a quick scan: she wasn't dizzy anymore, and her hands and feet seemed successfully reattached. The center of her body felt empty and destroyed, but she kind of knew that was a feeling she would need to get used to.

"Yeah," she almost whispered. "Yeah. I can drive." Walking, swallowing, thinking a coherent thought that didn't involve wishing someone was dead: those were more difficult. But driving? Yeah, Asha could drive.

"Do you have friends or family members you can spend the rest of the night with?" The cop's question caught her up short, again. Thinking about what was to come was just beyond her ability at this point. Yeah, I can drive, she repeated silently, but where should I go? She had no idea. Her blank expression said it all. The officer opened the front passenger door and produced a water bottle. He fished around a moment longer and came up with a small Dixie cup. The sound of the plastic seal being broken had a three-dimensional quality for Asha; she felt a bit as though her ability to perceive was becoming both impaired and fluid, like a psychedelic experience. Had she any access to the therapist part of her brain, she would have known that it was a reaction to the trauma, but she was held together only by shock and adrenaline. There was no thinking, no memory, no sense of identity or past. Just the current moment and pain.

He handed her the Dixie cup, half full. She sipped. The water nauseated her a little. She looked up at this young man standing over her, witnessing the ruination of her life, and met his gaze.

"Ma'am," he began, a touch self-consciously, "you can go whenever you feel ready enough to drive. The gentleman," the officer made no effort to conceal his distaste, "will be here for a while." Asha's expression formed the question. "We need to take care of some paperwork." The officer let his eyes travel to his partner, who was now checking Rob's tail lights and brake lights. "This could take a while."

She nodded, then asked, "Can I speak to him?"

A brief shadow of worry passed the young man's face. "I guess."

Asha drank the rest of the water and handed the officer back the cup. "Thanks," she murmured.

She approached the Jeep and cleared her throat. The officer working his way through all the possible ticketable offenses stepped back about a half-stride, giving her both space and protection. Rob's eyes seemed glued to the ground. The woman was edging away from Rob, looking as if she could disappear if she wished hard enough.

Asha spoke quietly. "Well, I guess this is it."

"This isn't how I wanted to say goodbye." Rob's voice cracked twice in the single sentence.

Asha didn't trust herself to answer. She was beginning to suspect that she might faint again.

"We need to talk," Rob quavered.

Asha willed Rob to look up, and when their eyes met, he winced in pain. She looked at the woman; she looked expensive, Asha decided. Expensive clothes, expensive haircut: she was going to be expensive to maintain. She also looked weak, spiritually anemic. Asha made up a story in a split second that allowed her to hate the woman and feel superior. She turned away.

The rookie cop fell in step beside her, and walked her to her car. He picked up her bag and lawn chair and loaded them into the back seat for her. As Asha settled herself into the driver's seat, he said, "I'm sorry."

She stopped what she was doing and looked up at him, standing alongside her car. She searched his face. He was sorry. It was genuine. He was truly sorry; Asha could see it. She stuck her hand out, somewhat awkwardly and he grasped it for a moment. She watched him walk away. She thought about how to drive. Put the key in the ignition, she told herself. Don't think about anything else.

It was late. Halia would be home. Asha drove there, the cop's suggestion that she not go home alone resonating positively within her. Halia. Emotionless, sensible, safe Halia; she would be a place Asha could collapse. Asha drove there with the quiet intensity of someone in the midst of a crisis forced to function. Brake, clutch, shift, high beams on, high beams off. She drove consciously, letting the driving keep her from thinking or feeling.

Halia had been asleep. Bezef's barking wakened her long before Asha's knock.

Asha's face told the story.

Halia hugged her briefly, as warmly as Halia had ever hugged anyone.

They sat upon the porch steps; Asha hadn't wanted to go inside. Halia listened; there weren't many details to explain. As Asha relayed the events of the evening, she was too deeply overcome with her own emotions to see the change coming upon Halia. By the time Asha described seeing Rob with the woman next to him, Halia was on her feet. Asha couldn't see her face, but she could see her fists clenching and unclenching.

Halia's gaze travelled to her front yard, to the gardens and containers full of flowers. Rob, in an early relationship fit of generosity towards Asha's friends, had landscaped Halia's front yard. A couple of raised perennial beds bordered by landscape ties and a couple of half barrels filled with annuals adorned the walkway to the mailbox. Halia seethed, looking at them and seeing only betrayal, wrong-doing. And the memory of Bones.

As Halia took off across the front yard, Asha shrank back involuntarily. With Herculean effort, and a shrieking grunt capable of disturbing the residents of the cemetery, Halia pulled loose one of the wooden borders. Wielding it sword-like, club-like, and just plain hooligan-like, she set about demolishing every last shred of evidence that Rob had ever set foot on her property. Crash. The half barrel no longer contained expensive annuals. Well, not live ones anyway. Crash. The half barrel was now more like a quarter barrel. Halia's rampage punctuated with roars of rage and effort became increasingly cold-blooded, as pure passion spent itself and considered fury took its place. She was about half done when Asha joined in, prying up another railroad tie and beating the contents of the perennial bed with it.

Both women were utterly oblivious to the noise level they were creating and the general ruckus being raised. Their tortured cries set Bezef to barking and hurling herself against the front door, desperate to protect Halia or join in the fun. The dull thumps of wood hitting earth were punctuated by cracking and splintering wood and occasional shouts of triumph. Both women, spent and exhausted and only marginally satisfied, eventually gravitated back to the front porch step. They looked like they'd put in a long day gardening, dirt, blood, and splinters forming their cosmetics. They shouldn't have been surprised when the state troopers pulled up.

The call had been made by the neighbors and the report was of a prowler or vandal. The pair of officers stayed in their car, scanning Halia's front yard with the spotlight. Both men felt their breath catch in their throat, and both right hands strayed to their holsters at the sight. "Multiple large angry men with intent is what we're facing here," murmured the driver, summing up the scene. They continued to observe, noting the oddity of the attack: two cars sat untouched in the driveway, garage windows weren't broken, but plants and planters were demolished. It was weird.

"Hey," the other trooper tapped his partner's arm. "On the front porch. Hit the porch with that light." The officers saw Halia and Asha, seated shoulder to shoulder, filthy, tear-streaked and emanating profound emotion. The trooper pulled off Nellie Hill Road, onto Halia's front lawn. Halia noticed and shrugged inwardly: it already looked like Beirut.

"Good evening, ladies," the driver called across the front yard. Both troopers advanced cautiously, flashlights held high and to the left. "We received a call about a disturbance here. Is everything alright?"

Halia had not realized the volume at which removing all trace of Rob from her front yard had occurred. Asha, as the overall situation from an outsider's perspective dawned upon her, had the presence of mind to be embarrassed. Her hands flew to cover her mouth as her eyes widened. With her bare sneakered legs dangling off the porch and dirt flecks adorning her hair, she looked a bit like an adorable ragamuffin kid caught playing with onion grass and making mud pies. Halia, of course, had returned to her pre-fury state of emotionlessness. She stood up, dusted her hands off, and extended one toward the officers as they continued to approach.

"I'm Halia Frank; this is my house." Halia offered, pre-empting their next question. The senior officer shook her hand, taking note of her firm grip and eye contact. "We had a little ..." Halia hesitated, seeking the right words. "We needed to kill some plants." She had no idea how bizarre that sounded, and continued on, matter-of-factly. "I'm sorry it got noisy. We apologize for disturbing anyone." Halia looked around and saw a stray nicotiana still hanging on, standing alone in what was left of a half barrel. She reached over, gave it a sharp yank, and dropped it casually to the ground. Her eyes, adjusted to the darkness, scanned effectively. Nothing remained intact. "We're all finished. It won't happen again."

The younger of the two officers slipped off toward the garage, surveying the damage. He approached Asha, still sitting on the porch.

"May I have your name, ma'am?"

Before Asha answered, his partner interrupted. "Did you say your name is Halia Frank?"

Halia nodded.

"Were you," he spoke to Asha, "in Cold Spring this evening?"

She nodded.

"You were married to Bones, weren't you?" The officer's voice contained a symphony of nuanced tones: admiration, awe, pity, and anger were all apparent on the surface. Compassion lay beneath.

Halia nodded again. Her face did not change.

The officer looked at the damage the two women had wrought. He looked over at Asha leaning against Halia's porch column, bare legs hanging there, pretty but now scarred. He felt his mood blacken, knowing what assholes do that makes the world of dating so hard for decent guys. Like himself. Like his partner. He gestured to the guy to leave Asha alone and return to the car.

"Are you okay now?" The question was addressed to both women.

Halia and Asha nodded once more.

"Anything we can do for you while we're here?" They hesitated, and he offered "Would you like us to secure the grounds? Check around a little? So that we can report that the prowler has gone?"

Halia shrugged. "That would be fine."

The two officers walked around Halia's garage, trying not to worry about the lack of maintenance obvious from every angle. They noted that the gutter grew plants as successfully as had the planters the women destroyed, and that Halia had a fairly sizable "Appalachian pile" behind the garage: no dead appliances yet, but an impressively red-necked conglomeration of items being held in solid waste purgatory. Behind the house, things seemed more tame: less garbage, no gutters. No evidence of prowlers or vandals. Just to be thorough, they checked the embankment leading up to the graveyard. And then they were finished.

Halia thanked them stiffly. The officer who knew Bones hustled his partner into the car, and then wavered. He considered offering the women an explanation; he felt that maybe leaving them alone was a better idea. He went with the latter. His face set with distaste at the memories of Bones, he got in the car and drove away. He steered the car around Nellie Hill Road toward Dunkin' Donuts, out on route 22. He avoided meeting his partner's questioning looks. He didn't want to get into it without something to sweeten the taste in his mouth.

Brulee was barking. Asha groaned and rolled over. A bleary one-eye-open glance at the clock elicited another groan and a petulant snatching of bedclothes and yanking them up around her

neck. 8:35 a.m. At six, she'd staggered downstairs and let Brulee
out to pee without waking up all the way. It was her intent to
ignore Brulee's barking in the hopes that she could repeat the procedure, but no. Asha heard the tapping on the glass of her front
door and realized someone was there.

She hauled herself to her feet and dressed herself in clothing collected from the floor and the foot of the bed. Probably
Jehovah's Witnesses, she thought. The way I look will scare them
even worse than Brulee's barking. It wasn't exactly true; on the
other hand, since the unveiling of Rob in the parking lot the other
night, personal hygiene was rather low on her priority list. As she
turned the corner on the stairwell and caught a glimpse of the huge
white bucket truck in her driveway and the large clean-shaven
man at her door, it fell into place. Thursday. The phone guy was
here.

Asha hung onto Brulee's collar with one hand, turning the
doorknob with the other. In moments like these, handling Brulee
was rather like wrestling a sixty-five pound angry greased mar-
lin. The phone guy stayed put on the front doorstep, waiting out
the struggle. Once all four of the dog's feet were on the floor,
he offered the back of his hand for her to sniff and crossed the
threshold. She couldn't help but notice that he used a hair product
to make his dirty blond crew cut spiky. How metrosexual, she
thought, and suppressed a grin.

"Good morning," he greeted Asha with professional cheerfulness. She immediately felt irritated and assumed he was either
happily married for 20 years or a philanderer. Or both. Brulee,
however, seemed satisfied, and wagged.

She let go of the dog and grunted, "Come on in."

"I just checked at the interface," he began, but she was walking away, headed for the kitchen. He hastened after her. "And the
trouble is inside the house."

Asha busied herself with filling the kettle for coffee, biting
back the words, "No shit, Sherlock." "The jack is right there,"
she indicated the offending item hanging pathetically alongside

the support column it was once duct-taped to. And then, so he wouldn't look stupid all alone, she said, "I just got up."

The phone guy looked up from the dangling phone jack, and assessed her bedraggled, mismatched appearance. He said nothing. His stock rose slightly. "You want some coffee?" she offered.

"No thank you." He hesitated, then added, "I'm Walter." Pause. "I'll be your phone man today." It was his standard line; sometimes it worked with cranky customers to get that first smile.

"Asha Jackson," she replied and grasped his outstretched hand. "This is Brulee. She'll act like she wants to kill you every time you go in or out the front door." Walter squatted down on his haunches and Brulee nuzzled her head into his muscular chest. He stroked her head, neck and back and she wagged. "Don't be fooled," she warned. "You start over at square one if you leave and try to come back in." The phone guy nodded.

She made herself some breakfast and sat out on the back porch eating and drinking her coffee. This was her last day to indulge in the insanity and bad behavior of bereavement: Pearl would be back tomorrow from her Fourth of July week with her dad. Asha had one more day to laze around, crying, emailing distant friends, talking on the phone, bemoaning her fate and wringing her hands. Literally and figuratively. This was her last day of privacy and absence of structure, and there was no one she was required to fake it for. Sorry, Walter-the-phone-guy, Asha thought, you just don't get a version of me fit for public display. Tough.

After several minutes it was hot enough and buggy enough to chase her back inside. Walter was not in her kitchen she noticed with both curiosity and relief. I can belch and fart in peace, at least for the time being, she thought. She put her plate in the sink and poured a second cup of coffee. Walter reentered the kitchen laden with tools and equipment, Brulee at his side. Asha narrowed her eyes at the dog, and Brulee approached Asha wagging and licked her hand. Okay, she relented. Go ahead and like him. I don't care.

"I'm going to take care of this," Walter informed Asha, gesturing at the tangle of wires. "The jack was broken, and I replaced it." Already, she thought. That was quick. "Are there other jacks in the house that give you trouble?" Walter went on. "I'm still getting a bad reading at the interface."

She grunted in the affirmative. There was a broken jack in the bedroom and an irritable, touchy jack in the computer room.

"If it's okay with you, I'll finish in the kitchen then take a look at the one in the bedroom."

She nodded, then said, "You know, I bet the problem is just bad placement. The feng shui is all off. The box on the outside of the house shouldn't be in that spot at all. No wonder none of the jacks work."

Walter looked at her. In fact, he stared at her. Asha was oblivious; she was already on to the next thing, in this case finding a couch downstairs to curl up on with her second cup of coffee and her depression. Considering what she said, Walter watched her walk away and remained looking after her for several long moments before turning back to the situation at hand.

For Asha, the situation at hand was a total mess. She experienced breaking up with Rob under these circumstances rather like being hit by a fragmentation grenade, and she found herself consumed by the task of picking out the shrapnel day after day. Her stomach boiled from the seemingly endless font of rage and hurt she had tapped into. Each discrete memory lodged like sharp hot metal in a limb or pierced an organ. Each hurt to grab hold of, seared to dislodge, and bled and ached once removed. She was on day four of this activity, punctuated by brief moments of functioning: speaking to Pearl on the phone, walking Brulee, scrolling through online help wanted databases. She found that she physically could not cry while running, and so she ran daily as a respite from the stinging eyes and aching throat.

The pain of the past was bad; the terror about the future was in some ways worse. As a break from crying over betrayal, she asked herself what the future held, and near panic accompanied that question. A homeowner, a single mother, unemployed, looking for a social work job that would keep her in the home-owning, single-parenting business; the prospects weren't good. Basically, only a school social work position would do the trick. She had already applied to all the openings in Dutchess, Putnam, Ulster, Orange, Westchester, and Columbia counties. All three of them. She had not yet received any invitations to interview. And it was July. School budget decisions were made in May, and openings were usually posted in June. It wasn't very likely that a whole lot more would be posted until the mid-August chaos of last minute retirements and new hires receiving better offers elsewhere. Unable to think clearly, she tortured herself with this knowledge and day-dreamed up increasingly negative scenarios.

She fretted and dozed and spaced out on the couch while Brulee kept tabs on Walter-the-phone-guy. Brulee did like him; it was true. From her perspective, what's not to like? All he did was pet her and fix things. Even Brulee could tell that that was a good thing. Walter finished replacing jacks (they were all bad) and then neatly tacked all the stray wires in the kitchen to the support column. He inspected Asha's telephone and answering machine situation and hesitated. Her telephone table was kind of crowded on top. The cordless phone base had I-holes for mounting. Walter looked at Brulee and said "What do you think?" Brulee wagged, started panting, and led Walter to Asha.

Her mood created an intimidating force field around her. Walter quailed. He cleared his throat as he approached the couch and carefully chose the volume and pitch of his voice. "Excuse me."

She turned to him and looked up. Walter spent much of his free time over the next three months seeking the right words to describe this moment. For him, it was all over. She was devastatingly beautiful, all tear-stained, red-eyed and bed-headed. He saw a gypsy princess, dark skin, dark eyes, dark hair, and a darkness of mood that both enticed and repelled. He made up a story right then and there that she had been wronged and victimized but was so obviously strong in her weakness. He felt his stomach flip and blinked hard and swallowed.

"What?" she hadn't meant to sound irritated.

"Would you like your phone in the kitchen to be on the support column so that it's up off the table top and out of the way?"

"You can do that?"

Walter, misunderstanding the import of her question, began describing the screws and the I-holes, and explaining how simple the procedure really was. She cut him off.

"No, no," she held one hand up – a truly regal gesture from someone whose blanket and clothing merged to resemble a pile of rags – and clarified. "Verizon will pay you to hang my phone on the wall?" She sounded incredulous but interested.

Walter's quick calculation was that this was not the moment to tell her the stories about all the different things Verizon unwittingly paid their employees to do. "Yeah," he assured her.

"Show me what you have in mind," she threw back her blanket and picked up her empty cup. She led the way back into the kitchen, Brulee and Walter at her heels.

His spot on the wall was too high. Asha, barely 5'3", looked at him with a self-deprecating smirk and reached for the phone, demonstrating that at that height it was a tip-toe effort. "My daughter needs to be able to get to it too."

"You have a daughter? How old is she?" Somehow Walter managed to make the question sound like he was making innocent conversation.

"Thirteen. She's coming home from her dad's tomorrow." Asha replied and left the room. Walter hung the phone alone, Brulee having followed her owner up to her bedroom.

It was well before noon when Walter felt like he had buttoned up the job to the best of his ability. Her kitchen now boasted a wall-mounted cordless phone, with all the phone cords, power cords, and answering machine cords neatly tacked on the column in organized straight lines. Her bedroom, the upstairs office, and for good measure, Pearl's room contained fully functional jacks. Everything tested fine. It was time to go.

Walter collected his tools and said a fond goodbye to Brulee. He was outside, packing up the truck and examining the location of Asha's junction box when she ventured out the front door. She was barefoot, but now dressed in an identifiable lawn-mow-ing-yard-work outfit: a pair of frayed Levi cut-offs and a bleach stained t-shirt.

"All done?" She picked her way toward the driveway.

"Yes."

"Thank you." Asha stood in front of him. She looked at him and let him look at her. He saw her. All of her: what she carried and what she had set down for the moment.

"You're welcome."

She smiled and Walter, a bit dazzled, returned the smile, offer-ing his hand once more. "Don't work too hard. It's hot out," she said and shook his hand. She turned away. "Gotta haul all these goddamned roses outta here…" she muttered to herself, press-ing her lips together at the inevitability of thorns in flesh. She stepped on a stray spruce needle leftover from this year's early spring cleanup. She winced but did not deign to yelp and headed indoors for boots.

Walter gave the placement of the box, the wires, and the over-all front of the house one last look, then drove away.

Asha attacked the diseased and defoliated roses with a ven-geance. They fought back, strong thorns drawing blood despite decent quality work gloves. The process felt good. The physical pain of thorn pricks along with the developing sunburn on her nose, cheeks, and shoulders focused her on something other than her psychic pain, now reduced to a dull ache at the back of her throat and a vague dread in the pit of her stomach. Work was healing on some level, so she abandoned the front beds once the dead roses were dragged off to the burn pit. She wheeled out the lawnmower and felt absolutely virile as she pulled the pullstart.

An hour later the gas tank was empty and Asha was flirting with dehydration. She dragged the mower to a level spot in the shade and went looking for a gas can. Empty. Her kneejerk re-sponse was to utter a fairly moderate string of epithets; she was too tired to vent more graphically. She carried the empty can up to the back porch and left it there for the moment. She slipped inside, the screen door banging shut behind her. The cold water tasted almost sweet, and she drank deeply. She located her wallet and took her VISA card out; why carry more than necessary on an already hot day? She checked her back pocket for holes before placing her card in it. She selected a carrot cake flavor Clif bar for lunch and gagged on the first bite. Too sweet. She headed out the back door leaving Brulee crestfallen in the kitchen. She picked up the red plastic five gallon can, purchased at a yard sale before she realized that she had inherited three others along with the house, and walked off to the gas station, a quarter of a mile away.

Watching from a bird's eye view, all that was missing was a plinky ragtime piano soundtrack to complete the appearance of a comedy of errors; as Asha walked north on Route 22, Walter pulled up from the south access on Nellie Hill Road, and slipped back into her driveway. Having consumed his lunch in the Dover Plains Library parking lot, Walter then used the resources for a little research on feng shui. The library ladies were charmed, intrigued, and delighted to help out a guy like Walter: he tickled their imaginations, with his odd request, ultra polite manner, and Verizon identification hanging around his neck. Having learned enough to be dangerous with a red ribbon and a mirror, Walter headed back to Asha's place, a pit stop at the local nursery on the way.

When she arrived home with the gas, she assumed Halia had stopped by. They had only spoken briefly and only a few times since the night of the fireworks, but Halia made it a point to swing by with some excuse or another almost every day. Yesterday it had been a vegetable lo mein delivery at dinner time, and the day before it was a package of Skinny Cow coffee-flavored flying saucers: Asha's favorite. So when she saw a flat of dwarf sunflowers sitting on her front porch, she just assumed it was Halia. The card neither confirmed nor denied her assumption: it wasn't signed. Just a poem by William Blake about sunflowers, clearly scrawled on one of those florist gift cards in what she assumed was florist-flunkie handwriting. That was sufficiently Halia-esque for Asha to smile and feel the momentary warmth of gratitude before returning to her more familiar (at least these days) experience of hollowness. Turning her back on the happy task that awaited her ("I'll plant you guys later when it's not so hot out" she told the flowers, running her gasoline-scented hand over the bright yellow petals), she picked up the gas can and lugged it over to where the lawn mower sat.

Around the side of the house, something red fluttered, catching her eye. The interface, as the phone guy had called it, had a red ribbon tied to its hinge. Huh, she thought, setting down the gas can and making her way through the lily of the valley to get a closer look. Sure enough, a red ribbon – a red silk ribbon – had been tied to the hinge, and a small rock pile had been placed on the ground next to the box. She squatted to examine these items more closely. Rocks. Earth energy, weight, permanence. And red, for fire, moving to catch the breeze. Air. "Hmmm..." Asha murmured aloud. "Maybe Grace was with Halia? She would know how to do a feng shui cure." Asha examined the red ribbon, and admired the hand tied good luck knot. How totally sweet, she thought, that her friends cared so much about her telephone woes. She'll have to tell them that the phone guy finally came and fixed the problem.

Asha had discussed her situation with her ex-husband over the phone when they arranged the logistics around dropping Pearl off the next day.

"So are you taking your house off the market?" Carl's deep voice formed the reasonable question.

"Uhhh, I guess so," was her halting response.

"Do you have a job lined up?" Again, a reasonable question.

"No." She didn't bother to attempt to hide the misery that answer unleashed.

"Any prospects?"

"No."

"Well," Carl's pause spoke volumes. "What are you going to do?"

"I don't know." The effort of fighting back the fear those words created in Asha exhausted her. The brief conversation was draining her dry.

"Pearl will be relieved." Carl's comment revived her slightly, although now guilt vied with misery for top billing. "Oh?" was all she could muster.

"I don't think she wanted to move or change schools."

"I guess not." I don't really want to move or change schools either, she screamed silently.

"You want me to stick around tomorrow when you tell her?" A kind and reasonable offer. Carl really wasn't a bad guy.

"Thanks, but I think it'll be okay just the two of us." A kind, reasonable, and totally inappropriate offer. He has nothing to do with this. I crashed and burned all by myself.

Somehow through the din of self-recriminations, she heard Carl say how sorry he was that she was in a tough spot, and that he hoped she'd find a decent job soon. Like an automaton, she went through the motions of social pleasantries. They completed the task at hand (arranging the time and place that Pearl would be returned to Asha) and hung up.

Pearl arrived back home in great spirits, and Asha found her *joie de vivre* infectious. She had gifts from extended family members on Carl's side and created a display on her bed of all her loot. Asha hung out with Pearl through all the trying on of new clothes and sprawled on her bed as Pearl rearranged dresser tops to accommodate all her new tchotchkes. Eventually Pearl's energy ran out, and she flopped down on the cheap twin bed beside her mom.

"So dad told me you have news?" Pearl asked.

"Yeah," Asha sighed and teared up. Pearl looked alarmed. "We're not moving. Not now anyway. Rob and I broke up."

Pearl studied her mother's face. "I'm sorry, mom," she murmured, wrapping her neither-teenage-nor-little-girl arms around her mother's neck. Asha hugged her back, careful not to feel too much.

"It'll be okay." They both spoke the words of comfort simultaneously, then unwrapped from the hug to grin at each other.

"What are you going to do?" Pearl asked her mother, fully expecting a sensible answer, all sewn up.

"I don't know," Asha answered honestly. Pearl's eyes widened. "I'll figure something out. Soon." Pearl looked only slightly mollified. "In the meantime," Asha wriggled up off the bed and onto her feet, "would you like an ice cream sandwich? Halia brought some over for us."

"Color me there," Pearl also found her feet and they headed downstairs together.

What the hell am I going to do? Asha asked herself as she wrestled open the plastic package.

What the hell am I going to do? Asha asked herself as she watered the gorgeous assortment of sunflowers cheerfully lining the front walkway.

"What the hell are you going to do?" Asha's real estate agent asked her when Asha told her she was taking her house off the market.

What the hell am I doing? Asha asked herself after she failed to apply for every single social work job opening advertised online, despite impossibly long commuting distances, insulting salaries, or terrifying clientele.

What the hell am I going to do? Asha wondered as she and Pearl tossed a softball back and forth in the backyard.

"Honey, just what are you going to do?" Asha's mother asked.

She avoided The Eft, Halia and Grace. Their pre-existing friendship with Rob made Asha feel awkward, and besides, she didn't think she could stand hearing the question one more time.

She discovered that no matter how hard she tried to come up with an answer and a plan, that thinking about it as an activity in and of itself was not fruitful. "I just can't come at this head on," she admitted to herself as she critically examined her resume one

more time. It's like writer's block, she thought. I need to open up
a new avenue, find a whole new approach. I'm just hamstering
away on my stupid wheel in here.

She found herself mouthing platitudes to Pearl: "You can't
push the river." "Every cloud has a silver lining." "Good things
come to those who wait." Pearl developed expertise with her eye
roll and heavy sigh.

Running helped. Asha believed in running. She let the pounding miles become her religion; she indulged in near ecstatic levels
of worship, upping her mileage, dropping pounds off her slight
frame, blissed out on the numbing that came with the increase
in endorphins. By late July, she was thin to the point of gaunt.
Brulee, ever in sync, followed suit.

And still the questions haunted her. "Any job nibbles yet?"
was one she dodged when neighbors ran into her on line at the
supermarket. Carl came to pick up Pearl, and swung by to drop her
off again, and Asha avoided his eyes and hid behind Pearl, making
sure that the questions hung in the air between them, unasked.

It was the third weekend after the fireworks when Pearl was
back at Carl's that Asha, home alone, reached her limit. Early
Saturday morning, she just hit her wall. She got fed up with wondering what to do, fed up with the ache in the back of her throat
and the dread in the pit of her stomach, the inaction and emotional
treading water that self pity had bred in her of late. She didn't feel
any better, but she found new energy in being sick of feeling so
bad.

"I'll go hiking," she decided. She spoke to Brulee, who
wagged and licked her bathrobed knee. "In the Catskills. I'll hike
a mountain with a fire tower on it, in the Catskills."

Asha had been up a couple of the fire towers in Dutchess County
and had visited Red Hill and Overlook with Rob. Finishing the
collection of Catskill fire towers was the thing to do. That much
was clear to Asha. Sometimes, Asha told herself, half apologetic
and half defensive, the answer is a small answer, not a big one.
I'm going hiking.

She was ready to go in minutes: directions, map, food, water, clothes, and Brulee ready to go and in the car in no time. She checked the clock on the dashboard as she pulled away from Nellie Hill Road: 7:15 a.m. She headed west.

It was a godforsaken long drive. West, all the way across Dutchess County, and then west again, all the way across Ulster County, and then southwest from Arkville, heading for Mill Brook Road. Asha's mind ran over the familiar hamster wheel, spinning pointlessly over well trodden ground: seeing Rob and his new woman standing there shivering in the parking lot, destroying every trace of his efforts at Halia's house, replaying the formal break-up conversation, picking away at the wounds it left open.

Rob had called Asha the day after being unmasked, and Asha had met him at the graveyard to have that final conversation. Rob had promised her that he just needed time to get his head together, that the other woman didn't mean anything, that he loved Asha, that he would get help and come back to her. He needed time, he said, "time to digest all that had happened since they first got together." It was a big commitment and he wasn't ready, but he loved her and wanted her and would find a way to ready himself.

Asha asked for couple's therapy. Rob said no. Asha, in a moment worthy of a bad reality TV show, demanded that he break up with the other woman on the spot. She had even handed him her phone, challenging him to call her then and there. He didn't. Somehow, boiling and destroyed inside, she managed to turn and walk away from him.

Asha replayed the whole thing over and over, searching in vain for a way to hurt less, to assuage the rage, and to rediscover the happiness that being in love with him had brought. Her obsessive scampering away on the hamster wheel like this would have been considered masochistic by any reasonably neutral observer, so she avoided most social interactions. The long drive to the trailhead, followed by a long solitary walk in the woods, and then the long drive back home alone met the need. She hoped no one else would be out hiking Balsam Lake Mountain today.

A green Jeep pulled up at the light by the Purple Palace Car Wash in Poughkeepsie. Her heart leapt, then tumbled back into place, hammering away. Oh yeah, she remembered. Being out on the roads of Dutchess County meant the possibility of seeing People, Places, and Things that would conjure memories. His car. Shit. She tried to sigh, to calm down the slamming of her pulse in her temple and her neck. If I had a nickel for each shotgun blast of adrenaline I get hit with every time I see a goddamn green Jeep, I wouldn't need to look for a job. Asha said a little prayer of hatred and ill will directed at the driver of every green Jeep in the Hudson Valley and tried to smile at her creativity with the range of disease and misfortune she wished upon him and all who were foolish and ignorant enough to have purchased the same vehicle as he had. Well, on the bright side, Asha found that the metallic taste and the concomitant nausea of let down interrupted the circular train of thought that was hurtling down the tracks toward certain misery.

Ulster County was better. She felt a tad safer farther from most places they had been together. Crossing the Hudson created a geographic boundary, a clear delineation between where he was, where they had spent their time together, and where she had seen him with Her. On the west side of the river, it was different: the Catskill Mountains were over here, as were her childhood home and her teenage haunts. She felt the river crossing ease her body, and she welcomed it.

Her mind continued to torture her, but less forcefully. Her attention wandered to the scenery as she rolled north and west following the Esopus Creek. The big cow atop the Reservoir Deli elicited a wan smile, and the huge eagle at the Route 214 intersection caught her eye. The hurt and anger slept just beneath the surface, and Asha kept both hands on the wheel, eyes on the road. She didn't see a single green Jeep in all of Ulster County.

Several miles down Dry Brook Road (named not for the seasonal quantity of the flow but for the three bridges spanning the creek), as the trailers became fewer and farther between, Asha was actually jerked into the present tense. She stomped on the brake pedal as a young bear crossed the road in front of the car, loping doglike into the field on the far side. Brulee had been lying curled in a tight circle on the back seat and sat up, blinking and stretching in response to the crisis. Asha was riveted. She looked around, relieved: no cars behind her. The valley ran north-south, with the Belleayre-Big Indian ridge to her east and Delaware County to the west. This valley was wider than the deep and narrow cloves up by Hunter and Halcott, and she was able to appreciate the closeness of the mountains without the drama and darkness of the forest pressing in on her. Asha sat in the car, stopped in the middle of the road, and looked around some more. Unbidden, as if the valley had reached out to her, interrupted her internal conversation, and asserted itself in her consciousness, she felt happy. For a few long moments, she felt protected from her pain, removed physically and encased in something different, a barrier made of earth and sky, water and views. She felt cut off, separated from all that hurt so terribly, and for those brief moments she even lost access to it. She inhaled the relief.

And then the moment was over. A crow flew past the sun, its shadow crossing the windshield, and Asha returned to herself. She tapped the blinker up, signaling the right turn onto Mill Brook Road. By the time she had climbed to the highest trailhead in the Catskills, she was once again fighting back tears.

She trudged up the wide stony trail. Her heart ached, her throat ached, and her mind, numb and empty, ached too. The trail was sufficiently undemanding as to require little of her in terms of effort. Keeping an eye on Brulee and placing one foot in front of the other were her only tasks. She cried most of the way up.

She wasn't expecting the cabin. Just shy of the summit, a tiny tender's cabin sat nestled under the balsams. The door was open and Brulee was inside, sniffing around when Asha caught up with her. Her assumption that the cabin was simply a display for tourist-hikers, with maybe a brochure rack and some maps inside, was incorrect. A spartan-looking cot and a pair of well-worn men's hiking boots placed neatly underneath it, and then a man's voice greeting the dog surprised and flustered her.

"Brulee! Come!" She sounded sharp, shrewish. "I'm so sorry," she called in through the open cabin door as the dog exited and circled her.

Rich, the volunteer fire tower docent, shrugged off the invasion. "It's okay," he waved her in from the "bedroom." "You can check it out. Everyone does."

Asha glanced around the room, leaning in from the stone stoop. It was cute in its rustic, state park way. And it was at least part display: the brochure racks were just hidden from view until you actually walked in. Okay, she thought. I didn't commit too major a faux pas.

She moved on to the summit and climbed the tower. She stayed up in the cabin for a while, Brulee curled in a tight circle at her feet. Hikers came and went, stepping over and around Brulee, who tolerated the stiff breeze and the intrusions without response. She looked at the views. She learned and instantly forgot the names of the mountains the other hikers shared with her and cried. She alternated between fighting bravely and surrendering to the swollen ache in her throat. Rich, the volunteer, came up to check on her, and after assessing that she was neither interested in chatting nor was she in need of emergency services, he left her alone again.

She didn't know how long she had been up there when she stopped looking and starting seeing. First the trees caught her attention, the sea of balsams that dominate many of the Catskill mountaintops. She saw them, black-green against the gray sky. They waved and whispered in the wind, close by, encircling the tower. She could see the roof of the cabin and the roof of the outhouse, partially hidden by the trees. She lifted her eyes, adjusting her gaze: out, not down. She saw the mountains that had been blurred when named a few minutes ago. She saw the contours of the cloves, knowing that water ran there. She saw layers, hills upon hills. She scanned the horizon, all 360 degrees, honoring the idea of a fire tower, and its tending. She saw no smoke; she saw no signs of civilization at all. She looked, she saw, and she knew. She wanted to be there, on top of that mountain and that one and that one and that one. She wanted to be here, in the woods. In the mountains.

And then she pulled her eyes away from all that to look down at Brulee. "Hey baby," she murmured to the dog. Brulee thumped her tail on the wooden floor. "Let's go."

Back at the car, Asha felt the pang of self-consciousness: it took longer to drive to the trailhead than to hike to the summit. Her stomach clenched at the recriminations she unleashed upon herself next. Was this a stupid thing to do? Was it wasting gas? Was it a waste of time? All the other things she could or should have been doing for the past six or so hours flooded in, threatening to drown her in self doubt. How could I have fiddled like this while the homestead back in Dover Plains was engulfed in unnatural disasters?

The hyperbole of the last thought, and its concomitant images of tornadoes whirling around the kitchen, wind shears demolishing the living room, a plague of locusts in Pearl's room: Asha almost smiled. Things are not so desperately out of control, she told herself. I have some savings, and enough from my last check to get me through September, maybe October if I'm really careful. Pearl and I are safe, the house needs nothing imminently (knock on wood) and we won't have heating bills for a while. She started up the Jetta and guided it out of the trailhead parking area, feeling something akin to optimism. Asha released the smile, and reveled in the momentary pleasure of certainty. "Fuck it," she said out loud. "I'm hiking. That's what I'm going to do. I'll hike the Catskill 35 while I figure out what comes next. Thirty-four more mountains is what comes next." The smile held a wicked challenge, a go-ahead-and-say-it cockiness, and she lifted her chin and sat up tall. She peeked at Brulee, curled up on the back seat. "Are you in?" she asked the reflection in the rear view mirror. Brulee wagged her tail.

During their good night phone call, when Asha told Pearl about the hike Pearl reminded her mother about her fascination with water towers when she was a toddler. "Wouldn't it be cool if fire towers held fire, just like water towers hold water?"

Hours later, Asha lay in bed imagining dipping into a well of fire and ladling it out. "I'd take a full measure right about now," she mumbled.

Several nights later, while Pearl slept Asha sat up at her kitchen table with a calculator, a legal pad, and a pencil. The phone was jammed between her left shoulder and cheek, tweaking her trapezius muscle into a mighty spasm.

"Halia? Did I wake you?" She threw a glance over her right shoulder at the clock, the phone sliding dangerously toward her collarbone. She shrugged it back up.

"No," the answer came back, despite the proximity to 11 pm. "What's up?"

"I've been thinking, and I want to bounce my plans off someone sane," she explained, laying down the pencil and taking hold of the phone.

"And you've exhausted your list of people who meet that description, so you're down to me?" Halia wasn't joking, but she also wasn't irritated.

Asha ignored the comment, and continued, "I think I'm going to have to liquidate some retirement accounts. I need enough money to keep me going here for a while and I don't know what else to do."

"That's a bad idea." Halia limited her response to what she saw as fact.

"I know," Asha agreed, dropping the pencil eraser-side down on her enamel table top and listening to the child-pleasing "boing" sound it made. "I know."

"No jobs?" Halia gave in and asked the obvious.

"Nothing that will work." Boing. "I've been applying for everything and anything that seems even remotely plausible." Boing boing boing. "I started looking back in May, as soon as the budget went through and I knew the position was ending. I've applied to, like, six or seven jobs, and I haven't been called for a single interview." She stopped boinging and began doodling in the margin of a list of expenses she'd made before calling Halia. "I guess this is going to take a while."

"How long can you go on like this?" Halia wanted to know.

"Well, I have enough from my summer paycheck to get me through September if I am really a fascist about money. Maybe a little longer," she looked at her lists, expenses and income. "I don't think I can shave my expenses any more than I already have. I need money. I need an income."

"Will you be able to collect unemployment?" Sensible Halia. That was a good suggestion.

"I think so. The districts hate to pay it, but I think they have to because they cut my position." She thought about it, and hit some buttons on the calculator with her eraser. "I think that will be enough to cover almost half of my expenses. I still need to do something else."

"Can you borrow from your IRA instead of liquidating it?" Another good suggestion.

"No. My IRAs and TSAs are all scattered because I've held all different jobs, so I couldn't ever roll one into another. I don't have one that's big enough to borrow from. Besides, I don't know if I could make payments..." she trailed off, scowling at her lists, and tapping the eraser against the pad.

"I'm not really helping, am I?" Halia stated the fact. "You already decided."

"Yeah," she admitted. "I just wanted to hear someone say it wasn't a bad idea."

"Well, it is a bad idea." Halia didn't sugar-coat it. "But it might be your best option compared to all the other bad ideas out there. You've ruled out racking up enormous credit card debt?" Now Halia was joking. At least Asha hoped she was.

"I've also considered going back to school, which is kind of like racking up credit card debt," she mused. "Living on student loans is my back up plan if I am still floundering around in a couple more months."

"What would you study?"

"Well, that's the problem." Asha boinged the pencil against her forehead. It didn't make the sound, and it hurt. She put the pencil down and sighed. "Physics. Quantum physics. The interface of psychology, physics, and consciousness." She hesitated. Halia was silent. "You see the problem."

"Liquidate your assets." Halia reversed herself on the matter.

Asha smiled. She knew she would have enough cash, even after the penalties, to buy herself a few months of hiking and licking her wounds. She had neglected to mention the hiking part of the plan to Halia, and Halia hadn't asked. It was the kind of project Halia just might understand, she thought. Either way, it didn't matter. She had heard what she needed to hear. It was time to call it a night.

"Thanks, Hali," she said. "Good night."

"See you Friday?" Halia asked. "At The Eft?"

"Maybe," Asha said, and then thought about it. "Probably not," she added.

"Maybe I'll stop by sometime," Halia offered. "Good night."

"Good night," Asha repeated and hung up.

It was going to have to be her IRA. A few minutes of recalculating monthly expenses to make sure she'd done all her math correctly and a few more minutes of racking her brains about potentially overlooked expenses and then she was done. The matter was settled. It was a terribly bad idea to gamble away years of retirement savings. It was the polar opposite of a financially savvy move. Asha knew this, but she also knew she had to do something. Without a miracle job offer riding in on a white horse, Asha had made her choice. Tomorrow she would make the arrangements.

It was Pearl who caught her red-handed. Asha continued to avoid The Eft and her friends as much out of habit and fiscal belt-tightening as anything else, so no one else was around to notice. She had been spending more and more time behind the computer, and guiltily minimized the screen whenever she heard Pearl approach. Eventually, emboldened by pure obsession, she began to indulge even when Pearl was in the room. It was only a matter of time before Pearl noticed.

"What are you doing?" she demanded.

Asha froze, realizing how it must look through Pearl's eyes. She failed to answer right away and Pearl got up and peered at the screen from over her mother's shoulder. "Are you thinking of getting another dog?" Her tone said it all: delighted, incredulous, and a touch condescending.

"Uh, yeah."

"Cool." Pearl studied the mug shots of dogs available through the Belgian Shepherd rescue organization. She pointed at her favorite. "Have you discussed this with Brulee yet?"

Asha grinned and said, "I know. Brulee will never forgive me. Just looking at these pictures makes me feel guilty."

Pearl giggled. "Are we going to get one?"

"Do you want another dog?"

"I want a horse," Pearl didn't miss a beat. Asha gave her the long suffering mom look. Pearl didn't let up. She adopted the tone usually reserved for a "how stupid grown-ups are" tirade: "Twice the amount of dog hair and mud everywhere. Great."

"Since when do you care?" Asha teased.

Pearl shrugged. "Yeah, let's get another dog. I think that one," she pointed at the screen, "is the one."

The dog's name was Lyla, the word for night in Hebrew. She was coal black, long haired and three years old. She was also in a shelter in northern Michigan.

Pearl lost interest once she realized that her mother was serious. As far as Pearl was concerned, they were getting another dog. The rest was just details.

Asha received her cash infusion, albeit at the expense of her future, and set about the task of recreating her life from the ground up. Questions of whether or not to move, where, how and when to get a job, whether or not to go back to school, and which mountain she'd climb next all percolated in the back of her mind as she moved through her daily summer routine. Take Brulee out early, before the heat and bugs become intolerable. Coffee and job searching before Pearl wakes up. Pearl and the day's adventures. Seemed like every day ended with long slow evenings that varied only in how sharp the pain that skewered Asha's organs felt.

Pearl. She hung suspended between childhood and teenagerdom, with Asha unable to predict to which side she'd fall day by day. Planning activities was an adventure in and of itself. Asha recognized that her window of opportunity to do things with Pearl was sliding shut, as friends and The Mall began to take on greater and greater importance. She put forth heroic efforts coming up with mutually satisfying days. Ice cream, as a destination or an ingredient, helped.

She found herself vacillating between huge bursts of energy and enthusiasm, and inertia and depression, usually at least in part depending upon how close by Pearl was at that moment. As the summer wore on, she found that she could add the miserable zap of adrenaline-powered dread, rage, and desire at the possibility of seeing him. She studiously avoided destinations that took her anywhere near familiar roads or old haunts. She wished every night, as her new bedtime ritual, that the entire village of Cold Spring would just slide off the Hudson Highlands, fall away into the river, and disappear.

And yet, she was unable to shake the urge to ask questions, to seek answers, to drive past his house, to delve, to stalk. On a Tuesday night in late July, she gave in. After dropping Pearl off at Carl's, Asha let it happen. She drove past Rob's house, telling herself "just this once" and "this will get it out of my system." His car was there, the lights were off, and Asha rated the overall experience a 9.2 on her emotional Richter scale. Rage, longing, self-pity, and a healthy dollop of shame collided in her chest, leaving her gasping for breath. She looked at her hands, white-knuckled on the steering wheel, and hurried back home, embarrassed but unfulfilled, knowing the urge would be back tomorrow. Her tears had dried up, but the deep furrow between her eyebrows was at risk of being mistaken for a coin slot.

Hating him didn't help. The memories would pop up, unbidden, triggered by a candy wrapper or the scent of gasoline, or some private joke. The daily walk with Brulee passed Halia's house: the ugly scars from that night remained visible, testimony to what he did and how she had reacted. But just beyond that, out of emotion's reach but not beyond memory lay the day Rob planted the half barrels at Halia's. He brought over plants, soil, and equipment; he worked all day on it. They spent the evening together afterward: they cooked a meal together, shared a bottle of wine, lit a fire… I guess there were some good times, she mused. Some really good times. That's what makes it all so much worse.

Pretending it was all going to work out in the end and that he would come back a changed man helped about as much as drinking: it made her nauseous and then regretful. The distraction of the project of getting a new dog helped more. Emails zipped back and forth: from Asha to Michigan, to the shelter where Lyla patiently waited, to the Belgian Rescue volunteers who put out the call to their network looking for folks to help. First order of business: bail Lyla out of the pound. Then volunteer efforts shifted to creating a canine underground railway system to transport her all the way to Dover Plains.

Finally Asha connected with Elsa, the Belgian Shepherd Dog guardian angel. After Elsa drove hours across northern Michigan to bust Lyla out of doggie jail, the emails evolved into phone calls and took on a new urgency. Elsa had Lyla at her home, and getting Lyla to Asha was a logistical nightmare. Finally, after three days and threats of divorce from Elsa's overwhelmed husband, Elsa and Asha gave up on the BSD rescue transport chain and decided to just do the drive themselves.

Driving halfway to Michigan to pick up a dog, a completely unknown dog, seemed like an extreme thing to do, Asha realized. Pearl had basically no response at all; she was pretty inured to her mother's extreme behavior. Pearl's father, also accustomed to Asha, agreed to take Pearl for the day so that she would not be subjected to the road trip. Grace, relieved to finally hear Asha's voice after her extended absence from The Eft and her failure to return phone calls, also agreed to help with Brulee.

"You really want another dog?"

"I know it's crazy." Her voice held that tight, frenetic quality of someone who is mono-focused to the point of near desperation. "But I've wanted a black dog my whole life, and now is, in some ways, a good time to add a dog to the household. At least I'll be around to help everyone get used to each other."

This is ridiculous, Asha thought. Tired from the hours she had already logged and sobered by the number of miles still to go, Asha dipped into energy reserves created by pure eagerness to see the dog. To see her, to pet her, to experience that thrill of relief and delight; Asha prayed that the trip was worthwhile, that the goal would be met.

"Why on God's green earth would y'all get another dog now?" Lukey Jane had blurted out last week at The Eft.

It had taken a lot to get Asha to agree to even set foot in the place. After all, it was Rob's hang out spot: it was where they first met. But Grace and Halia had set Asha straight one evening when they decided enough was enough. Sick and tired of Asha's self-imposed exile from The Eft and her penchant for stewing in her own juices, they marched to her home last Friday evening and insisted she return with them to "get right back on that horse."

Lukey Jane had been there, ready to make all of them laugh, albeit unintentionally. It was her hollering about getting another dog that Asha replayed in her mind as she rolled down the highway. She couldn't explain to Lukey Jane why she wanted Lyla. She couldn't find the words to explain the need for this stupid excursion; it all paled in contrast to the purity of need she felt. It was like teenage lust. She needed a hefty dose of unconditional love – love that hits like the first bite of a homemade brownie still warm from the oven, or even better, the memory of such a treat from back in time: pre-calories, pre-zits. She craved to be obliterated by love, to have a vessel into which she could pour all her rejected love. A love that wouldn't fight back. Asha in her pained, cloudy wisdom knew that as ferociously as she loved Pearl, she couldn't dump this need on her daughter. Only a dog could heal this kind of wound. Only a dog, and only the right dog. Which is exactly what awaits me in a motel room in Falconer, NY, she hoped fervently. Lyla, the black dog from Michigan.

Melons Need a Long Hot Summer to Grow

The dingy-white bucket truck rumbled to life. Walter reviewed his first job and guided the truck onto Route 28 West, which is actually north, through the Shokan area. Makes for exciting navigation – between the mountains and the reservoirs and the dearth of roads in the preserve, nothing is intuitive. Roads head north by running east or take you west by dipping south, and half the time you can't get there from here. "Back to Flushmanns," Walter grinned to himself, using his private name for the village named after the margarine magnate. He shifted his weight, settling in and pressing his big shoulders back against the seat. He was glad he'd taken this truck on his brief out-of-town assignment last week: no need to adjust all his settings again. Mirrors, tools, even the sunglasses holder was just as Walter preferred it. Not that I'm getting all OCD about my truck, Walter thought as he pulled way over to the right to let a hot shot tourist zip past. Just organized. A place for everything and everything in its place made the day go smoothly.

Since returning from the out-of-area assignment in eastern Dutchess, though, Walter found himself wishing he could arrange his social life with the same efficiency he inflicted on the rest of his life. Lonely, bored, and fed up with the nice but uninspiring women he seemed to attract online, Walter found his thoughts wandering back all too frequently to the customer in Dover Plains with the dog. He wondered what was wrong that day and indulged in a wide variety of fantasies in which he could be helpful. He laughed at their male simplicity; they all boiled down to sex or violence. Often both. Violently destroy the offender, then seduce or be seduced by the beloved. Walter enjoyed the delicious torture of playing and replaying scenarios with ever increasing creativity. He enjoyed his long evenings home alone a whole lot less.

The truck rolled along Route 28, heading nominally west, but magnetically north, past Mount Tremper and Mount Pleasant, criss-crossing the Esopus creek, and eventually, Walter always joked, stopping of its own accord at The Dancing Bear: his favorite breakfast joint.

As a utilities worker, Walter had sampled delis and cafes up and down the Hudson Valley, from the Bronx to Saugerties and then west over to Halcott (over time, the right to pronounce it "Hawk-itt" must be earned and then brandished as a symbol of localdom). Walter had learned in his early 30's to drink coffee, and now in the later years of that decade developed a connoisseur's taste for the beverage. The Dancing Bear boasted organic, fairly-traded, shade grown, songbird certified, full city roasted, strong coffee. He was hooked.

The breakfast crowd consisted of working men like Walter, seeking to fuel up for the day ahead, hikers on their way to the many trailheads to the west and south, and a fair number of self-employed consultants who appreciated both the coffee and the free wi-fi.

"Where's Kip?" Walter ordered his egg wrap and helped himself to coffee. He directed his question regarding the café owner-chef's whereabouts to Kip's wife, Wenny, who sat at the counter helping her two year old feed herself pancakes.

"Good morning Walter," Wenny enunciated extra clearly and loudly.

"Good mawning Wa-Wa," Fiona repeated after her mother. Both giggled.

"Good morning," Walter replied. After selecting the stool next to them and savoring his first sip, the waitress returned with Walter's wrap. Fiona turned on him like a baby bird in a nest, all open mouth and huge eyes. His potatoes were not safe. He picked one up in his fingers, juggling it and blowing on it until it was cool enough to handle, and then popped it into the child's mouth.

"Kip's actually trying to take his day off," Wenny answered Walter's question. "He left to go running a little while before you got here."

He nodded, chewing. He checked his watch and checked his wandering thoughts. That woman in Dover Plains looked like she might be someone who runs. He had noticed her muscles and her springy step. Mostly her muscles. He shook his head and began fussing with another forkful of home fries for Fiona.

"You're distracted," Wenny observed. "At this rate, Fiona's going to have to eat her own breakfast this morning."

Walter reddened and waited until Wenny's attention focused on Fiona's attempt to direct a fully loaded forkful of maple-drenched blueberry pancakes into her own mouth. "I guess I do have more on my mind than usual."

"Who is she?"

"I don't know." His answer stole Wenny's attention at a critical moment, and the pancake bite landed on Fiona's bare leg. Wiping it up and smearing it around with sticky fingers became the next activity for the little girl. Wenny watched but did not interfere.

"That sounds really romantic," she told Walter.

"Or really pornographic," Kip bellowed from the front doorway, laughing and breathless.

Both Wenny and Walter turned to greet Kip, the black-haired Irishman with a talent and penchant for inappropriate remarks. He scooped up his daughter and she squealed and giggled. He leaned in for a kiss from Wenny and clapped Walter on the back. Releasing the child, he adjusted the bandanna on his head and wiped his sweaty face with the back of his hand. "I gotta go get showered up," he said. He lingered for a moment, squeezing Wenny's hand, and then let go to tousle Fiona's hair. "You kinda need a shower too." He took note of the maple syrup, butter, and squashed blueberries that decorated Fiona's hair, face, hands, and clothing. Then Kip disappeared behind the door marked Private.

"Breakfast can be a tough meal." Wenny handed Fiona a napkin, but its use seemed to smear the stains more widely and grind them in more thoroughly. Wenny and Walter shrugged. He got up to go.

"Is there someone?" Wenny asked him as she collared Fiona before the child could wreak maple-blueberry havoc on the dining room. She sat upon Wenny's skinny hip, sticky knees hugging her mother's midsection. Wenny found a damp rag and began cleaning their spot at the counter.

"Well, no," Walter answered. "Not really. I mean, not exactly. I guess maybe not yet."

"Okay," Wenny laughed. "I'll take that for a yes."

He paid for his meal and left.

It was a hot, steamy, humid July day that offered little by way of breezes and haze instead of views. Before finishing his first repair, Walter's blond crew cut was spiky with moisture, and thunderstorms were booming somewhere off in a clove to the north. He picked up his next job from dispatch and discovered that there would be overtime offered tonight up by Halcott Center. These summer thunderstorms were helpful for catching up on credit card debt; they promised overtime even after the busy season's overload dried up. Good, Walter thought. I can end my day in Halcott and go check on Charlie before I head back to Shokan.

Checking on Charlie had become part of Walter's routine a good fifteen years ago. When they first met, Charlie had been in his late sixties, spry and tough, full of backwoods fortitude and attitude. His telecommunications knowledge, however, was woefully inadequate and his do-it-yourself efforts had made a royal mess of things up at his cabin at the tip of the tail of the Vega-

Denver valley. It had taken Walter half a day just to figure out what Charlie had been trying to do.

The two had hit it off right away for no good reason. Charlie Voss was mean and tough and "stringy like an old bobcat after a bad winter," or so he claimed. But he earned Walter's respect with the western Catskills know how he'd managed to scrape from the rocks and wrest from the forest itself. He'd been managing on his own for decades, working for the town's highway department, hunting deer, turkey, and bear, and drinking shitty beer. He lost his wife, Virginia, to a blood infection when the boys were still in grade school, and both boys were gone before they saw a legal drink or got to vote in a presidential election, one to a logging accident his first year on the job, and the other to alcohol and a motorcycle.

Alone in his hunting cabin on the southwest slopes of Bearpen Mountain, Charlie chose to do without a phone for the summer months up until a few years before he met Walter. After a few missed opportunities for overtime and fishing trips, Charlie gave in and installed the mess Walter ended up fixing. Ambivalent about having a phone at the cabin from the get-go, it wasn't until last summer or so that Charlie could be counted on to answer the thing with any reliability. The typical pattern was that after days of calling and receiving no answer, Walter would disable the GPS unit on the truck and lumber up through the Vega Mountain Valley to the end of the road. He'd rumble up Charlie's long dirt driveway in the phone truck, wondering what he'd find at the cabin: mountain lions, bears and heart attacks vying for top billing. Charlie's hunting cabin squatted at the edge of one of the most remote patches of private land the area had to offer. Back in the day, that made good sense; Charlie had fed his family from the bounty of that land. Charlie had turned eighty-six last spring though, and these summers at the cabin were becoming increasingly worrisome to Walter. He hoped that perhaps this year he would be able to cajole or bully Charlie into heading back down to his village home in Halcottsville before the first snowstorm.

At 5:00 p.m. it was still hot as hell. Despite desperately needing a thunderstorm to break the hold the humidity had upon the
Catskills, there was neither threat nor promise of a good storm out
by Bearpen. Walter's truck door banged shut as he plodded up
the dirt path, feeling all of his 200 lbs in this heat. A bachelor's
hunting cabin built for temporary housing, Walter appreciated that
Charlie and his father had followed the old adage: do it once, do it
right. Though simple, the cabin was solid and sensible; the porch
faced the sunset and allowed just enough room for two chairs and
a cooler. Inside, the luxury of indoor plumbing attested to the
fact that at one time Charlie had been thinking of using the cabin
for family vacations or at least to make sure it was a comfortable
place for Virginia so that she could join him during the long, over-
lapping hunting seasons.

Charlie was not on the porch. Not a good sign, Walter thought.
To be damn near anywhere else on this property involved too
much exertion in this heat, age notwithstanding. Walter's work
boots clomped across the wooden decking, echoing in the heavy
damp air.

Walter inspected the screen door as he headed inside. It
looked like it was holding up just fine; his stealth installation four
summers ago (with old hardware to make it look as though it had
always been there) showing no signs of age or wear. Walter had
needed to fix the previous door one time too many; Charlie had
a bad habit of kicking it open when his hands were full. The
replacement had been found leaning against a dumpster in Pine
Hill, and Walter had wasted no time in making the switch. Maybe
Charlie bought Walter's feeble lie, that it really was the same door,
he just "fixed it better" this time, or maybe Charlie stopped carrying a beer in one hand and the old Winchester in the other when he
was heading out. Either way, the door held up and Charlie's pride
remained intact.

Listening hard once in the cabin, Walter heard all the expected
sounds of the neighborhood: birdsong, insects, distant generic ma-
chinery (a gravel mine? Walter wasn't sure), and then honing in

on it, he heard what he was listening for: snoring and the whir of a fan.

"Charlie?" he called toward the open bedroom door.

No response.

"Charlie!" Walter called again.

Nothing.

Walter walked slowly, heel to toe, trying to quiet the step of a large man in work boots. Three steps to the doorway of the bedroom and there Charlie lay, clad in boxers and an undershirt, an oscillating fan gently ruffling the old man's white hair every 2.7 seconds. His breathing sounded normal. Walter exhaled.

On his way out, Walter checked the apartment-sized refrigerator and found milk and beer, venison chops in the freezer, bread in the bread box, and bananas on the card table. Walter had long since given up the fresh fruit and vegetable fight and just satisfied himself that Charlie ate regularly. At least he always drank the well water up here, Walter conceded. That's probably what's kept him alive this long: Bearpen water, venison, lousy beer, worse coffee, and a failure to smoke. Satisfied that Charlie was indeed alive and adequately stocked, Walter checked to make sure that Charlie's phone was working. Dial tone was clean as a whistle. An answering machine or voicemail was just not worth the battle, Walter had decided long ago. At eighty-six, Charlie was entitled to some veto power. Maybe his recent phone answering strike was his way of expressing his frustration with the modern world. Walter shrugged. Compromise.

He peeked in on Charlie one last time before leaving. Charlie stirred slightly, then resumed his rhythmic snoring. Walter trod quietly across the porch and headed home.

The gang at The Eft was right there where Asha had left them. Or so it seemed to her when she dragged herself in that Friday night after arriving back home with Lyla. Lukey Jane sat at the bar with AnneMarie, her hair arranged in some sort of naturalistic sculpture on top of her head, ostensibly to fend off the heat. The corners of AnneMarie's lips kept twitching each time Lukey Jane looked away. All that hair piled up on her head made Asha think of a badly balanced triple scoop ice cream cone. She caught AnneMarie's eye and grinned.

Halia and Grace shared a table for two near the back wall. Asha almost gave up looking for them, figuring they had missed each other. Larry at the bar saw Asha's tense scan underway and jerked his thumb toward the back corner where her friends were camped. Halia had her back to the room, but Grace faced the crowd. She saw Asha and waved her over.

"It's hot," Asha murmured to no one in particular and fanned herself as she approached. Halia grasped a chair from a neighboring table with her right hand and pivoted it around. The borrowed chair spun and landed between Halia's and Grace's chairs as if it had been set there for Asha all along. It dropped into place as Asha arrived. "Wow," Asha muttered. "Nice timing."

Halia shrugged at Asha. "I could see you in the reflection off that print on the wall over there –"

"Don't bother trying to explain it away – I'm still going to be impressed," Asha cut Halia off. As if it were no big deal that in the dimly lit pub Halia picked up a reflection from across the room, calculated the reflection and refractory angles and the distortion inherent, corrected for them, anticipated Asha's precise momentum, including her momentary hesitation to avoid colliding with a waitress, then reached out, grabbed the chair, spun it on one leg, and made it land precisely as Asha arrived... Anyone could have done the same, right? Asha chose to be impressed with Halia. Grace just wanted to hear about the dog.

"It's uncanny," Asha gloated. "Brulee is just fine with having another dog in the house. So far it has been wonderful."

"No accidents?" Grace, the veterinarian, could be counted on to take the discussion in an earthy direction.

"Nope. No apparent distress. Both dogs sleep in my room, so they let me know if they need to go out. And I get up early anyway."

"How about with Pearl? How does she get along Lyla?" Grace had fallen completely into her clinical role.

"Fine. Pearl is great with dogs. She's been super with Brulee since day one, and I think Brulee is a more difficult dog overall." Asha paused to give her drink order to the waitress. She ran her hands through her hair, finger-combing her curls away from her face. The ring Rob had given her caught what little light there was, the stone and metal glinting briefly. "Lyla seems to be a normal dog. No major issues, no baggage. She's not trained at all, but she seems smart and sweet and absolutely velcroed to me." Her drink arrived, an alizarin smoke, and she took a sip before continuing. "She has just settled right in and we love her. She's great."

Grace seemed satisfied. The doctor in her had heard all she needed to hear. Of course both Grace and Halia had stopped by to welcome Lyla and check in with Asha, but not since last week when Asha had driven out to Falconer to pick her up. Hearing that things were fine with Lyla and Brulee freed the women up to chat about other things.

Halia was off for the summer, the blessing and curse of the life of a public school teacher. This summer she did not claim to have a major project underway, and that boded ill. Hali was at risk for becoming even more eccentric when she had the time to indulge. Grace was also enjoying her summer, juggling her husband's and her ten year old son's schedules to allow for meals and sleep squeezed in between work, camp, softball league for the adults, and summer baseball for Andrew. A mini-van mom at heart, Grace just seemed to get more energetic and happier the more she had to manage.

Asha, totally distracted by the blast of serotonin she received in the form of Lyla, forgot that she hadn't told her friends about her decision to extend her time of not working and to hike in the Catskills as a way to figure out her next move.

"I'm taking Pearl and the dogs with me tomorrow when we go to Giant Ledge," she remarked casually.

Halia perked up. "Giant Ledge? On a Saturday? Are you sure that's wise?"

"Uh, what am I missing?" Asha asked. "I thought it would be perfect. Not too far, not too steep, not too far from ice cream afterwards, great views... I thought it was gonna be a great introduction to hiking in the Catskills for Pearl." Her voice thickened with angry tears threatening to erupt. *Why does Halia have to know more than everyone about everything all the time? Why does she have to ruin my day with Pearl before it even starts?* Asha had just enough self-awareness intact to realize that although she was better than a few weeks ago, she had not yet regained an emotional resiliency necessary for social interaction. She swallowed hard, pulling herself together a little. *Fuck it,* she thought, her lips pressing themselves into an ugly thin line. *Halia's superiority complex isn't what's pissing me off.*

"Well, yeah," Halia tried to tone down her voice of authority. "That's the problem. It is short, and it is pretty, so every non-hiker and their great-aunt Sally 'hike' up Giant Ledge on a pretty Saturday afternoon in the summer. It's a friggin' highway. You might want to save that one for mid-week when it's less crowded. That way you can have the dogs off the leash without having to deal with so many strangers."

Damn. She was right. It was good advice, Asha acknowledged. It would be stressful to deal with two dogs on leashes and tons of strangers everywhere. And Lyla was an unknown, both on the leash and in the woods. She realized that she had pictured this hike in her mind as she and Pearl having the place to themselves and both dogs running free. *Shit,* Asha cursed silently as she sighed. *Oh well, better to rethink it now than when I'm sitting at the trailhead.*

"The Denning trailhead is a lot quieter," Halia was saying. "Maybe you could do Table."

"Maybe. I'll have to look at my map. How do you know so much about hiking in the Catskills?"

Halia smiled and shrugged. She doesn't mean to be annoying, Asha told herself.

"Do you have maps?" Grace asked. "Because you could borrow ours. Eddie and I have the New York-New Jersey Trail Conference set. We have other stuff too. Do you need anything? Backpacks? Hydration system? Compass? Binoculars? GPS unit?"

Asha and Halia laughed. She really is a Minivan Mom, like a thirty-something version of Barbie, complete with her "camping set," Asha thought. The laugh was affectionate, but Asha declined everything. "I think I've got what the modern girl needs to bring on a hike: Pearl has her iPod thing for the car ride, her cell phone, her camera, Luna bars, Vitamin water," Asha trailed off, Halia and Grace shaking their heads at the list of Pearl's requirements. "Whatever," Asha's smile was a little shaky. "Just as long as she comes with me…"

Halia's face flashed a brief frown and she looked away. Grace sought and held Asha's gaze for a moment and reached out, covering Asha's hand with her own. She gave her a smile and squeezed and released her hand. There was nothing to say.

"Mom," Pearl managed to give the three letters multiple syllables and an impressive diphthong whine. "How far is this place? This is taking forever." She pushed her bangs out of her eyes with her left hand, working the controls of her MP3 player with her right.

Asha rolled her eyes, exaggerating the gesture as much as possible while driving. "I don't know," she whined back. "Who put the stupid trail in the woods, so far away from, like, the main roads?"

Pearl grinned and took the bait. "Who put the stupid mountain in the middle of the stupid woods?"

"Actually, it's not a stupid mountain," Asha couldn't resist interjecting some education. "The Catskills are an eroded plateau, geologically speaking. Do you know what that means?"

"Yeah!" Pearl hollered back, getting revved up. Asha winced in anticipation of the volume at which the response would be delivered. "All the stupid dirt got washed away over a few million stupid years, leaving behind big tall stupid rocks."

"Damn straight," Asha said, and took her right hand off the wheel to offer a high five. Pearl tapped her mom's hand perfunctorily.

They continued north on Denning Road, Asha as impressed with the remoteness of the trailhead as Pearl, minus her judgment about how annoying it was. They passed the YMCA's outpost, the Straus Center, and continued on, the pavement fading away into a dirt track.

They slipped through a dark stand of evergreens and exchanged a comic "uh-oh" look. Before either one of them voiced the fear or asked the question, the road emerged in what looked suspiciously like someone's front yard. Asha slowed down, beyond dirt-road speed to where-the-hell-am-I, and then to is-this-right speed. The dogs in the back seat began to dance around, eager to get out and confront all they detected through the open windows.

"Sit down," Asha yelled at them. Both dogs ignored her, but Lyla at least had the decency to look remorseful and worried. Pearl snickered but took over the job of yelling at them so that Asha could focus on wondering if they were where they wanted to be.

To the right, open fields were bordered by woods. To the left, the mowed fields contained rock cairns and sculptures and fell away towards an enormous pagoda-roofed mansion. The road curved past some barns and other out buildings and appeared to continue past this estate. Okay, thought Asha, maybe this isn't a driveway. Undeterred, she drove on.

As they approached the barn, a man and a dog stepped out of the shadows and into the sunlit dirt road. Both Asha and Pearl instinctively examined the dog as closely as possible, and both reached the same conclusion after the initial once over. "That's a Groenendael," Asha murmured, knowing that Pearl already knew. She slowed to a crawl and hit the electric window button as she drew up alongside the pair.

"Good morning," the man said. He looked as if he could have stepped straight out of the Sundance catalog: ageless and all understated quality and country elegance from his haircut (long enough to look tousled) to his footwear (handmade Italian leather "work" boots).

"Hi!" Asha responded, feeling acutely aware of her own appearance: a pink fleece pullover recently liberated from the Salvation Army was all that guy could see of her. "Is that a Belgian Groenendael?"

"Uh-huh," the guy nodded. "This is Star." Simple. Nice.

"We have one too," Asha jerked her thumb towards the back seat, as if the rocking of the entire vehicle from the vigorous tail-wagging wasn't a dead giveaway. "That's Lyla and Brulee. Brulee's a Malinois."

"Cool."

Asha suddenly felt as if she were intruding. This road to the trailhead practically runs right through this guy's front yard, she realized. That must suck.

"Going hiking?" he asked.

"Yeah," Asha grinned with relief. She shaded her eyes, scanning in the direction the road seemed to go, and asked "The trailhead is up this way?"

"Yup. You're almost there." The guy pointed but Asha couldn't really tell what he was pointing at. Whatever, she thought; at least we're still on the right road and not trespassing on some pretty rich guy's private property.

"Thanks," Asha smiled. He returned the smile, and she put the car in gear and began to pull away.

"No problem," the guy smiled back. "Have a great hike."

As they rolled away, Pearl answered her mother's unspoken question. "No way. Absolutely not. Too old."

Asha laughed.

Table Mountain from Denning has its good points. The trail never turns into a miserable slog, its elevation being spread out over several miles. One way. Although both Asha and Pearl were in great shape overall, the hike was probably at least a mile longer than Pearl could do comfortably as a first time out. Asha knew this, having studied the map the night before, measuring her thumb joint against the scale and guesstimating along the twisty parts. After rounding up a little she gulped and decided not to tell Pearl just how many miles were on the agenda. If we have to cut it short, so be it, Asha told herself. It will still be a lovely walk in the woods and ice cream.

Although the first mile was uneventful, Asha worried about the distance, worried about Lyla becoming a good trail dog, and worried about Pearl having enough fun. She developed a face-ache from the tense expression she knitted into her brow. It took most of that first level, wide-trail mile to relax. Pearl seemed fine, the dogs seemed fine, there were no other hikers, and they were making good time without any real effort. They reached the trail intersection and headed east to cross the Deer Shanty Brook and the Neversink River before starting their ascent.

Pearl was completely charmed by the bridges; she ran ahead and riled the dogs up, throwing sticks for them off the bridge and into the river. Lyla joined right in, enjoying chasing Brulee as much as she enjoyed chasing the sticks. Asha took advantage of the brief rest to marvel at the bridge's construction. She realized that she was standing more than a mile from the nearest roadway: all of the materials and lumber had been carried to this spot by volunteers. She wondered how to become one of those volunteers, imagined the camaraderie of hard physical labor out in the forest, and imagined laughing together over a beer at the end of the day. She shook her head, waving away bugs and fantasies, reminding herself: I need a paying job back in Dutchess County, not a volunteer gig several hours' drive from my home. Nevertheless, the allure of being out here, often, with a purpose… it worked on her, and she indulged in dangerous thoughts of real estate prices and employment prospects in Ulster County.

"Stupid trees everywhere," Pearl taunted her mother, interrupting her reverie.

"Mmmm?" Asha looked at Pearl and then remembered. "Indeed. Who put the stupid trees in our stupid way?"

The top of Table Mountain is flat, like a tabletop. Pearl was singularly unimpressed, as she had envisioned a mountaintop more along the lines of the Himalayas, or at least the Rockies. The balsams were okay, but Pearl wanted snow-capped peaks. The lack of a distinct top – no specific spot, no rock outcropping, no signpost – irritated her further.

"Well, do you want to keep going?" Asha offered. "I read that Peekamoose has a distinct summit with a glacial erratic on it."

"A what?" Pearl spat the words at her mother.

"Big rock," Asha said lamely.

"Does it have any snow?" Pearl asked through clenched teeth. "Is it craggy and sharp? Does it have views?" She emphasized 'snow', 'craggy', and 'views' with such vehemence that both she and Asha started to laugh.

"None of the above as far as I know," Asha admitted. "But it's got a big rock."

"No thank you," Pearl clipped the words short. "No rocks. No trees. But I'll settle for a view," she said, looking down her nose at her mother. "If you can provide one."

Asha pulled the dirty, creased Tyvek map from her pocket and consulted it at length, her face stiff with concentration. An asterisk, the symbol indicating a view, looked to be less than a quarter mile up ahead, just off the trail to their left. Asha looked up and squinted into the woods. Then she shrugged. "Follow me," she commanded.

The dogs, antsy with human indecision, crashed into the forest with reckless abandon. Asha followed suit. Pearl hesitated, then sighed and plunged in after her mother. Five minutes of stumbling through trailless thick forest later, and Asha and Pearl arrived on the ledge.

The view was worth the price of admission – east, past the great bowl of peaks visible from the reservoir and north to the Devil's Path and beyond. Pearl gazed, lips parted, until she realized she must have looked a little slack-jawed, and grinned self-consciously. Asha also gazed to the east, the early afternoon sun lighting up Lone, Rocky, Balsam Cap, Friday, and Cornell Mountains. Slide, the tallest mountain in the Catskills, stood off to the north, close and inviting, beckoning to Asha. She looked, and consulted her map and then looked some more. Binoculars revealed Hunter's fire tower. Silently, Asha handed them over to Pearl, who looked for several minutes before handing them back. "Stupid view," she murmured to her mother.

Asha smiled.

The way back down was uneventful until somewhere in that final mile stretch when Asha and Pearl realized that Lyla was no longer with them. Both dogs had been staying close, with occasional forays off the trail to chase rabbits or chipmunks. Apparently Lyla had not returned from one of these excursions.

Asha and Pearl called and clapped their hands. Brulee wagged and jumped up on Asha, but Lyla did not appear. After several moments of straining and failing to hear her distant footfalls, Asha decided to continue on toward the parking area. They walked slowly, scanning the woods, and Asha kept shrugging her shoulders and saying something cheerful that Pearl didn't believe.

Asha's mind worked overtime on how to look for Lyla without alarming Pearl or leaving her alone. She would not be up for a quick two mile run out to the bridges and back, checking for any sign of Lyla on the trail they had already walked twice. Asha was trying hard not to worry, but they were far from home, and, Asha admitted while mentally kicking herself, Lyla wasn't wearing any identification tags. Shit. Asha indulged in cursing up a storm silently.

Be positive, she reminded herself, checking her deep frown and affixing a plastic smile to her face. She stole glances at Pearl, who wore her worry with a little more honesty. They had reached the trail register. No Lyla.

"Let's open up the car and get our packs off," Asha suggested. They headed across the grass and gravel parking area, Brulee running ahead. Asha heard the familiar growl Brulee reserved for greeting Lyla in play. Asha charged over to the car to find Lyla sitting next to the driver's door.

"What are you doing here, goofball?" Asha tousled the dog's head.

"Yay!" yelled Pearl, dropping all preteen pretense of cool. She threw her arms around the dog and hugged her hard. Then she submitted to an equally hard hug from her mother and hugged her back. They both petted Lyla for a moment without saying anything.

"Okay guys," Asha opened the car doors for herself and the dogs. "Let's go get some ice cream." As she and Pearl buckled their seat belts, she corrected herself. "That's stupid ice cream for you."

"I'll take stupid chocolate with retarded sprinkles," Pearl ordered.

Stupid fucking lost and found chocolate, Asha thought. Goddamned dog. Aloud she added, "You scared the crap out of me, Lyla."

Pearl slipped into iPod world, wrapping her long hair around her fingers and looking out the window. Asha reviewed the hike and began lusting after the next one. I guess that's how it is, she decided. As soon as you check one off, you hunger for the next one. In some ways, she admitted, having the list might be better than finishing it.

"Hey Walt," the old man's voice rumbled through the phone lines, competing with impressive bursts of static for Walter's limited hearing in his left ear. "You heading up this way any time soon?"

Walter switched the Verizon-issued Blackberry to his other ear. "Yup," he answered. He knew the drill; Charlie wouldn't ask for the favor he needed unless Walter said he'd be out that way anyway. "What's up?" When Charlie was a little younger, Walter applied gentle teasing, asking questions like "What tools should I just happen to have in the truck when I stop by this weekend?" Charlie would redden and stammer a little, but over the past couple of years as his age advanced and his health declined, his ego developed a new fragility. He no longer took kindly to the ribbing, and Walter, quick to pick up on the difference between tolerant embarrassment and true discomfort, dropped the banter.

"Need to make a doctor's appointment," Charlie growled. Doctors were one of the few reasons Charlie left the cabin on the southern slopes of Bearpen Mountain. Doctors, the rare beer out in Roxbury or Margaretville, or the even more rare shopping trip to Kingston or Delhi. Otherwise, supplies were brought in, mostly by Walter. Charlie still held a valid driver's license and his eyesight was better than Walter's hearing (at least in Walt's left ear), but he knew his limits. Other than the twice yearly pilgrimage to and from the cabin, the old Ford sat still in the driveway, just another element in the landscape, like the huge white pine that exhaled pollen every spring or the slanting rock slabs out in the field that usually housed a woodchuck family. With each passing year both Charlie and the ancient truck had increasingly grave doubts about the safety and wisdom of making the trip one more time.

"Sure, Charlie," Walter pulled the phone truck over and began rummaging around for his calendar. "Do you want me to call and make the appointment for you?"

"Yeah. I got the name and number right here."

Walter took the information from Charlie and recognized the doctor's name, a fairly well known cardiologist in Kingston. Walter made the call and was surprised to find a convenient appointment readily available. He called Charlie back and made the arrangements. "You feeling okay?" Walter let his concern show. "Is this just some sort of checkup, or is something wrong?"

"I'm old, you jackass," Charlie roared through the static, laughing, coughing, and then spitting. "That's what's wrong. I feel like shit. Same as always." Charlie relented, the bravado established. "Just keepin' an eye on the same old problems," he offered.

"Okay," Walter allowed. Without his own parents to chauffeur around, playing the role of dutiful son to Charlie would have to suffice. Walter grinned to think of his own parents and Charlie in the same sentence. Mom and Dad were too polite to actually use the label "redneck," and they certainly wouldn't ever call anyone "white trash," but they would have been sorely tempted by Charlie. My folks would be proud of my kindness to a lonely old man, but I think they wish I'd found a better educated, less "rustic" old man to help out, Walter chuckled after hanging up. Rustic is definitely a word mom would use.

Charlie's social graces had been soaked in gasoline and lit up long ago, and what remained was charred but pure. As Charlie aged, he lost whatever shards of subtlety he may have had as a younger man; his opinions and their delivery were hardened by years of not giving a damn what anyone thought. He shot deer and bear out the bedroom window of his cabin if the mood struck him, in and out of season, without regard to laws or convention. He was as likely to eat venison chops for breakfast as he was for dinner, the main difference between the two meals usually being that Charlie drank two beers at dinner. Charlie toyed with the complete abdication of his role as an adult member of society, indulging in the nihilistic hedonism of advanced age. He seemed to delight in the feral behavior he'd kept at bay for decades, narrowing his eyes at Walter as if to invite the rebuke, hungering for the opportunity to abuse Walter's patience and insult his senses.

And then there were good days when that wasn't true at all, and Walter would find every evidence that Charlie had eaten oatmeal for breakfast, washed his clothes, and even seemed to listen when Walter spoke. Walter chose to keep coming back, ready for whatever version of Charlie the day would offer. He didn't have a whole lot of other places to go.

Annie… where was she these days? Last Walter heard, she'd been passing through Colorado with a new guy. The asshole she'd been cheating on Walter with had been unceremoniously dumped soon after he had assuaged his guilt about the affair by telling Walter. Seven years was long enough to be over her, but there's some parts of getting over someone that just can't really take hold until the next relationship kicks up those vulnerabilities again. I'm as over her as I'm going to get, he told himself, driving down Route 28 on autopilot, mind wandering over familiar landscapes. I've plateaued.

Annie. She was a piece of work. Walter smiled, remembering her gorgeous red hair, her raucous laughter. She was so lively, so spontaneous, so different from me and everyone I'd ever known. Walter sighed, revisiting the summary for what seemed like the millionth time: it was a clash of cultures. He had applied Polish immigrant upbringing logic to what she approached as a post modern adventure. The end had torn him up bad.

The years of licking his wounds coincided with the deepening of his friendship with Charlie. Charlie took up available time and, despite the gruff delivery, would offer nuggets of wisdom and solace from time to time. He had known his own hard times having lost Virginia and both boys before he hit forty and long ago faced the demons the long, dark Delaware County winters threw in his path. Anticipating where his relationship with Walter was headed and knowing that he would one day have to tolerate a one-sidedness that would only increase, Charlie did what he could to pay his future debt up front, a small gift here or there and the passing on of frontier lore whenever possible. None of that mattered to Walter. He wasn't keeping score.

When Walter arrived at Charlie's cabin to pick him up for the doctor's appointment, Charlie was dressed and waiting. Walter needed to take the whole day off to work around the 11:15 a.m. appointment, but he thought lunch out in Kingston might be nice for Charlie, and he didn't have any other use in mind for his personal days.

Charlie had done a lousy job shaving, as usual. Walter made a mental note to give Charlie an electric razor at the next appropriate gifting occasion. Not that Charlie would use it, but it was worth a try. The short sleeved plaid shirt Charlie had selected was clean, and he had found the pair of khakis Walter put in his dresser drawer several months ago when he removed the threadbare pair Charlie had used as his "going out" pants for the past twenty-five years or so. Charlie looked about as presentable as ever, the effort expended in clean clothes and hacked-at facial hair couldn't conceal that Charlie's once beefy frame was now gaunt and his clothes hung on him, scarecrow-like. Walter appraised Charlie carefully and worried a little. Shedding all that weight bodes ill, especially at Charlie's age. Age hadn't erased pride, though; Walter wondered if Charlie would like to stop in at his barber's for a haircut and shave. He ran his hand over his own close cropped hair, an involuntary gesture. Guess I could stand a trim too, he decided.

"You ready?" Charlie had located his wallet and was gearing up for a tirade about being late.

"Sure," Walter answered. Not wanting to get barked at, he hid his efforts to help the old man out. "Age before beauty," he joked as he held the screen door for Charlie. Charlie threw him a look that forty-five years ago would have sent his own sons scurrying for cover and took his time making his way down the steps and across the grass to Walter's truck.

Walter squinted at Charlie's limp and rubbed his head one more time. Just how lame and slow Charlie really was, Walter didn't know. Last week, this same frail-looking old gentleman, half staggering in his bad imitation of an arthritic old geezer, managed to drag a good-sized white-tailed doe he'd illegally shot from the edge of the woods to the shed out back, a distance of at least one hundred yards. Walter let out a quiet sigh, knowing that trying to make Charlie's actions make sense was just shoveling sand against the tide. Charlie was old enough to have become a caricature of himself, hamming it up for the audience as the opportunities arose. Who knows? Walter shrugged. Good days and bad days. We all have 'em. And if I ask any questions, I'm bound to get hollered at, he reminded himself. I already got The Look. With a grin creasing his handsome face, Walter strode off after Charlie.

They drove most of the way in silence. Walter's thoughts, after making their usual rounds, sought to go over one more time just how he might meet that beautiful, sad woman with the dog. Charlie read it on his face, the distant look in his eye, and the smile he hadn't realized he was sporting.

"Who is she?" Charlie demanded.

"This is a disaster," Grace said cheerfully, retrieving a green-inked gel pen from deep in her ponytail. "This is so negative! She has to be positive, about herself, about her hopes and dreams, and about who she's hoping to meet."

Asha had stopped in at the animal hospital to pick up heart-worm pills for the dogs and drop off a hard copy of her Match.com profile for Grace to edit. "I'll meet you and Halia at The Eft later this evening. Just go ahead and edit it for me. I want it to put out the right vibe, y'know?" Grace was delighted to take on the role of energetic consultant for Asha's dating profile and took the job seriously.

Grace began crossing off sentences on the print out. Halia read Asha's profile upside down, from across the table.

"Maybe she wants it to be negative, to scare off anyone who just thinks she's cute," Halia suggested.

"Maybe." Grace didn't look up. The pen hovered above the page for a moment. Grace reread a phrase, frowned decisively, and the pen struck. Another adjective bites the dust. "I'll need to see the photos she decides to put on here. She is really pretty," Grace mused, sounding concerned. "You're right, we'll have to choose the pictures carefully."

Halia nodded and looked away. The conversation was making her feel queasy, like cheap fried food.

Grace sized Halia up, and for once it was Grace who read her friend's thoughts from the look on her face. "Hali, she doesn't want to be alone."

Halia swallowed and looked at the ice cubes melting in her glass.

When Asha arrived, Grace was telling Halia about her most recent astrology reading. Asha looked okay, the heroin chic look she'd been sporting of late giving way to a more chronic-illness-in-remission look, complete with a highly suspect level of cheerfulness. She limped slightly as she made her way to the table and greeted her friends with hugs and kisses. She collapsed onto the free chair and ordered a seltzer with lime to drink.

"Did you have a chance to look at my profile?" She asked Grace as she reached for the empty fourth chair at their table. She pulled the chair closer and placed her right foot upon the seat.

"Jesus Christ!" Grace exclaimed. The bruising and swelling on Asha's ankle reached religious proportions. "When did you do that?"

Halia looked over at Asha's ankle. Her eyes swept over Asha and her belongings before she got up and headed for the bar. Grace and Asha watched her go without asking.

"Yesterday." Asha fussed with the position of the chair for a minute, then continued, offering answers to the rest of the inevitable questions. "I was running on the Appalachian Trail out by the Housatonic. I turned my ankle on a tree root."

Grace made little grunts of sympathy as she examined Asha's ankle. "Did you go to the ER?"

"No. After a couple of minutes I could stand on it, and then I could walk and even run on it a little."

Grace geared up for a massive tirade about responsibility and self care, but Asha cut her off. "I had to get back to the car. I iced it as soon as I got home."

On cue, Halia returned with ice in a ziploc bag wrapped in a napkin. "Have you been doing twenty minutes on once every hour?"

"When I remember," Asha grinned.

Halia arranged the ice pack on Asha's ankle, using the napkin to protect her skin. She glanced at her ugly black thrift-shop watch, and sat down.

"Thanks," Asha swirled her lime around in her glass. "It's okay. It doesn't hurt that much, and it'll heal. No big deal." She looked from Halia to Grace and back again. "Are you guys okay? You look all serious."

"We're fine," Grace said, realizing that she and Halia had visibly tensed upon seeing Asha's elephantine ankle. She leaned back and crossed her legs, physically breaking the tension in the air. Halia moved her chair a little to face both Asha and Grace better. Grace's smile was tired but genuine, and Asha felt herself relax as well. The "let's worry about Asha's ankle" moment had passed.

Asha reached for the sheet of green-inked paper on the table, raising her eyebrows at the number of cross-outs. She scanned it. "That bad, huh?"

"Yeah." Grace paused, and then shrugged. "It has to be positive, the whole thing. If you present yourself in anything other than a positive light, who knows what kind of creeps and weirdos will take notice."

Asha didn't respond right away, her brow knitted as she leaned over the sheet of paper. She had picked up Grace's pen and was twirling it between her fingers. "So you think this line about enjoying old black and white tearjerkers while eating stale popcorn is negative? I though it was kind of clever and funny. The kind of guy who gets what I mean is the kind of guy I want to attract."

"Nice idea," Grace was diplomatic. "But I don't think it works. It makes you sound depressed and depressing to be around."

Asha cocked her head and looked at Halia, hoping to mount an argument. Halia shrugged.

"And this line about spending a lot of time alone and quiet," Grace pointed to the paper, indicating a sentence with a neat green line through every word. "It might as well read 'Favorite pastime: brooding' to a fun-loving guy."

"I guess I was trying too hard to be honest," Asha agreed.

Halia spoke up. "If honest sounds like your hobbies are staring at the phone and sighing, and your favorite pastimes are unfolding paperclips and alphabetizing your spice rack," both Grace and Asha began to snicker at Halia's exaggerations, "maybe the whole endeavor is a little premature."

"I'm getting it," Asha grinned mischievously. "Reading between the lines, this profile actually sounds more like 'Self destructive OCD bitch seeks abusive asshole for self-fulfilling prophecy.'" She was laughing but her eyes began to fill.

"Easy, there," Grace instinctively patted Asha's arm. Halia checked her watch and removed Asha's icepack. "Create a profile that doesn't focus on who you are or how you feel now. Create one that manifests where you want to go. What kind of relationship do you want to be in? Who do you want to be? How do you want other people to see you? What are the qualities you've relied upon so far to get you through?"

"Sheesh, you sound like a social worker." Asha continued to teeter on the verge of tears, teasing Grace in the hopes she could get a laugh and change the subject.

"Or you could just wait until how you feel and how you want to feel are a little more in sync," Halia offered quietly. Grace shot her a look, which Halia ignored.

"I know I'm not ready to get involved with anyone," Asha admitted. "But I've spent a month moping around, doing nothing, licking my wounds, playing out the whole stupid cliché, pints of Ben and Jerry's and all. I'm sick of myself and fed up with being a lousy mom to Pearl. It's just that I'm still so angry," Asha covered her eyes for a moment with the heels of her hands, wiping away the tears she squeezed through pinched shut lids. "I want to feel happy again. And for now, I'm willing to take the fake happiness of just being distracted. The whole online dating thing could be a real distraction. I'm ready to re-make my self on paper.

Enough of this sitting at home, leaning on Pearl for support, nursing all this misery. I'm done with that. It's time to get moving."

Halia checked her watch again. Not quite time for the next ice pack.

"Y'know, Walt," Charlie was in a talkative mood after lunch, a full stomach and a beer loosening his tongue. Walter knew whatever it was that Charlie had to say, he'd say it quick, get it over with, and then sleep the rest of the way home, once again the beer and the full stomach to blame. "I ain't gonna be around forever."

"That what the doctor told you?" Walter joked.

The corners of Charlie's mouth turned down. "I ain't in the mood, Walt. I got some stiff thinkin' to do."

"About what?"

"About my place. The house. The cabin, stuff like that. There ain't no one to leave it to."

Walter was silent.

"You don't need it," he said, his voice rough. Walter tried to catch his eye. Charlie brushed away some imaginary crumbs from his shirt front, his hands busy while his eyes looked straight ahead. "You got a place to live. A decent place. You did good for yourself. I want to give the cabin an' all the land up on Bearpen to someone who needs it. Someone who's struggling."

Walter kept his eyes on the road, hands on the wheel. Uptown Kingston with its narrow one-way streets and busy lunchtime traffic would have required it anyway. Charlie looked out the window.

"Or maybe the state would want the land. Make it part of the park or something." Charlie continued, thinking aloud, his customary growl conversational in volume at least. "It ain't no good to me once I'm gone, but someone should get some use out of it." He rubbed his barber-smoothed chin and thought about taking care of loose ends. "Someone should benefit from it."

"I never heard you talk like this before," Walter observed. "Did the doctor tell you something that's got you worried?"

"Naah. I'm in great shape," Charlie hollered at Walter. He laughed angrily, a barking laugh that turned into a cough. He waved away the concern on Walter's face and explained, "When you get to my age, it's just time to make sure yer papers are in order. I bin ignoring it fer years, but I guess I'm finally ready to take this on. What the hell do old coots like me do when they ain't got family? How do I take care of this?" The last question was clearly directed at Walter with the expectation that, like a doctor's appointment or a leaky faucet, Walter would just fix it up nice and neat.

"I guess you'd talk to a lawyer. You could put some kind of conservation easement on your land to protect it, maybe set up some sort of trust to deal with your assets..." Walter realized he didn't know much about this topic at all, but shrugged, knowing that he was about to find out.

"Make me an appointment with a lawyer," Charlie ordered. The altruistic uncertainty that had been so unfamiliar to Walter was gone, and Charlie was firmly back in character. On the long drive back Walter wondered about Charlie's intentions for the cabin and the house in Halcottsville.

As Walter had predicted, snoring commenced shortly before they reached Shokan, and he didn't even begin to blink blearily until they hit the tiny dirt road at the north end of the Denver-Vega valley.

"Virginia wanted it, y'know." Charlie was picking up the conversation where he left off, oblivious to the intervening hour or so nap.

"Oh?"

"She wanted to do good for other people. She cared about folks that needed and didn't have." The truck rolled to a stop outside the cabin. Charlie didn't move to get out, but instead turned to Walter and grabbed his arm hard. Hard enough to make Walter draw back and tense up. "Sometimes I think she knew they'd all leave me alone. Like she had the sight, y'know? She died when the boys were little, but I think she knew I'd end up like this – all alone without them. She told me what she wanted for the house and the land as like a dying wish, y'know? I gotta honor that. Else what kind of man am I?"

Charlie released his grip on Walter's arm. He turned his back to Walter and struggled with opening the heavy truck door. Walter thought about Virginia and Charlie as a young couple back in the 1940's or '50's. Virginia has been gone at least fifty years, Walter calculated. That, he thought, is a very long time to carry around someone's dying wish.

They entered the cabin, Walter carrying his canvas shopping bag with a few staples, picked up while they were out. Beer, bananas, sardines, and in a fit of goodwill toward the doctor, Charlie had allowed Walter to buy apples. Warm from the sun at the farmstand, picked within a day or so, they perfumed the small cabin with the scent of autumn.

Walter went for a knife to cut up an apple, and the kitchen drawer's old knob dove enthusiastically into his hand, the screw stripped from decades of lousy repairs. Walter sighed softly, not really irritated. He squatted down, peered at his culprits, and pried the drawer open. After a snack of cheddar cheese and apple slices, he'd head out to the truck for his tools.

Asha limped with Brulee and Lyla through the Valley View Cemetery, stopping every twenty yards or so to rest her throbbing ankle. She had a thin-lipped smile to offer at the blackly comic thought of her dogs killing squirrels or rabbits right here in the cemetery and kept her eyes peeled for visitors that might take offense at the dogs' joyful exuberance. She failed to notice a small divot and twisted her bad ankle again. Not enough to do more damage; just enough to bring tears to her eyes and transform the marginal smile into a grimace.

Last night's first online dating experience hadn't gone so badly. He was a perfect gentleman, despite having lied about his physique: "athletic and toned" really precluded a beer gut in Asha's opinion. He was nice, he was kind of cute, and he had a tolerant mutt that Brulee and Lyla thoroughly terrified. Asha made her slow way along the aisles of gravestones, replaying the date in her mind, analyzing, searching, explaining to herself why she wasn't ever going to see him again. She threw a stick for the dogs and watched them race for it, their muscles rippling. All business. Brulee got there first and snatched the stick at a dead run, Lyla only a half step behind. Asha watched, leaning on a gravestone, emptied out and wrecked.

The email had been there, waiting for her when she had gotten home last night. Perfect. As if her efforts to move on somehow traveled through the ether and reached his cheating bastard consciousness just in time to cast another line. Another apology, an invitation to call. Carefully worded baited hooks. Asha's heart had stopped slamming away after a few minutes, and she composed a response that shut the door as firmly as she could.

It is a cliché to say that the truth shall set me free, but it fits. I know that you lied to yourself and all those around you about who you were to me and what we were. I know that you spun a web of lies around my actions so that you could justify lying and cheating. I do not forgive you. I was open; I was vulnerable. I trusted you. I trusted us. You betrayed that trust. I am angry now, but one day that anger will fade and in its place will be a small dead place in my heart. A scar. A black mark on my soul. For me, these final words of truth have meaning and substance. They are ugly; they are honest. These are the words that define our connection. These are the words that complete our story.

That tight, why-am-I-not-surprised smile accompanied the tears – both last night as she wrote and sent the response as fast as she could, and now, in the graveyard.

Asha replaced the cordless phone in its base on the kitchen column. It is handy there, Asha thought, and appreciated that phone guy's efforts to tidy up and unclutter her kitchen. The top of the telephone table looks nice now. And the phone seems to work reliably. Asha shook her head with a smirk; could she really credit Grace's feng shui cure?

A job interview, the first one to pop up in weeks, and Asha's gut reaction was to recoil as if it were poisonous. Yes, the phone call had interrupted a much more pleasant project: poring over maps of the Catskills, lusting after peaks and considering just how many she could bag in one day from a single trailhead. She was lost somewhere in the Neversink basin, measuring miles with her thumb and fantasizing about the smell of balsams when the phone rang.

The call came from a scheduling secretary at the Bedford Hills prison, a maximum security women's facility about one hour away by car. The commute would be long, the work deeply traumatizing, the schedule difficult, but the pay was good. Better than good: the salary was comparable to what she made at school. And it was the first nibble she'd had in weeks.

And yet, pushing her maps away and opening up her calendar to schedule the interview, she felt revulsion, the way that bad meat makes you involuntarily pull your head away when you smell it.

"Quit being such a baby," she told herself, pushing the calendar out of the way after hanging up the phone. "An interview is like a first date. I get to say "No" too. I get to choose whether I even want a second date."

That helped her push the whole subject out of her mind and return to the map reading. The peaks around the Neversink seemed a little intimidating: no trails, miles away from places to leave the car, deep wilderness far from roads. Even with two dogs, Asha quailed at the thought of managing the navigating and staying safe. She had read about Friday's cliffs claiming the lives of experienced hikers. She chewed the inside of her cheek and folded up the map, reaching for another one from the Ziploc packet. She selected the map that included Hunter Mountain and the rest of the Devil's Path and spread it out on the kitchen table. The Becker Hollow trail doesn't look all that long, Asha decided. And Southwest Hunter is right next door. Asha reached across the table for her guide book to look up the bushwhack information. She stopped chewing her cheeks as she read the route description.

The answering machine message light blinked its "3", indicating that things had been busy while Asha was out running.

"Pearl?" Asha yelled up the stairs, gearing up for a tirade.

"I let the answering machine pick up because I was doing my nails," the preteen yelled back down the stairs. "Dad wants you to call him back, Grace wants to know if you have plans for this Friday night, and 'Romantic Dover Dude' wants a date."

"What?!" Asha's heart rate surged back up to its mid-Benson Hill sprint level. How could her phone number have become available? She stood at the bottom of the staircase clutching the banister, sweat springing from her hair follicles. Shifting gears from preparing a parenting lecture at top volume, she entered a full blown privacy-emergency-freak-out. Head upstairs for the computer or around the corner for the phone? She hesitated long enough to see Pearl's head pop out from her closed bedroom door and call down the stairs, "Just kidding. It was Grandma, just checking in."

Laughing and furious, Asha strode into the kitchen and listened to the messages herself. I'll deal with her later, she promised, considering just how best to exact revenge upon the thirteen year old.

Carl's message was unlike him. He generally didn't call, preferring to handle any business they had in person at drop off and pick up. Carl was, or at least used to be, a phone avoider. He was probably the one who suggested to Pearl that she let the machine answer the phone. The telephone answering machine was Carl's favorite invention.

"Hello?" Carl has a nice voice, Asha admitted to herself.

"Hi, it's Asha," she said, her words sounding shiny, metallic – hard and bright. Something about his tone on the answering machine made her nervous.

"Hi Asha," he answered. He always sounded in control. Why didn't he ever sound excited or nervous?

"Is now an okay time to talk?" Be polite, Asha coached herself.

"Sure." Carl didn't continue.

Asha waited. Okay, you were the one to call here and leave a message asking for a call back. What's with the one-word answers? Cleansing these thoughts and their emotional counterparts from her voice, Asha gave in and reminded Carl: "You left me a message? You asked that I give you a call?"

"Oh yeah," Carl answered.

Okay, Asha relaxed. He's going to stop making me drag it out of him. Good. "Pearl told me that you have a job interview coming up."

"That's right."

"She told me that it's at the prison."

"Yeah." Asha wondered where this was headed.

"Don't go. Well, I guess you can go if you want, but don't take the job. I mean, do whatever you think is right, but I don't think you should even consider this job." Carl spoke quickly, the words tumbling out. "Do you really think you can handle it? Don't you realize what it'll be like? What you'll hear? Who you'll be alone in a room with?" Carl drew a quick breath. "It won't be good for you and it won't be good for Pearl. Besides, is this really the direction you want your career to go? Wouldn't a school job be better?"

"Yes." Asha's struggled to speak through clenched teeth. "Yes, a school job would be better, but there aren't any. A clinic job might be better too, except that the hours suck and the pay is worse." Breathe, Asha told herself. Don't fight with Carl. It's not his fault. None of this is his fault, even if sometimes he is a cold, controlling bastard. "Yes, I've applied to every sensible and plausible option in six counties," Asha counted on her fingers after blurting that out, ready to defend what sounded like hyperbole. "This is the first bite I've gotten since the end of the school year. I was thinking I'd be irresponsible not to at least interview."

"Don't."

"Don't?"

"Don't interview. You don't want this job." Carl took a sip of something; Asha heard him swallow. "I mean, do whatever you want, but my opinion is don't do this. Don't interview. Don't waste their time and yours. Don't even think about spending forty hours a week in a maximum security prison. That won't be good for you or Pearl."

"And when I'm facing foreclosure?" This time it was hyperbole.

"You won't. You'll find something. Something else will come up." Carl stopped talking and let out a long breath. "Look that's what I think. I just felt like I owed it to Pearl to at least say what I thought. You'll do what you want…"

What the hell do I say to that? Asha's desire to end the conversation guided her toward placating. "Uh, okay. I'll think about what you said. I have some time to think about it."

"Okay. Just think about it, okay?" Now Carl sounded like he was talking to Pearl. Sometimes he was really annoying, even when he was trying to be considerate.

"Okay, Carl. I will. Have a good night." Asha used the universal conversation ender, and it worked. Asha hung up and sat there in her kitchen, sweat drying on her arms and legs, cotton t-shirt cold and clammy against her belly and back. She got to her feet, muscles stiffening from the post-run chill and lack of motion. She replaced the phone in its cradle and began her stretching routine, her thoughts returning to the happier landscape of devising sweet revenge upon Pearl.

"I'm ready."

Walter had barely creaked the top porch step when he heard Charlie's gravelly voice from inside. He's in righteous form, Walter inwardly groaned. I hope I've appropriately prepped the Margaretville lawyer for this encounter. Walter called a greeting through the screen door and entered the cabin. Sometimes Charlie's notion of "ready" needed a few adjustments.

"'Afternoon, Charlie," Walter said warmly.

"'Afternoon, Walt." Charlie's pale blue eyes roamed over Walter's appearance, apparently sizing him up for something.

"How ya feeling today?" Walter checked his watch – they had fully fifteen minutes to spare. He launched into his quick once over: check the fridge, check the infrastructure, make the mental list of items to grab while they're out.

Charlie's answer came in the form of a throat clearing growl. He strode out the screen door and spat. "I'm fine," he bellowed through the screen. "Feel like shit. Like an old man should." Relenting, he re-entered the cabin and went looking for Walter, who was checking on his supply of toilet paper and soap. "Think we could stop for a beer after this damn appointment?" Charlie was actually making a request. "You ain't got a date or anything?" This was an impressive display, recognizing that it was indeed a late afternoon appointment on a Friday and realizing what that might mean to a young unmarried man like Walter.

Walter's dates were few and far between, but there had been occasional Friday nights when Walter had been unavailable to Charlie. Charlie's response had always been the same. He'd narrow his eyes and measure Walter up and then deliver the same speech: "Choose carefully son. A good woman's worth her weight in gold. You pick the one that's right for you, and then you treat her like gold 'cause that's what a good woman is." Then his face would darken and he'd warn, "Don't settle. Settlin' on the wrong one will make you a miserable son-of-a-bitch." And,

Charlie added silently, then you won't be welcome around here anymore.

"No, Charlie, I don't have a date tonight. A beer on the way home sounds fine." Walter's date dials all spun to point to Asha Jackson, the customer with the dog back in Dutchess County. He wanted her badly enough to have developed a superstitious belief that he couldn't think of her by name. Like it was a jinx. For now, he was seriously stuck on Her, and that put a crimp in the ol' dating habits.

"Yer still sweet on that one you told me about last week?" Charlie looked pleased. "That's good, Walt. That means something." Charlie glanced at his watch. "You about done poking around my bathroom? Can we go now?"

Soon Charlie's rhythmic snores offered counterpoint to the hum of road noise. A 4:00 p.m. appointment had meant that Walter was able to put in a half day and not burn a whole vacation day on the project. It also meant that the drive coincided with Charlie's afternoon nap. Walter had been freshly prodded to think about Her and the comfortable solitude of the drive was a fine opportunity.

How to meet her without doing anything unethical, illegal, or against company policy provided the constraints. There was an upscale-looking bar down the street from her house. He could go there and hang out and hope she walked in. She was clearly a runner; he could see that from her physique. He could take up running and start running the local roads in her neighborhood. He could ask for another out-of-area assignment in Dover and do a follow-up check on her line to make sure it was still clear. All the way to Margaretville Walter continued to generate scenarios and then shoot them full of holes. He was honest enough with himself to admit that all he really wanted was to ride into Dover Plains on a white horse (his white Toyota pick up truck would have to suffice), kill whatever was making her sad, preferably in front of her and with his bare hands, and then profess his undying devotion to her. The whole meeting, dating, courting, modern way of doing things just felt cumbersome to Walter. He wanted to get to the point.

The lawyer received a slightly less ornery post-nap version of Charlie. Walter ducked away from the young man's invitation to join them, feeling strongly that the business Charlie needed to conduct was private. The waiting room at Haynes, Rusk, and Halcott, LLP offered a spotty collection of outdated magazines but mercifully, a slick stack of Catskill Mountain Guides sat near the door. Walter learned about the notion of terroir as it applied to maple syrup production in the Spruceton Valley until the hour and the warmth of the sun through the window caught up with him and he found his mind drifting back along now familiar tracks. Does she like maple syrup? What would he make her for breakfast? Did he own a proper breakfast-in-bed tray? How about a bud vase? Walter rummaged around in his memory for the location of the equipment he'd need once he was at the dating stage with her. These thoughts rapidly deteriorated into imagining pre- and post-breakfast activities. Walter dozed off with a smile on his face.

He awoke with the slightly sour taste of nap in the back of his throat and Charlie standing in front of him.

"Gotta ask ya somethin'." Charlie broke into Walter's sleepy twilight state with his abrasive growl.

Walter blinked and rubbed his hand over his head and face, rubbing his brain into alertness. "What's up?"

"You want anything? After I'm gone, y'know? Anything special of mine you gotcher eye on?"

Walter swallowed. The nap taste was tinged with a metallic saltiness at the thoughts the question raised. Walter hadn't ever really thought about Charlie's stuff leaving Charlie's control. Someone else using Charlie's truck or his hunting knife just felt wrong to Walter. He saw his role in Charlie's life for the past fifteen or so years as all about making sure that Charlie remained in control of all his stuff. Now that he was being invited to take something, he felt his stomach flip-flop at the thought. It all belonged with Charlie.

He swallowed again and looked forward to that beer to wash this taste out of his mouth. He studied his feet for a moment, then looked up and met Charlie's eyes. "I don't know, Charlie. Is there anything you'd like me to have?"

"Ayup." Charlie's voice was a little softer, almost as if he didn't want the lawyer, standing a respectful distance away, to hear. "I want you to have my hunting rifle. The Winchester. My pa bought it back when he first built the cabin. It put food on the table for us kids and then for Virginia an' the boys and me. Damn thing'll last forever. About time you took up hunting. You won't have me to shoot deer for ya forever."

Walter smiled, felt his eyes well up, and coughed hard to cover it. Charlie seemed to have breathed in the same specks of dust, as he coughed the moment away too. He stuck out his hand and Walter stood up, seizing it. They pumped each other's hands for a moment, then pummeled each other's backs with their free hand in a classic "I-ain't-gay" men's hug. Charlie turned to the lawyer. "I'll come back after you write it all up and sign everything. Make sure you put in the part about the gun goin' to Walt here. It's a Winchester 30-30 lever action. Got that?" The man nodded. "Good." Turning to Walter, Charlie apologized. "I'm still using it, Walt. I'm still gonna need it, or I'd give it to ya today."

Walter's eyes seemed glued to the buttons on Charlie's flannel shirt. He wasn't sure if he was going to succumb to the seriousness of the moment and need to clear his throat some more or if the jog to his memory about Charlie's use of the gun would break the mood and set them both laughing. This was the gun Charlie had taken to bed with him the year he caught a nasty cold in the middle of hunting season. Walter walked in one morning to find Charlie picking slugs out of the window sash and wall because he'd missed the window, aiming for deer in the meadow outside. Walter had demanded then and there that Charlie promise never to hunt from his bed again, and Charlie had laughed so hard he damn near needed to go to the emergency room.

Walter lifted his eyes to search Charlie's face. Eighty-six years worth of life and death met his gaze. "Let's go get a beer, Walt." And Charlie patted Walter's shoulder once more.

Up early and out the door on time, Asha shrugged off the anticipation of a long drive. Her mind was occupied by what would soon be demanded of her, so mentally rehearsing responses to challenges helped the time pass quickly. Having scheduled this event for a day when Pearl was with Carl meant that Asha didn't need to figure out a safe and entertaining place for her to spend the day, but it did mean that she wanted to be sure that she had her cell phone with her to call her daughter if and when she was triumphant.

Carl's admonition that she reconsider the only job interview she'd been offered in weeks had echoed in Asha's conscious (and probably in her unconscious) mind for days. Asha went through several developmental stages: 1) questioning Carl's motives; 2) indignant self-promotion, as in "I'll take the job just to prove I can handle it"; and finally 3) miserable negative self-projection, as in "I can't handle this job and I won't get any other offers." Finally after bouncing around, mentally reacting to Carl and to her own fears and anger, she settled down to think rationally. Looking at the financial situation, Asha figured she had about another month left of earning no income at all. Pearl would be back at school in two weeks, so Asha thought about maybe getting a part-time job during school hours and postponing the whole career-next-move decision a while longer.

Her time was spent each morning at the computer, scrolling through want ads; her coffee growing tepid as her wrist grew numb. A disturbing pattern revealed itself: the social work jobs just didn't seem to grab her. She found herself yawning and clicking "next" over and over again while she daydreamed about being a forest ranger or a librarian. Most of the social work jobs she read descriptions of sounded like nightmares: low pay, high case-loads, no support. Just not appealing.

But it was deeper than that. Something about losing her position at the elementary school after seven years... after all the glowing performance evaluations, all the effort to create a real place for herself in the school, all the cheerleading she'd done for the kids and for her profession... Asha just felt kind of deflated about the whole thing. Emptied out. Done. She clicked away, chin in one hand, eyes tearing from skimming the entries too fast. She wanted a reprieve from being responsible, a respite from the heaviness of her profession. Morning after morning, she tried to find something online to get excited about, but seemed to keep coming back to the same thing, admitting to herself that all she really wanted to do was go hiking.

The job search process found its soul mate in her online dating experience. Mornings were want ads; evenings, after Pearl went to bed, were Match.com profiles. Asha watched thumbnail after thumbnail slide across her screen. No one caught her eye. No one even made her slow down. After only a couple of weeks, Asha threw in the towel. No more searching. She left her profile up, as much out of lethargy as hope, and let it go at that. If only I could just chuck job searching too, she mumbled at the screen, clicking the "x" to bail out of Match.com for the last time.

And then this opportunity came along and Carl was telling her not to take it. The idea, when Asha first rolled it around in her mind, gave rise to alternating waves of panic and relief (and a healthy dollop of irritation at Carl for spitting in her first sip of success at job hunting). The internal argument lasted a couple of days, the sensible "just go practice interviewing" versus the "don't waste anyone's time, if you're sure you don't want the job, don't go." But, Asha whined to herself, how do I know I definitely don't want the job if I don't go on the interview and check it out?

Asha teetered back and forth until she finally teetered farther to the relief side, and fell. It was a soft landing on the idea of hiking instead of interviewing on the same day. A message to the universe: this is where I want to be. This is what I want to be doing. Hiking was the affirmation she offered up in the face of prison. She hoped the universe was listening.

The idea gleaned from the hiking book was to hike up the Becker Hollow trail to the summit of Hunter Mountain (yeah, Asha laughed off the idea of taking the chair lift and hiking over to the true summit at the fire tower as cheating), then head over to Southwest Hunter to bag her first bushwhack peak. Looked pretty straightforward. Armed with maps, extra water, and Clif bars, Asha set out.

All this driving to the Catskills, Asha realized, was going to cost more than she typically budgeted for fuel. I'll just have to hike more efficiently, she told herself. More peaks per outing. She did the math in her mind as she drove headed steadily north and west across Ulster County and into Greene. Number of daylight hours, driving times, number of miles, elevation changes. Sheesh, Asha giggled to herself, this is one way to take all the fun out of this project.

The parking area held a few cars, all Subaru Foresters. Asha shrugged. A diesel Jetta and her ancient Ford F150 made up her fleet. The diesel was for human transportation, the truck for everything else. The dogs burst from the car as if Asha had hit an eject button; Asha emerged more slowly, the two hour drive stiffening up her muscles more than usual. She stretched and got organized: daypack swung into place, map into the accessible front pocket, keys clipped to the fob inside the pack, and a quick emptying of her bladder in the bushes. All blessedly un-witnessed. The Subaru crowd apparently gets an early start.

Heading up the trail, Asha had a moment of omniscient self-awareness. Pink daypack, matching pink socks (so lucky to find pink Smartwool hiking socks at the Salvation Army!!!), two insane dogs racing around, hiking all alone... I am such a dingbat, Asha decided. What the fuck. I should be interviewing for a social work job right now, not pretending to be Hiker Barbie. She shook her head and trudged onward, self conscious and uncomfortable. Whatever, she snarled at the defeatist attitude. I'm doing this. I'm seeing it through.

Asha let her mind drift away into more familiar territory: worrying. Once she was finished chiding herself for choosing to hike instead of interview, she moved on to worrying about what to do for dinner tonight after the hike, whether or not she was carrying enough water for the dogs, whether or not the dogs would bark at other hikers, how hard it would be to find the canister on top of Southwest Hunter, and if there were rattlesnakes on top of Hunter. She started worrying about whether or not she would pick up Pearl on time and then realized she was a day ahead of herself – that was on the list to worry about tomorrow.

Lyla slipped away first, lured by the gurgling of the stream. Brulee followed, and Asha called them back before realizing that there was a waterfall, just a small cascade, only a few yards off the trail. Asha followed the dogs through the woods, over to the stream and stood on the remnants of a small concrete dam, watching the dogs swim.

After a moment, they moved on, the dogs shaking on Asha so that she was freckled with wet spots and mud. Asha felt quieted. The proverbial splash of cold water in the face (well, in this case on bare legs) helped shut off the noise. And in the relative silence, Asha heard the next truth: she missed Rob. She knew that the silliness of the pink socks would have been a delightful private joke, something they would have giggled over when they reminisced about the day they hiked Hunter. She knew Rob would have wanted to make love by the waterfall, and afterward she would have hiked on rubbery legs with mosquito bites in awkward places. Asha smiled a bittersweet smile as she continued on the trail, feeling all that, knowing its truth, and yet knowing that all she believed she had lost was a lie.

Hiking took over. Her thoughts ceased to come in words. Just ache. The trail got steeper and the footing over loose rock required attention. Asha and the dogs settled into work mode, trudging up, minds empty, breathing hard. Finally, after what felt like a mile of climbing a steep staircase Asha took a break. She turned her back to the summit and looked east, the trees too thick to allow for a view. The dogs stopped too, shoving their heads under her palms for a pat. "Good girls," Asha panted. "Good dogs."

Asha pulled the map out of her pocket and checked distances. This trail doesn't look all that long, she thought. I figure we should be coming up on a junction soon. This Becker Hollow trail ends and I pick up the Devil's Path. No, Asha corrected herself, I pick up the dinky little yellow trail to the summit, then grab the Devil's Path to head over to Southwest Hunter. A loop, Asha grinned. She liked loops. She turned back uphill and surged on, eager and impatient.

Asha liked this part: the huffing and puffing, the work, the pushing hard and feeling the effort. The part that most people hate. She lost herself in the sweat and slamming of her heart, rhythmic footfalls, rhythmic breath, and no room for anything else. It was pure work, and even the dogs had slowed down. She covered ground.

And then the yellow-blazed trail to the top was there. The sign at the junction indicated .35 miles to go. She kicked it into high gear, her energy reserves replenished by excitement. The balsams smelled so fresh and the trail narrowed, becoming delightfully rocky and "interesting" (i.e. dangerous). Each scramble over boulders promised the she was almost there.

Popping out into the meadow-like summit was almost anticlimactic. She was just there. Like Balsam Lake Mountain, there was a cabin at the top, but this one was all locked up. Some hikers were up in the fire tower's cabin, and more sat at the picnic table down below. Asha had her hands full keeping both dogs close, getting herself out a Clif bar, and changing out of her sweat-soaked t-shirt. Used to this routine from running, she anticipated the need to change into dry clothes at the top or freeze. She threw a dry thermal long-sleeve on, her nylon anorak on top, and waited for the folks up on the tower to come down before she made her way up, both dogs in tow.

It was an excellent view day, clear and remarkably not hazy for August. She shivered, the wind undoing all the good the sun tried to do. Despite the summer's heat the only part of her body that felt warm was her hair. She didn't last up top too long.

A little water, an apple, and that was enough staying still. She set off for Southwest Hunter. The guide book gave pretty clear instructions: head for the red-blazed Devil's Path, hang a left, follow the old railbed, and up the drainage to the canister. Sounded easy enough. She headed south and then west at a good pace, excited by the treasure hunt at hand.

A small cairn marked the turn off from the trail. "Thanks," Asha muttered, offering up her little prayer of thanksgiving to the cairn gods. Following the old rail bed posed no real challenges although she did a fair bit of ducking and dodging around branches. "So this is why they call it bushwhacking," she acknowledged out loud after a few minutes of pushing through some thick stuff. "Ow," she complained, her bare legs cross-hatched with scratches. Consulting the book frequently, she found her left turn and plunged into the dry ditch. The dogs were in their element, crashing through the woods, chasing squirrels and chipmunks. She was alive, aware of everything, alert for anything. Every sense fully absorbed, her mind taking in, processing, and planning. This was it. Asha had found her drug.

She fought her way up the last quarter of a mile or so, trying to discern a herd path from a vague maze of deer trails. After a few minutes, the drainage ditch leveled out and she found herself on an unmarked trail. She strode forward, joyful at the relative freedom of movement, and excited. She had to be close now.

When she saw it, she let out an involuntary whoop of pleasure. She crashed through the balsams into the clearing, shrugging off her pack and dropping it onto the forest floor. The canister was nailed to a tree, just a little higher than comfortable for Asha to get at. She stood on her tiptoes and worked the thick plastic lid off the PVC pipe. Inside, a Ziploc bag held a spiral memo pad and a pencil. She signed in and stood there, her hip against the tree, reading the few entries before her. Not as long nor as colorful as the entries in the Appalachian Trail logbooks, but charming nonetheless. She replaced the pen and pad after several minutes and sat down, taking a long drink of water.

"Well, ladies," she addressed the dogs that lay in the clearing, panting. "This bushwhacking is pretty easy, isn't it?"

Charlie wasn't really waiting for Walter, just kind of thought he might show up, unannounced-like. It was a glorious late August day, the kind of day that used to make Charlie sad, back before his emotions became arthritic. Charlie puttered around the cabin, touching things that didn't need touching, and thinking about dying. He could feel it coming on, like winter. He could read the signs. And just like bringing in some extra wood or filling a few extra jugs before a storm, Charlie wanted to take care of those last few chores so that he'd be ready for what was clearly headed his way. The unfinished state of his affairs was just plain stuck in Charlie's craw.

He shuffled out onto the porch, boxers, undershirt, and boots on. He slurped instant coffee from an old diner mug and surveyed the front yard. Gonna need some tree work, he decided, narrowing his eyes at a few saplings at the edge of the meadow and a middle-aged maple growing too close to the cabin. Not this year, Charlie acknowledged, but soon. That damn maple was too close to the roof, but oh, she was pretty in the fall. Now sweet gum, Charlie remembered, that was Virginia's favorite tree for autumn color – she used to go on and on about the rainbow on every leaf. I'll have to plant one up here, Charlie thought. Got a nice one, down at the house, but I never did plant one up here. He slurped, swallowed. Charlie passed his hand over his brow and spat. Hot day. Not gonna get much done today.

He pulled the screen door open and clomped back inside. He made his way over to the spartan table and set the mug down. He frowned at the old telephone for a moment, then picked it up and dialed Walter's cell phone number.

"Walter?" He barked. Barely waiting for the reply, he continued. "I got tree work needs to be done. You headin' up this way today?"

"That old man again?" Kip asked, having heard Charlie's trademark growl from across the counter. Walter's bad ear necessitated the highest volume setting his cell phone offered. May as well have had it on speaker phone, apparently.

Walter confirmed Kip's guess with a nod. "Charlie," he mumbled through egg and potatoes.

Breakfast at Kip and Wennie's was such a ritual, Walter occasionally extended the indulgence to a weekend morning. As often as not, Kip wasn't working and had a moment or two to sit with Walter and catch up. Often Wennie joined them, the babysitter offering a brief respite from the relentless stickiness Fiona's care involved.

"What's the deal with that guy?" Kip wanted to know. "Doesn't he have any family?"

Walter shook his head, chewing.

"Does he bug you every weekend?" Kip sounded critical, but Walter heard the concern behind it. He swallowed, noting that Kip's homemade salsa was just a little more salty than usual and arranged all his disparate thoughts and feelings before responding. Wennie slid onto a nearby stool, both hands wrapped around a mug of coffee.

"Yeah, Charlie leans on me now, but he knows there are limits. Actually a call on a weekend like this is unusual." Kip's face registered relief. "Y'know, he's eighty-six years old. He's mean and crude and nasty in every sense of the word, but he's also an amazing person. He has heart, and he goes deep, but he's so crusted over at this point it's kind of hard to see that part of him." Walter paused and thought about all the things he never put into words about Charlie. "I guess it just gets to me, him being all alone like that. The way I see it, maybe if I help him out here and there, it'll preserve his dignity and independence." Walter wiped his mouth with his paper napkin and crumpled it up thoughtfully. "He's been carrying around his wife's dying wish for something like forty-five years. The way he talks about her," Walter's eyes misted over. Both Kip and Wennie raised their eyebrows. "He's just from another world. When his generation is gone, there won't be any men like that anymore." Kip and Wennie exchanged a glance, and Walter could feel them thinking "hmmm, no more chauvinist, racist, nasty, rude, red-necked, undereducated, opinionated alcoholics with chips on their shoulders. Not such a bad thing." Walter could see their point. Charlie certainly had the capacity to embody the stereotype fully at times. Well, okay, most of the time. "I guess I figure if I give him the chance, he'll take the opportunity to show who he really is. Who he really was, I guess. There's a part of him that's wise and generous, alongside all that other crap."

"But Walter," Kip leaned on the counter, adjusting his weight to ease his aching back, "what about you? Your life? What are you doing? Seems like all you ever do is work and run errands for the old geezer. Are you even checking your emails anymore?"

"Why? Are you sending me love notes?" Walter tossed Kip the bait.

"Yes, honey," Kip played along.

Wennie scraped her stool loudly as she hopped off. "That's enough for me," she said.

"Oh come on, honey, you know you secretly wish Walter and me -"

"Ding!" Wennie raised her voice over Kip's and turned on her heel. Still chewing, Walter looked at Kip.

"My inappropriate bell just went off," Kip grinned.

"Must sound like a cathedral in here when you're cooking."

"Only when I'm thinking of you, honey," Kip teased, and Walter laughed his 'good sport' laugh. Kip switched gears. "Are you seeing anyone?"

Walter shook his head, the orange slice garnish suddenly compelling.

"You still thinking about that one over in Dutchess? The one with the dog?"

Walter nodded, looked at Kip and shrugged, big shoulders lifting and falling heavily back into place. "Yeah. I think from the first glance it was real trouble, but there was this moment when she was lying on the couch, and I had to interrupt her. When she looked up at me from under the blankets, something happened." Walter paused, swallowed hard, and shrugged again. "That was it. Go ahead and stick a fork in me 'cause I'm done." Walter brightened a little as he said those words, as if finally saying them out loud made it all a bit more real.

"So what have you done about this? Have you called her?"

"I can't."

"What do you mean, you can't? You're telling me you fell in love with her, love at first sight, and you can't call her? You have to do something." Kip was moments away from reaching across the counter and shaking Walter by the lapels. He shifted his weight and gave Walter an exasperated look.

"I can't call her. It's against company policy. A huge bozo-no-no. I'd be fired within the day if anybody found out." Walter continued to push around what was left on his plate, not hungry anymore.

"So find another way to track her down and meet her. Look, you can't just pine after her." Walter didn't look up, not wanting to meet Kip's insistent gaze. Kip's dark Irish features were focused on Walter with an intensity that was starting to make him think about tree work in the Vega Mountain valley. "Walter, that would be masochistic, to label this chick the love of your life and the do nothing to actually connect with her?" Kip threw his hands in the air and spun away, heading for the kitchen. "The only masochism you're allowed to indulge in needs to involve me and the gorilla mask."

"Ding ding ding!" Wennie walked through the dining area, having caught only the last sentence. She stuck her fingers in her ears and continued about her business, liberally ringing Kip's inappropriate bell.

Walter laughed and laid down his fork. He reached for his wallet and thought about Kip's admonition. *I do need to do something; otherwise I am setting myself up.* On the other hand, Walter admitted to himself, *sure is a safe way to avoid disappointment.*

"Yer chicken!" Charlie roared at Walter. "Ya goddamn fool! Call that girl up. Use any damn excuse, but call her up. Trust me, real women are much better than being all alone with yer imagination."

Walter cringed at the thought of Charlie's imagination. "This damn tree work is what's imaginary," Walter retorted.

Charlie looked away and said nothing. He coughed, spat, and went back inside, leaving Walter to his chainsaw.

Waitressing. *At a decent place on a good night, I could make some money,* Asha thought. *Sometimes waitresses make enough to hold together a home and family. Don't actors rely upon waiting tables?*

Asha gave up and clicked the 'x' on the top right of the screen, shutting down her internet connection. Her coffee was still hot. She took stock: It was Sunday, she had no plans for the day and no commitments anywhere until tomorrow morning when it was time to pick up Pearl. Asha headed downstairs, through the kitchen and out onto the back porch. Both dogs followed.

Asha sat on the back porch steps, drank her coffee, and considered her options. "What the hell," she decided. "Knock off another one. Today let's go try Bearpen." She spoke out loud, addressing her comments to the dogs and the weeds crowding around her back porch steps. The dogs wagged their tails at her voice, and the weeds breathed a sigh of relief, knowing another weekend of being ignored had been achieved. She went inside and collected up hiking gear and equipment.

The trailhead was at the end of a dirt road. She read and reread the directions and description of the road a few times before sighing and snapping the book shut. She strode out the front door and slung her day pack into the tool box in the bed of the truck. Yes, the truck. Old Bessie would have to be impressed into duty for this one. Asha didn't think the Jetta's clearance was high enough to manage what she assumed the condition of the dirt road would be. "This is going to cost a fuckin' fortune in gas," she mumbled as she struggled with the door handle. Stumbling backwards when it relented, she instructed the dogs, "Hop in, ladies."

They leapt simultaneously, and Lyla bounced off the steering wheel and fell back onto the driveway. "Good thing you're pretty," Asha soothed her, stroking her soft black fur.

Dogs loaded, directions to the trailhead on the dashboard, and a second cup of coffee in her purple travel mug (a gift from Pearl and Carl that first post-divorce Christmas), she headed out to the western Catskills.

Driving old Bessie gave Asha plenty to worry about, as she watched the gas gauge march steadily toward 'E'. Bessie hadn't ventured more than about fifteen miles from home in years. She was a '71, and she was a beast, but even Bessie-beasts have a lifespan. Asha didn't know just how much life she had left in her, and since her odometer stopped working the last time she drove her, Asha wondered if that meant they were on borrowed time.

So Asha took it slow, choosing back roads, worrying about whether or not the gas gauge still worked or if the tires would hold their pressure. The truck had been her father's, and she seemed to remember a problem with overheating back in the late 1980's. He got that fixed, she decided. A new radiator and hoses were installed as a parting gift. *To Bessie, or to me?* She wondered silently, thinking about her dad and his beloved truck. He missed the truck. Asha missed him.

Focusing on Bessie's performance and what-iffing her way across Dutchess County got boring. Her mind wandered. Windows open, Asha's curls danced wildly in the wind, and the dogs' tongues dripped on Bessie's floor. Blessedly, the dogs did not fight over the window seat although equally blessedly the bench seat in a '71 Ford F 150 is big enough to accommodate two sixty pound dogs and Asha. Brulee took the window seat, and Lyla curled up in the middle. "That seat belt thing isn't poking you, is it?" She felt around with her right hand, helping Lyla arrange herself more comfortably.

Asha considered her hike. So, it's a trail-less peak with no canister, she mused. How'm I going to know when I'm done? she wondered. She giggled about the wish for an "X marks the spot" type indicator. Will the list police accuse me of cheating if I fail to set foot on the precise summit? How will they know? She shrugged it off. From the description in the book, it sounded like the ski equipment leftover from Bearpen's days as a ski slope would kind of be a dead giveaway that she was at the top. Sounds like I can't miss it, she thought.

Bessie's old bones groaned over the washed out and deeply rutted jeep road. She plunged and bucked a good bit before settling down to rest at the parking area. Asha and the dogs tumbled out, cramped and sweaty from the long ride. No other cars in the parking area, she noted. Good, she thought. I like the idea of having this big old mountain to myself. She and the dogs slipped into the woods to empty their bladders. Asha giggled again at the sight of all three of them squatting to pee.

The trail was really a continuation of the jeep road, and it was much easier walking than driving. That was fine with Asha; contending with the heat and the bugs was enough. Here and there locust trees gave evidence to the lateness of the season, their leaves already autumn-brown from the leaf borers. Not knowing whether or not they'd find much water along the way, she carried enough for all three of them, her pack heavy and damp. Swatting at the mosquitoes, she strode on, picking up her pace a little, hurrying.

After a fairly arduous climb, she paused to catch her breath and take a drink. Brulee had charged into the woods a few minutes before, and Asha was also figuring now would be a good time for a break, to give Brulee a chance to rejoin them.

The water tasted good, a sure sign that Asha was dehydrated. She drank, and then shared some water with Lyla, pouring it into her cupped hand for the dog to drink. After a Clif bar and some more water, Brulee still hadn't returned. Asha called and whistled and started to get annoyed.

Lyla watched Asha intently.

After about ten minutes, Asha was too impatient to just hang out and wait for Brulee to reappear. She shifted her weight from foot to foot, smacked herself in mosquito-eradication efforts, and weighed her options: continue on and assume Brulee will just catch up or set off in the direction Brulee went. She stood there, waffling, not liking either option.

"Brulee-eee-eee!" Asha drew out the name, cupping her hands around her mouth and adding a silent prayer for good measure.

Lyla whined.

She reached out and buried her fingers in the soft black fur of Lyla's ruff, offering and receiving comfort. Lyla sniffed the ground, then sniffed the air. Then the dog turned to her, looked right at her, and whined again, louder.

"Okay," Asha decided. "Go ahead. Lead me to her."

Lyla started off, heading downhill to the south. Due south, Asha noted, checking the compass. Okay, to get back to this spot, she told herself, all I have to remember is to head north until I hit this trail. She kept the compass out and hurried after Lyla, who moved easily through the thick underbrush.

Time and distance were tricky enough to keep accurate account of while hiking, but after a while of this bounding through the woods, Asha began to worry. She chided herself for making a potentially dangerous decision based on impatience and a dog's whine. It seemed as though they had been heading south for at least half an hour with no sign of Brulee. Asha continued to yell for the dog, her throat getting scratchy and painful. Keeping up with Lyla, hurrying downhill for a solid thirty minutes, she decided that they had to have covered a good mile. She pulled out her map and studied it, Lyla dancing around her and whining.

"Okay, I have no idea where I am," Asha admitted to the dog. "All I know is that the truck is back up over that hill." With that, Lyla took off, nose down, stretched out in full stride. Despite her worries, Asha couldn't help but notice how beautiful the black dog was. Lyla rippled and gleamed, a black flash in the sunlight. Asha sighed and hastened after her. She had to half-jog, leaping over rocks and logs, to keep Lyla in sight. "This will be amazing if I manage to not fall," she muttered between clenched teeth as she righted herself after a tricky landing. She could see open fields ahead, and wondered what that would mean. Private land obviously, but friendly-helpful private land, or deep-shit dangerous private land? Her worries multiplied.

Lyla shot out of the woods into an unmowed field. The late summer wildflowers: turtlehead, purple loosestrife, and cardinal flower over by the streambed, black-eyed Susies, corn cockles and Deptford pinks dotting the drier spots, bowed and parted before Lyla's sixty-five pounds of forward momentum. Asha followed in her wake.

She saw the cabin, and then she saw the old man. His posture wasn't promising, thin arms folded over his chest. As she got closer, she could see that he was wearing generic old man pants: dun-colored work pants, stained and greasy from years of use. Then she saw Brulee, tail wagging, trot around from the far side of the cabin. Lyla saw her too and shifted into overdrive. The dogs split the remaining distance, Brulee charging across the old man's field as if she were protecting her own home.

"Hello!" Asha called out, waving to the man. He didn't respond. She could see his face and quailed. His arms were still crossed over his undershirt, which, she couldn't help but notice, looked remarkably new and clean. Perhaps it was just the contrast with the pants, the cabin, and everything else. Upon closer inspection, all of it gained decades. Brulee came flying up to Asha, crashing into her, the canine equivalent of a huge hug. She responded to the dog, petting, stroking, talking, all the while wondering why Brulee had taken off and come down here.

"That yer dog?" The man's voice from across the field made her almost smell cigarette smoke. The man coughed and spat, the effort of raising his voice apparent. Asha straightened up and headed toward him.

"Yes, she's mine," she called as she approached. "I'm so sorry she bothered you. She's never run off like this before." Asha swung her pack off her shoulder and began rummaging around inside for leashes.

"She ain't no bother," the old man said. He squinted at Asha and chewed his lower lip. Well, she ain't a girl, he thought. Too old. But she's all clean and cute like a girl, with all them curls and those big brown eyes. She ain't white, he decided, but she ain't black neither. What the hell, he wondered. She's wearing expensive-looking clothes, out running around in the woods with these dogs. What the hell was she doing out there anyway? He peered at her, suspicion evident in his narrowed eyes.

Asha stopped pretending that she was going to find leashes and stood up. She was still trying to determine the relative level of danger inherent in her situation, and so far this guy was not giving anything away.

Curiosity got the better of him. "What the hell were you doing out there? You all alone with them?" he exploded, his voice raised with concern and bewilderment. He just couldn't make it add up; she was not so young as to be a kid that didn't know better, she was alone, deep in no-man's-land woods, with two dogs. "You sure as hell weren't hunting." He voiced the only explanation he could come up with, ruling it out in defeat. He rubbed the five, six, and seven o'clock shadow decorating his cheeks and chin and waited for a satisfactory answer.

"I was hiking," Asha tried to relax her shoulders. They slid half an inch away from her ears. "I'm doing the Catskill 35. I was trying to get Bearpen Mountain for the list. I parked over on the jeep road off of Route 23."

"Hiking on Bearpen?" He considered her answer. "Now? Why? The blackberries ain't ripe yet. Besides," he started to chuckle, looking back in the direction she had come from, "you jes' climbed over Roundtop." He gestured with his thumb.

"I did?" Asha pulled out her map, not sure whether or not to believe the old man.

At that the old man started to laugh. He laughed hard enough to cough, and coughed hard enough to scare Asha. This time he didn't spit.

Asha looked back over her shoulder at the hill she had climbed. Roundtop indeed. Shit, she thought. I'm gonna end up climbing that stupid thing twice today.

The old guy watched her, followed her gaze, and read her thoughts. Brulee left Asha's side, circled him, then leaned against his right leg, asking to be petted. He looked down at the dog, ruffling her ears and grunting, "Hey there." Then he bent down and called to Lyla, "C'mere, you. Lemme pet you too." Lyla stepped away from Asha's side, barked once, and held her ground. The old guy wasn't put off. "You scared? C'mere, ya big baby," he cooed. Lyla hung her head and took a few steps forward. After being stroked by his big rough hands, Lyla gave a hesitant wag and retreated to Asha's side. Brulee shoved her head under the old man's now available hand.

"My dogs like you," Asha smiled her winning smile, having decided to put a little effort into making friends with the apparent property owner. He didn't seem terribly dangerous or truly threatening. Just old. The longer Asha stood there trying to figure him out, the older he seemed. At least sixties when she was across the field had at closer inspection become at least eighties.

"Yep." He nodded, looking at Brulee. "This here's a fine dog." He looked at Asha, a final piercing squint, and relented. If this is her dog, she can't be all that bad. She didn't look like a "citiot" but she looked like nothing the old guy understood. Not black, not white, not urban, but not local, not hunting, but hiking from some damn list. He didn't know what to make of her, but here she was at his cabin with these dogs. Damn fine dogs, both of them. "You want some sardines? Or a beer? You must be hot an' thirsty, after running over ol' Roundtop chasin' yer dogs."

Asha's initial pre-programmed childhood response: refuse out of both etiquette and safety. She did her own last ditch check-in with her gut. Is this guy dangerous in any way? Her internal magic eight-ball said no. "Sardines, eh? I haven't eaten sardines since I was a kid." She smiled her I-still-am-a-kid smile and said, "Sure."

The old man turned toward the cabin, both dogs taking up positions at his sides. "What's yer name?" he barked at her.

"Asha."

"Ashes?" He repeated, making no effort to conceal his distaste, evident in the turned down corners of his mouth. "Ashes? That's a stupid name for a girl." He paused, thinking, while she struggled to come up with a fitting response. While she absorbed the affront, he decided. "I'm jes' gonna call you Smokey." He looked over his shoulder at her, and she could have sworn she saw a flash of youthful jauntiness cross his creased and stubbly face. "That okay with you?" he challenged.

Asha nodded. Who cares? She recovered quickly. "What's your name?"

"Charlie."

Walter finished closing out his last job of the day and leaned back in the old metal desk chair, tipping the chair up to balance on its back legs. Verizon's Shokan central office was small, and Walter wanted privacy for his next phone call. The other Universal Outdoor Technician who worked out of Shokan, Steve, had finally stopped dicking around on the computer and left for the day. Good.

Walter stretched his arms back, expanding his chest. It hurt so good; he had just upped his pull-ups to fifteen two days ago and he felt it. Felt good, felt strong. Walter felt like he could face damn near any challenge, whether it was hanging from a pole, reaching out of the bucket for the splice case in high winds out in Big Indian, or beating the crap out of Big Al in jiu jitsu tomorrow night. Damn near any challenge but knowing what to say to Her… Walter swallowed and acknowledged his weakness. In this situation, he realized as he bumped the chair down to level ground, he felt like a skinny little boy with a bunch of weeds plucked from the end of the driveway. Outclassed.

That damn phone number had been burning a hole in his shirt pocket ever since he got it from dispatch this morning. Once again he went over it in his mind. It was pointless; it achieved nothing. It was fully legal, ethical, and would not get him fired, but it was also hopelessly ineffective at making any progress in terms of a social relationship. His plan, the one he had been obsessively rehearsing since 9:00 a.m. when it dawned on him, was to call her up and do a routine customer feedback survey with her. Does your phone work now, ma'am? Any further troubles I might be able to help you with? And then say thank you, have a nice day, and hang up. Unless, of course, she says, Wait, don't hang up, aren't you that beefy blond that hung my phone on the kitchen column for me and made friends with my terrifying Cujo-esque beast? Let's meet for coffee and get to know each other. Walter shook his head. It wasn't even funny anymore.

He reached for the phone. Now or never. Although it seemed like half his body was overproducing moisture, the place where he needed it most was as dry as a bone. He attempted to clear his throat, but that didn't help much. He swallowed and dialed.

He was glad she didn't pick up on the first or second ring; his heart was pounding loudly enough to make hearing her over the still static-y phone connection difficult. Three rings. Disappointment entered his bloodstream alongside the adrenaline. Four rings. It was the dreaded answering machine message. Walter was about to panic when he heard her voice. The outgoing message on her phone, recently changed to accommodate job searching, was Asha speaking slowly, clearly, and Pleasantly. Walter was taken aback. What a beautiful speaking voice. He left his professional checkup message, finishing with the invitation that if she experienced any further telecommunications needs, she should call them in to the repair dispatch. He hung up, knowing it was clean and above board, but utterly unhelpful. And yet, he had heard her voice. Not her first thing in the morning, I am sad and angry voice, but her public voice. She sounded cultured, professional, intelligent, and Walter had to admit, really sexy. It was the depth of her voice and the patience with which she spoke. The words rolled off her tongue as if they were rolling out of bed after deep and fulfilling... Okay. Walter interrupted himself. Get a grip. She's got a deep voice; it's very attractive and it's time for me to go home.

Walter stood up abruptly and checked his watch. He'd have to hustle to make it to jiu jitsu on time. Adding an extra class tonight felt like a good idea. Hopefully, he could spar with the instructor and get totally exhausted. That would help a lot.

Brulee seemed to know her way around the tiny cabin, nosing the cabinet door open to expose shelves neatly stacked with sardines tins and bottles of grape juice. Charlie jerked his thumb toward the juice. "Can't stand that stuff. Friend of mine bought it; guess he thought it'd be good for me. Some damn article he read." Charlie managed the sardine tin deftly, his callused old hands repeating movements that no longer required thought. He handed each dog a slimy fish.

Amid the smacking of dog lips, Asha giggled and commented, "They are going to have awful breath."

"So will you," Charlie stated, plunking the open tin and a fork down on the card table in the kitchen area. The cabin was clean and mostly empty, and it smelled of dry wood, old man, and sulfur. Asha was trying to decide if Charlie actually lived there and, if so, if he lived alone. The place had an air of being cared for that didn't mesh with Charlie's age and attitude. Asha entered a touch tentatively, but it was cooler inside, the screens kept the bugs out, and she was grateful for the respite.

After a snack of sardines and saltines, Asha was powerfully thirsty. She declined the beer but accepted a bottle of water.

"Water here changes. For a few years it was nice – sweet even. Now it's sulfury as all hell. Can't drink it." Charlie took a swig of beer. Budweiser, Asha noted. Yuck. "But it'll change again. Maybe next spring, after the snowmelt."

Maybe, she thought. She wondered about climate change and acid rain and the impact they had on Catskill aquifers and springs. The world Charlie came of age in was a very different world compared to the one he would leave. Ideas of nature, wilderness, the mountains … Asha saw the look of incomprehension on Charlie's face when she said she was hiking. It wasn't only the fact that she'd made a ninety degree turn and failed to notice, thus climbing the wrong mountain; it wasn't only that she was hiking to complete a list. It was deeper, more fundamental, she figured.

"Do you live here year round?" She asked.

"No," Charlie growled through his last swig of Bud. "I got a place over to Halcottsville. This here's my hunting cabin." Charlie thumped the empty bottle on the table suddenly enough to spook the dogs. Both leapt to their feet and Lyla barked. "Hey there," Charlie rubbed Brulee's head a touch clumsily, his voice more tender than his hand.

Charlie stood up and looked at the clock on the stove. It was a beauty: a 1970's harvest gold electric with an analog clock. "Listen Smokey," he turned to her and addressed her as if they were something other than strangers. "You ain't hiking back over that mountain now. You'll getcher self lost or something." He rubbed his bushy stubble and said, "I'll give you a ride back to yer car." She started to protest, but Charlie snarled and held up one of his big tough hands. "I still have a goddamned license and the ol' truck is registered and inspected. Runs fine." She looked uncertain but she shut up. "That's better Smokey." He turned to the dogs and said "Go! Git in the truck!" Both dogs raced out of the cabin. Asha watched their tails disappear down the front porch steps. "You too, Smokey. Go get in." Asha felt just a touch of a chill, not from his words but from the momentary lack of grit and gravel in his voice. He sounded kind and almost fatherly. She moved quickly before the other Charlie returned.

Charlie's truck was Bessie's cosmic twin, a 1971 Ford F150, ancient but well cared for. Asha wondered if Charlie had bought it brand new, like her dad had done. Charlie drove okay: He took it slow and talked to himself at intersections, but he seemed all right. Asha decided that she didn't have to worry about his driving on the way back home.

When Charlie saw Bessie, he was pretty well floored. He tried hard to take it in stride and not show it, but Asha's stock rose immeasurably. He repeated, "That's your truck?" twice, but after Asha produced the key, he nodded his acceptance of the fact. "Listen Smokey," he spoke quickly, the words tumbling out and running away before Charlie could take them back or undo them with a snarl or a biting laugh. "You need to git up Bearpen to finish yer list?" Asha nodded. "Come back to my place in about three weeks. Blackberries will be ready for ya then. I'll show ya the trail up on my land. Takes ya right up to the top."

"Thank you," Asha answered, her hand on the door.

"Bring them dogs. Bears hate dogs." Charlie reached for Brulee on the seat beside him and scratched her ears one last time. "Now go on. You gotta git back home." Asha scrambled out of the truck and let the dogs in Bessie. She turned to wave goodbye to Charlie, but he was already off, navigating his own lurching way back to the cabin.

Kip was laughing, leaning forward, one forearm supporting his weight, while he searched for a way to arrange his hips that would ease his back. Walter chewed his pancakes stoically, ignoring his friend's amusement.

"So you called her in your capacity as a phone man? Three weeks after you were there fixing her phone? Isn't that a little weird?"

Walter finished chewing and swallowed. He looked at a nice bite, right there, all syrupy with a mango chunk perfectly centered. He considered taking another forkful before responding. Kip was relentless, and Walter was feeling a little sensitive and defensive about the whole thing. He looked up from his pancakes and met Kip's piercing black-browed eyes. He sighed inwardly. "Yup."

"So what happens now?"

"Nothing."

"But – but -" Kip sputtered, shifting his weight and switching arms. "How do you get to meet her again?"

"I don't know."

"So what did calling her accomplish?"

"Nothing, I guess."

"Walt! Come on, man," Kip whined.

"What?" Walter wasn't exactly feigning innocence, just playing for time. How the hell was he going to say, "I just wanted to hear her voice. That was enough." He knew how lame and pathetic that sounded, and he was heartily embarrassed. But not so embarrassed as to be cured. Oh no. If anything, this just made it all worse.

Kip was talking. Walter was almost finished with his pancakes. He focused on drinking his coffee. The mug felt solid and sensible against his normally equally solid and sensible hand. The coffee was strong, bitter, and sweet. It helped. "... driving me crazy!" Kip finished with a dramatic crescendo, straightened up, and stormed back into the kitchen.

Walter checked his watch and poured himself another cup of coffee. Hopefully his first job would be something straightforward. Maybe a simple service order or a No-Trouble-Found up to the house. Walter gave himself ten more minutes and settled a little more comfortably into his blue collar slouch at the counter. He enjoyed his second cup thoroughly.

"Hey, y'know what?" Asha sat cross-legged on the bar stool, Grace and Lukey Jane in agreement that there was no way that could be comfortable.

"What?" Lukey Jane had become Asha's adoptive big sister and social guard dog in the aftermath of Rob. Her tone took on that father-of-a-teenage-daughter edge whenever she mentioned dating. Natural suspiciousness told her Asha's next words were bound to be trouble.

"That guy that fixed my phone last month called me."

Lukey Jane's protective hackles rose.

"He just left a message," she continued, oblivious to Lukey Jane's concern. "Just checking that my phone worked now." She paused to take a sip of her Wingnut Ale. In a piece of diplomacy rivaling the Camp David accords of the 1970's, the owners of the two competing pubs, The Blue Eft in Dover and the Power Plant in Wingdale, reached détente. The Power Plant's renowned libations, Wingnut Ale and Swamp River Porter, were now available at The Blue Eft. May peace prevail in Dover. "Isn't that sweet?"

"Probably not. It's probably some new company policy." Grace suggested. She wasn't typically cynical, but her latest tarot reading had ended with the suggestion that she take off her rose-colored glasses from time to time, just to try seeing the world as it is. She glanced from Lukey Jane to Asha to see how this version of herself went over.

"Oh." Asha's reaction was minimal. She sipped her beer and tried to slouch, but the posture was so alien she gave up. "Well, he sounded like he genuinely cared..."

"They probably hired an actor." Lukey Jane offered her attempt at cynical. Grace considered it, but Asha snorted and changed the subject.

"I met someone." Asha's lips twitched, and her eyes flicked from Lukey Jane to Grace and back again.

"Do tell." Lukey Jane's invitation came out as a threat.

"Well, he's older than me," Asha began, "and he's really good with dogs." Lukey Jane relaxed her jaw muscles, but her eyes were still hard. "He lives kind of far away, but he's got a really beautiful spot."

"What's he do for a living?" Grace asked.

"Nothing," Asha grinned. "Retired."

"Retired?" Lukey Jane exploded. "How the hell old is this guy, Asha?"

Asha relented and told Lukey Jane and Grace about her aborted hike up Bearpen (well, Roundtop, actually. Asha left that part out, figuring Lukey Jane wouldn't let her try another bushwhack alone after hearing that she'd climbed the wrong mountain, even if it was Brulee's fault) and the story of meeting Charlie. During the telling, Halia arrived and was seamlessly absorbed into Asha's audience.

It seemed that the more Lukey Jane heard about Charlie, the more she relaxed. "You're a dang fool, wanderin' around all alone up in them woods," Lukey Jane criticized Asha affectionately in her Oklahoman twang, "but he sounds like yer guardian angel. There when ya need him with sardines, beer, and a ride back to the trailhead." Lukey Jane meant to pat Asha on the back to give her a supportive, sisterly gesture, but the impact necessitated a rescue by Grace and Halia. "Sorry," Lukey Jane muttered.

"Reason number thirty-seven why it's not safe to sit cross-legged on a bar stool," Asha joked, untangling her legs and hooking her sneakered feet around the bottom rungs of the stool.

"You plan to take him up on his offer?" Grace wanted to know.

"Yeah," Asha answered. "I think so." She stood up, wiggling her hips and legs. "Wedgie," she explained. "I figure I'll head back up there on Labor Day. Carl asked to take Pearl to his sister's for the day for their pool party, barbeque thing." Asha's face clouded over. "I don't want to be home alone on Labor Day."

"You won't be alone." Lukey Jane informed her. "The town's doin' fireworks that night, settin' 'em off right across the street from yer house. You'll have half the town for company right on yer perennial border if yer not careful to chase 'em off."

"Ugh." Asha was new enough to owning her home to not yet know all the subtle, intimate details specific to that spot.

"Just you wait til Santa comes to town." Lukey Jane and Grace laughed knowingly. Halia looked thoughtful and Asha looked as if she might start to cry, thinking about Rob and fireworks.

"Why don't you bring the dogs over to my house in the evening? I'll have tranquilizers for the dogs and ear plugs for us," Halia offered.

Asha looked at her, her eyes dangerously full. "Okay," she agreed. "Good idea." Asha couldn't think of anyone she'd rather avoid fireworks with.

Walter showed up unannounced early Saturday morning, reckoning that all the tasks of the fall season would start breathing down his neck soon enough. There would be plenty of chores and errands ready for him: ones that Charlie had thought up and was getting ready to ask for and ones he hadn't realized needed doing. Best to get a head start, Walter figured.

"Yer here." Charlie's statement gave little away, but his eyes lit upon Walter and the truck almost greedily.

"Yeah." Walter examined Charlie. The once over to check for physical illness, mental illness, senility, dementia, the I-haven't-been-here-in-a-while once over that Charlie and his homestead received each time Walter arrived had become second nature to Walter. The longer it had been since the prior visit, the longer and more studied the glance. This time Charlie met his eyes.

"Well?" Charlie challenged Walter.

"You look good," Walter admitted. He strode past Charlie into the cabin, the screen door banging behind him. Walter hesitated, listening to the door slam. I could change that, he thought, looking at the door frame and thinking about a hydraulic door stop.

He shrugged. There was something old fashioned and charming about the slam, and Charlie didn't seem to care. And there were a hell of a lot of other, more pressing tasks. The cabin received the same once over, all-encompassing glance and earned the same response. It looked good. It looked like Charlie had even swept recently. What the hell?

"What's on yer list fer today?" Charlie asked. His eyes roamed the room, then rested upon Walter's truck, visible through the open window.

"You planning to stay here for hunting season this year?"

"Yep."

"Then I guess cleaning the chimney is on my list." Walter clomped out to the truck to get his brushes. He passed the bowl Charlie had set on the floor for Brulee. "Why is that there?"

"Fer a dog." Charlie made his way over but stopped short of picking up the bowl, morning stiffness preventing him from bending down to the floor. "Some damned fool hiker lost her dog. One of her dogs. She used the other one to lead her here." Charlie rubbed his unshaven cheeks and chin, then ran his hand over his white tufts of hair. "I was thinkin' mebbe we could head into town. I need some things."

Walter nodded, hesitating before heading back out to the truck. He looked at the Corelle bowl on the floor, then bent over and picked it up. Charlie took it from him and carried it to the sink.

Chimney cleaning didn't take all that long. Checking and re-placing the weather-stripping around the front door didn't take long either. Convincing Charlie to close up the cabin earlier this year and head down to the house in the village before the snow flies: now that would take a while. Walter didn't engage in that battle, knowing that winning would be losing. Charlie would drive up to the cabin daily during hunting season, regardless of the weather, the road conditions, or the number of beers he'd con-sumed. No, having Charlie stay at the cabin 'til December was going to have to be okay. Walter clenched his jaws in response to his next realization. It wouldn't be something he'd need to worry about for many more years.

Charlie puttered around getting in Walter's way, trying to participate. After the chimney and the door were done, Walter told Charlie to get ready to go.

"Awright, Walt," Charlie disappeared into the bedroom and reappeared moments later, ancient blue workpants over his boxers and a blue and white striped short sleeved shirt over his guinea tee. "Ready," he tried to sound like his querulous self, but his pleasure at going out ruined it. Walter pretended not to notice.

Walter scratched his head, dust and sweat itching his scalp. He followed Charlie out to the truck. It was hot again, hotter than late August up in these hills usually got. Just to remind everyone how short summer can be in the western Catskills, late August nights get downright chilly and daytime temperatures hover right at that edge of "No, I don't think I'll go to the swimming hole today." Well, not today. Today was Brooklyn hot, baked asphalt with seaside humidity hot. Cooling off in a creek on the way home sounded damn good to Walter.

"So what do you need in town?"

"Socks," Charlie barked over the engine starting. "Boxers. Ammo."

"Anything else?"

Charlie hesitated, long enough to draw Walter's gaze away from the driveway. "Mebbe check a bookstore."

"Okay." Walter knew that Charlie would either explain or not. Asking was irrelevant.

"Wanna look at a book on dogs."

Walter drove, eyes on the road, jaw muscles twitching.

"That hiker's dog…" Charlie's gruffness returned. He cleared his throat noisily and rolled the window down. Dust plumes followed the truck down the hill. "That dog …" Charlie felt obligated to explain. After all, Walter was taking him on this manufactured errand just so Charlie could try to figure out what kind of dog Smokey had. He figured Walter had a certain right to know why. "It was a good dog. A damn good dog." That should satisfy Walter, Charlie decided. Walter was the kind of man who would grasp the value of a good dog.

Walter had no idea what Charlie was talking about but let it go. Charlie hadn't had a dog of his own for decades. Not since Virginia's dog, the boys' childhood pet, died back in a different millennium. He'd had that stupid thing for years after Virginia and then the boys left him. A young man alone, he watched that dog grow old and die, the way Charlie supposed he should. "Don't want no damn dog," he'd snap, when Walter noticed how much he seemed to enjoy other people's. "Damn things scare away all the deer, and doncha know bears hate dogs," he'd complain. And then walking down the street in Margaretville he'd get downright misty over some stranger's mutt. This particular hiker's dog was just the most recent one to catch his eye.

"Hey Charlie," Walter changed the subject, "do you remember when you last had your eyes checked?"

"I can see just fine," Charlie countered.

Walter considered teasing Charlie with a version of how many fingers am I holding up, but thought the better of it. "Charlie. You are eighty-six years old and I'm taking you to buy shotgun shells. It is my civic duty to make sure you can see." Walter caught Charlie's eye and added, "Now what you choose to aim at is your responsibility."

"What – are you gonna start arguin' fer gun control next?" Charlie baited Walter.

"Yup." Walter smiled, knowing Charlie anticipated the response. "My idea of gun control is being able to consistently hit your target." He paused for effect. "You need to be able to see to do that."

Charlie grinned appreciatively. Walter was powerfully reminded that he needed to schedule a dentist visit for Charlie.

They rode on mostly in silence. Charlie returned to napping and Walter made a mental list of items to check for in the clearance department at Home Depot and Lowe's. Stuff for Charlie's house in the village, stuff for the hunting cabin, stuff for his own home. Walter wasn't exactly in need of much, but running through the major systems at each location and troubleshooting what they might need over the next few months was a decently distracting enterprise. It helped to pass the time and it helped Walter avoid the unwanted thoughts that were beginning to get annoying. Well, not exactly annoying, Walter hastened to correct himself. Thinking about Her wasn't annoying at all. It was the hopelessness that was starting to bug him, the obsession without being able to take action. The stuckness. Walter wasn't really a fantasy addict. He actually preferred the real thing. This relentless unfulfilled longing, while delicious and compelling, was starting to turn the corner for Walter and feel too pointless and frustrating. And yet the idea of giving up and moving on was even more distressing than all the longing. So Walter tried to just change the channel. Set it on the back burner, think about something else, he told himself. So far, he was not particularly successful.

Charlie was able to get all he set out for at Gander Mountain. He chose replacement socks and boxers, same brand, same colors Walter imagined he's been buying for decades. And it was one-stop shopping; eye exams were available at the rifle counter. Guess Walter wasn't the first person to worry about the combination of hunting and poor vision. Charlie checked out fine: 20-20 in both eyes. Charlie shot Walter a gleeful and triumphant glare as he picked up his boxes of shells.

Damn, Walter swore silently in awe of Charlie's perfect vision and delight at getting a dig in at Walter. That man never lost an opportunity to take pleasure in having a go at me, Walter acknowledged to himself. That's how he shows love. Asshole. Walter smiled. Walter walked alongside Charlie, available just in case. But Charlie didn't need any help walking. Charlie was a little slow and plenty stiff, but he was still fully functional. Hell, apparently he can see and hear better than I can, Walter realized. Charlie got tired and he got cranky, but he was made of rawhide and pure attitude and nothing more. He would attack, berate, or belittle Walter as soon as bat an eye, then turn around and ask for something in the same breath.

It seemed like maybe it was Charlie's one concession to aging. He probably had some semblance of social skills back in the day, but they were long gone at this point. All that remained was essence, like the shore temples in south India, all details, all finery erased and pure essence remained. Statues finely carved, scrubbed by wind and sea into ideas, suggestions. Charlie had been honed down to a single point by age, loss, loneliness and the elements. Just an idea, a suggestion of what it means to be a man.

Walter sighed and reminded himself that despite all of Charlie's bullshit, he really needed Walter and, underneath the bravado, really appreciated him. Shit, Walter suppressed the chuckle: Charlie even handled the electronic checkout all by himself.

Walter guided Charlie to the dog book section at Barnes and Noble's and helped him find an inches thick tome describing and depicting dog breeds. Charlie began leafing through it, standing there.

"C'mon, I'll buy you a cup of coffee," Walter offered. "You can take a load off your feet and take your time going through it."

Charlie looked up from a pageful of schnauzers and nodded absently, his gaze somewhat unfocused. "Yeah, Walt. Thanks. That'd be good."

Walter hesitated, trying to read Charlie's expression.

"I'm jes' tryin' to picture that dog again, git 'er real clear in my mind, so that I'll be able to tell," Charlie trailed off, Walter leading the way to the coffee shop.

Walter chose an expensive, sweetened, elaborate drink with a foreign sounding name. Charlie wrinkled his nose and frowned. "Jes' plain coffee," he growled at the barista.

At the small round table, Charlie pored over the encyclopedia, turning pages with a snap. Toy breeds, terriers and hounds – snap, snap, snap. Snow dogs. Snap. Working breeds. The snaps slowed. "Look at this one," breathed Charlie, jabbing at a color plate of a Doberman pinscher. "What a beauty."

So Charlie was a real dog lover. Walter absorbed this new information about Charlie slowly, watching the old man's face change as he gazed almost tenderly at the animals he clearly approved of.

Snap. Pages turned, but now appreciative grunts preceded each snap. Great Dane. Sigh. Snap. Komondor. Snort. Laugh. Turn the book sideways to show Walter. Comment: "Looks like a mop." Snap.

Walter sipped his macchiato and burnt his tongue. Charlie's good mood was infectious. Walter set the cup down without cursing, even silently.

Snap, snap, snap. The non-sporting dog section offered Charlie the opportunity to pick up speed again. Walter watched, relaxed, and tried carefully slurping another sip. The hot liquid tasted good.

Australian cattle dog. Snap. Bearded collie. Snap. Belgian Malinois. Walter saw Charlie's face change, and could have sworn he heard the screeching of brakes.

"Uh-huh," Charlie said, nodding. His face softened, remembering Asha's dog. "A damn good dog," he murmured, pushing the open book toward Walter.

And suddenly Walter felt the electricity of universes colliding in him. There, on the page, was the spit and image of Her dog. Right down to the face that looked as if it had peeked up the chimney and the coat the color of perfectly browned toast.

"Tell me about this hiker," Walter strove to sound casual.

"You wanna come hiking with me again sometime?" Asha asked Pearl over a waffle and peaches late summer supper.

Pearl laid down her fork and chewed thoughtfully, giving her mother's question fair consideration. "Maybe." Always the diplomat. Such is the life of an only child of a divorced social worker.

"What if it included a stop at an ice cream place afterward?" Bribery, deal-making, and the occasional threat made up the menu of parenting persuasions.

Pearl raised one eyebrow. "How long a hike?"

"Short." Asha crossed her fingers behind her back.

"How long a drive to get there?"

"This trailhead also happens to be located in the woods," Asha began.

"The stupid woods," Pearl reminded her mother, stuffing another forkful of waffle into her mouth.

"Right," Asha grinned. "The stupid trailhead does happen to be in the middle of the stupid woods again. Coincidence, I guess." Asha had finished her waffles and watched Pearl eat. Boy that kid could eat slowly. Just like her father, she couldn't help but recall.

"Seriously mom," Pearl's words were muffled by half-chewed waffle. "Is it that same trailhead?" Just a hint, a mere smidgeon, of whining complaint was detectable in her tone.

"No honey, it's not. That one trailhead we went to that day was much farther. That was a really long drive," she remembered, agreeing with Pearl. That really was totally in the middle of the stupid woods.

"Is there a waterfall?" Pearl wanted to know.

"Nope. Just views this time. Totally killer awesome views."

"Fine." Pearl swirled a peach wedge in her maple syrup. "When?"

"Soon." Asha's smile reached her eyes. She looked almost relaxed for a moment, unguarded and happy. "We should pick a day based on the weather. That way we get the killer awesome views, not just mist and clouds."

Pearl had speared another slice of peach and was busy drawing hearts in the remaining maple syrup on her plate. Her failure to answer right away drew Asha's attention. She looked at the plate. "Grab a piece of peach, Mom." Pearl drew a tic tac toe board on her plate, using a peach and the puddle of maple syrup.

Asha hesitated. Pearl gave her an exasperated look and scolded, "C'mon, mom, before the board melts."

Asha picked up her fork and selected a sturdy-looking slice. She drew an "o" in the center space.

"So you think the old guy met her?" Kip's tone said it all – incredulous, delighted and many things in between.

"Well, I can't be positive," Walter hedged, "but it sure sounded like her. And the dog sounded exactly like her dog."

"Yeah, except you said there were two dogs that day." Kip pushed his baseball cap back and scratched his head. "You said she only had one dog."

"Yeah," Walter agreed. He didn't know what to make of that. Maybe it was her. Walter squinted involuntarily as he tried to picture her deciding to go out hiking. He could see it. She looked like she could be the hiker type. She looked really fit; Walter remembered taking notice of that. She had incredible shoulders. When she reached up to show that he'd positioned the phone too high, he saw sculpted arm, shoulder, and upper back and couldn't help but wish he saw more.

I like to hike, Walter mused, picturing her out in the woods. Maybe one day we could do some hiking together. I could show her the swimming holes deep in Platte Clove, take her up Overlook in the winter when there's no one there, or show her the quarry on Sugar Loaf. Maybe we could discover stuff together, do some bush whacking and finally complete the thirty-five. I've been meaning to finish that list for ages. He shook himself, trying to bring his thoughts back into The Dancing Bear and the conversation he was having with Kip. Yeah, she was believably hiker-ish.

"Why don't you go check out Charlie's cabin again?" Kip was talking. Walter beamed back in, seemingly mid-sentence. "Search the place. See if she left anything there." Kip rearranged his baseball cap, smoothing his hair underneath. He added, "She sounds a little like a ditz if she was lost and hiked the wrong mountain. Maybe she was ditzy enough to leave something lying around with her name and number on it?"

Walter opened his mouth to defend her, to argue furiously against calling her a ditz. He caught himself and grinned. Kip grinned back, getting it. "Yeah." Walter took Kip's suggestion, since it was the only concrete action either one of them came up with. "Yeah." Walter repeated, still smiling. "Good idea."

Labor Day dawned like a throwback to July: hazy, hot and humid, without the promise of a thunderstorm to clear things out. Just hot and muggy and unappealing. Asha reconsidered. Perhaps it wasn't a great day to hike a 3500 footer. For most women my age, she thought, this would be a perfect mall day: air conditioning, sales, and a day off from parenting. She poured her coffee right into the travel mug. She fed the dogs, the dry kibble pellets loud against the plastic bowls. No, she thought as she caught a glimpse of her face reflected in the cabinet's glass door, I'm just not that kind of girl. Haven't had a hairdo since 10th grade (more of a "hair don't," she giggled to herself), haven't worn makeup since my wedding, and that was an anomaly back then. Naaahh, she shook her head, shaggy curls swinging left and right. No interest in heading over to the mall. I prefer the woods: bugs, sweat, and that cranky old weird guy. My kind of day.

Not Pearl's kind of day, though. Somehow I spawned a mall rat, Asha admitted to herself, dropping an apple and a Luna Bar into her day pack. Today would not be a day to drag Pearl out on a hike. Good thing she's busy with her dad and his family today. Asha pictured the backyard, filled with wet children screaming and splashing and adults with drinks in their hands, lounging poolside. Carl's sister and all the sisters-in-law had hairdos and breakable nails. She knew Pearl would have a great time. Asha also knew she belonged somewhere else, somewhere far, far away from recreation that included chlorine and concrete.

Chasing after that early start, Asha allowed herself to skip the job search ritual. She drank half of her coffee at the kitchen table, eating a bagel and watching hummingbirds visit her bee balm and rose-of-sharon. One male, one female. They bickered, squeaking at each other when they got too close. She grinned, enjoying them. Small but feisty to the point of obnoxious, and completely unafraid of humans, Asha admired the tiny birds. Why am I charmed by miniature cranky tyrants? she wondered, and swigged the remains of her coffee. A glance at the clock elicited a colorful curse: no time to make a second cup.

She shifted into high gear, wrestling her curls into two short ponytails. The dogs wagged expectantly and paced as she finished packing her pack. The drive across the two counties was unremarkable. She chose the Jetta, having seen Charlie's road and driveway, she knew she didn't need the truck. Save gas, save money.

She had been toying with applying to random jobs she wasn't even interested in, just to say she'd done something. Made an effort. Over the past two weeks, she hadn't seen a single job she would even consider. There was just nothing out there. The process was feeling so stagnant Asha knew she had to do something, but hiking was the only activity that held any appeal. Knowing rationally that her choices were irrational and yet feeling at peace with the chaos; that was the best summary she could come up with to describe her current state. They were the words she repeatedly silently in answer to the completely rational questions she kept asking herself: What the hell am I doing with my life, my career, my financial security? And all that came back from the place within her where she held all her answers was: "I'm going hiking." That's all.

This inner dialog was sufficient for most of the way. Navigating those last few turns, heading up the clove between White Man Mountain to the west, Roundtop in front of her, and the long spine of Bearpen, huge and curving to the north and east, rooted her in the present tense. She pulled up to Charlie's cabin and cleared her throat.

The dogs bounded up to the screen door, unaffected by the heaviness of the muggy soup they were breathing. She followed behind them.

"Hey there," from Asha's angle all she saw was his hand reach out and pat Brulee's head. She smiled. "Smokey?" Charlie raised his voice, then stepped onto the porch to spit.

"Hi." Asha greeted the old man. She hung back and hovered on the porch.

Charlie was up and dressed for the day, white undershirt, blue workpants, and, as a nod to the weather, brand new Teva sandals. She noticed them but said nothing.

Charlie examined her too. He couldn't decide just what he thought of her cockamamie outfit. Who the hell wears shorts to walk in the woods? Unable to hold back, he grumbled "Yer legs are gonna git all scratched up from the blackberries." And what did she do to her hair? It looked like two brown pom-poms got stuck to her head. Charlie squinted at her and unconsciously ran his hand over his own bent and lumpy hairstyle. She was clearly a grown woman, he decided, but she looked like such a little kid. It wasn't just that she was clean, and it wasn't that all her clothes looked new and modern and full of crazy colors. Even her socks were some damn shade of purple, Charlie noticed. Was it that she looked kind of innocent? Nah, Charlie corrected himself. Not innocent. She just didn't look mean. She looked like life hadn't shit on her yet, and she hadn't turned mean because of it. She lacked the meanness Charlie knew so well. It was what helped folks survive out here, where the soil was thin, winters were long, and when the black flies were bad, they could damn near carry off children or livestock. Life was hard and beautiful and mean, and the only response that made any sense to Charlie was to give it right back, to dish out as much meanness as he received. Smokey looked soft and pretty and nice. How the hell did she do that, Charlie wondered, since she ain't no kid no more?

"Ya ready to head up?" he asked.

"Sure," Asha answered a little too quickly.

"Follow me," Charlie pushed past her and headed, stiff-legged, down the stairs. Both dogs flowed past Charlie and raced into the tall bluestem meadow behind the cabin. Charlie walked much the same way he drove, slowly, carefully, and occasionally talking to himself when things got tricky. He led Asha through the tall grasses to the opening in the woods at the northeast corner of the meadow. She did not attempt a conversation along the way.

"Should take ya a coupla hours ta git up top," Charlie jerked his thumb in the general direction she should go. "Take yer time, there ain't much water out there this time of year. Don't git over-heated, 'cuz I ain't gonna be much help comin' after ya."

"I should be okay. I have plenty of water." Asha gestured at the pack on her back. "And I have more in the car if I run out."

Charlie looked at the car, one hundred yards away, and frowned. "Ya got a map with ya?"

Asha nodded and produced a folded up piece of paper from her back pocket.

Charlie pored over it for a minute then rubbed his jaw. "This looks like a piece of the USGS map…" he mused. "Where's the rest of it?"

"I printed it out on my computer at home, using a USGS software program."

Asha's explanation looked like it put lemons in Charlie's mouth. His frown deepened into a look of utter distaste. "Okay, well I guess it'll work." Charlie tried to move on, shaking off the unpleasant experience. So you don't need to buy maps anymore. Just buy a computer, software, a printer, ink, and tinker around with it when it don't work right. Nah. Charlie thought he'd just buy himself a map. Save himself all that trouble and nonsense. He showed her where they were on her piece of paper and traced the route with a wrinkled finger up to the summit. "There's an old trail," he offered, "that I used to take to go git blackberries. It'll take ya right up to the top. Then," Charlie smiled broadly, "follow the same trail back down here. There ain't no old geezer on the other side to give you a ride back over here." At that Charlie laughed, wheezed, coughed, and spat. She took it as her cue to leave.

"Bye, Smokey. See you later."

Asha was back in Charlie's backyard three hours later. She was strong, fit, and a touch lonely out there, so she moved fast. Charlie would have been impressed.

The dogs bounded up the porch steps and through the screen door ahead of her. Charlie stumbled out, clearly having enjoyed a beer or two with lunch and a post-lunch nap. His white hair would have given it away, flattened to the left side of his head and sticking straight up on top, if his blinking and stumbling didn't. He squinted at Asha as she approached, "Well, Smokey, how was ol' Bearpen?" Sleep and bleariness softened Charlie, his squint and growl toned down to mere grumbling.

She responded by smiling a wide toothy grin, spreading her extended fingers for him to see and sticking out her tongue. Blackberry juice had stained her tongue purplish-black, and her fingers, legs, and clothes were decorated with deep magenta blotches. Charlie laughed appreciatively. She braced herself for the coughing and spitting that seemed to reliably accompany Charlie's expressions of mirth.

"Didja bring me some?" he managed to wheeze.

She produced a quart mason jar, minus the rubber gasket, full of berries. "These are for you."

"Thanks Smokey." Charlie took the jar and headed inside. Lyla and Brulee flanked him, Brulee taking the side with the available hand. He petted her and fussed over the dogs as he shuffled across the cabin. Asha followed them in. "Have a seat, Smokey." Charlie was back to yelling and growling. She sat. "Wanna beer?"

"No thanks," was her automatic response. A beer actually sounded good, she realized. Not some pisswater, mass-produced crap, but something that actually tasted good. Asha knew better than to ask Charlie about choices in that area. She'd seen what he drank. She tried to remember if she had one Dogfish Head Brown Ale somewhere in the back of her fridge back home. Not likely, she decided.

"You sure? I got a bottle of this stuff my friend made." Charlie pulled a Grolsch bottle out of his apartment sized fridge and held it up for her to see. "I can't drink it." Charlie pulled a face. "All full of flavors." He exaggerated the look of disgust, hamming it up for her. "You might like it." Look at what yer wearing and what ya did to yer hair, Charlie added silently. There's no accountin' fer taste.

"Okay." Asha flashed her I'm-a-good-guest smile. Charlie shoved the bottle into her hand.

"Hold on." Charlie handed her a glass. "My buddy says ya gotta drink it out of a glass. Says it tastes better that way." Charlie cracked open another Bud.

Maybe it was the heat, and maybe it was that she was already a touch dehydrated, but the beer tasted fantastic. As good as her beloved Dogfish Head, or better, it was a beautiful rich red-brown color, sweet and complex. Slow down, she told herself after the first sip. Got a long drive home and this stuff is strong.

And so, each with their own version of hops and malt Samadhi, they began to talk. They talked about Bearpen, or, more to the point, Charlie talked about Bearpen. He told Asha about the forests in the 1940's and '50's. He regaled her with tales of bears and blackberries, both in the woods and in the kitchen. He bragged about his prowess with a bow and arrow and he waxed nostalgic about Virginia's venison stew and blackberry pie.

"Virginia?" Asha spoke the name gently, reverently. "Your wife?"

"Yep." Charlie looked past Asha, focusing on something behind her on the kitchen counter. "We got married in 1943." He paused, glanced at Asha, then gazed at the handle of the drawer behind her. She followed his gaze, then looked back at Charlie. "That handle fell off mebbe ten years ago. My buddy, he's a real handy guy, comes up here all ready to put on a new one. Gonna replace the old worn out one, right?" Charlie shook his head. "Virginia picked out them handles. She liked 'em. Said they made this here cabin look like a woman had been here too. Can't replace 'em, jes' 'cuz they're old."

"You're alone now?" Asha asked.

"I been alone for damn near sixty years." Charlie spat the words at Asha, angry with her for not knowing, then angry with himself.

"I'm alone now too," Asha offered, then pressed her lips together. It paled in comparison.

"Why the hell are you alone, Smokey? You could be real pretty if you didn't look so…" The alcohol loosed Charlie's tongue just enough to leave the rest of that sentence hanging in the air between them. Without the words to explain further, his voice trailed off.

"I'm alone now. There was someone. It didn't work out," Asha reddened slightly and looked out the window, feeling like she might start crying. Goddammit. Brulee got up and clicked steadily, confidently, over to her. She sat at Asha's side and leaned in gently. Asha stroked her head without looking at her. Lyla, curled up at her feet, didn't move.

"That is one damn good dog," Charlie stated. "It's a Belgian Malinoise, isn't it?" Charlie puffed up a little, proud of his efforts.

"You say it mal-in-wah," Asha corrected, and then immediately regretted doing so. "Yeah." She looked down at Brulee and her eyes filled. "Yeah, she's a good dog. She's been there for me through everything. I got her after I got divorced. I've had her for four years now, and I guess we really know each other inside and out." Asha blinked hard and swallowed harder, then met Charlie's eyes. "You can love a dog in ways that you just can't love a person. A dog can take it."

Charlie finished his Bud and set the empty bottle down on the table with a clunk of agreement. "What happened? What'd he do, cheat on ya?"

"No." Shit. She clenched her teeth to stop the tears. "He didn't. It was the one after him that did." Charlie pulled a ratty bandanna out of his pocket and pushed it across the table. Asha dabbed at her eyes, grateful that it didn't smell like gasoline or anything worse. "I found out I was losing my job. We had only been together a few months. He kind of offered the rescue," she looked up at Charlie to see if he was getting this. His eyes locked on hers. She dropped her gaze to her hands and continued. "He suggested that we live together, that we buy a place together over by Warwick."

Charlie nodded familiarity. "They got the black dirt over there. He a farmer?"

She nodded. "Kind of. Anyway, the more we made plans and started making it real, that I was really going to sell my house, that we were really going to move in together..."

"Where ya live now, Smokey?"

"Far from here. Dutchess County." Charlie nodded again. She continued. "Then things started getting strained. Tense, I guess. He started working late a lot, and getting headaches when we had plans. Then he made plans to hang out with other people when we had time alone planned. I should have seen it coming."

"Ye only see whatcher lookin' at, Smokey. I bet you were lookin' at land and houses over in Warwick, thinkin' happily ever after thoughts." Charlie shook his head. "That bastard was lookin' fer a way out."

"I found him with her, out, at a spot we used to go to. A special spot," Asha wept openly, saturating the red rag.

Charlie sat silently for a while, watching her cry and thinking back on things. "Times like this, Smokey girl, I ain't proud to be a man. I tell ya that true, as true as them dogs there. Men do some bad things, and then, when they think they ain't gonna git caught, they turn around and do some'n worse." He got up, and headed out the door to clear his throat and spit. On his way back to his seat, he patted her shoulder, a little too hard and a little too awkwardly, he realized, but it was the first time he'd touched a woman in damn near twenty years. "So how long ago didja find 'em?"

"About six weeks."

"An' how long you say you were with 'im?"

"Almost a year."

"Well, it's gonna take some time, Smokey. I always say ya gotta times it by three. Ya think it should take about two months? Plan fer six." He sounded confident. She stopped crying. "I loved Virginia to a degree you can't know about yet, Smokey. I loved her when I first saw her, and I kept on lovin' her after she passed, and after both my sons passed, and a long time after I thought I should git going myself. Fer a while there, I was mad, too. She up and left me with two little boys, and what the hell good was I at being a mother and a father to them boys? No damn good at all. I hurt bad when she left, but I hurt worse after both my boys were gone. The one thing I had to do after she was gone was to raise them up right, and I failed. They were wild stupid boys, and they died because I couldn't teach 'em how to be men." Asha raised her eyebrows at him, awaiting an explanation. "Liquor and a motorcycle took one; loggin' accident took the other." He reached over to the counter for another rag, and wiped his face.

"You want to move on, to stop hurtin' and find someone new, butcha can't, right?" Charlie predicted. Asha nodded. "An' ya don't know how to let go, right?" Again she nodded. "An' people keep tellin' ya that cha gotta fergive, right?" This time he didn't wait for the nod. "Fergiveness – I heard an awful lot o' that shit when I was mad as hell and hurtin' like a baby back then. Preacher would talk about fergiveness to me. Hell, one day that crazy ol' man drove way the hell out here to try to tell me some nonsense about fergiveness. I think they thought I was gonna blow my brains out after my second son died, so they sent the preacher up here to talk me out of it." Charlie laughed. Asha didn't. He continued. "They'll tell ya that ya can't move on til ya fergive that bastard, but don't believe 'em. That's horseshit. You ain't never gonna fergive that bastard fer what he did, an' ya shouldn't. But yer gonna have to git back in that saddle and ride, girl. This is yer life, and ya gotta ride it out. Like a damn TV show, this episodes over. It mighta stunk, or it mighta bin great, but what the hell, time's up, and it's over. Next." Charlie blew his nose and mopped his face again. "Yer sufferin' ain't worth shit. It's part o' last week's episode. This week somethin' else is gonna happen. You gonna sit this one out, sufferin'? Bad move. You keep that up and y'know where you'll end up? Old and alone, girlie. Old and alone jes' like yours truly here."

Asha wasn't sure what to make of his words, of his story. She sat silent for a moment or two, absorbing it, crumpling the bandanna in her hands, and keeping her eyes lowered. She spoke without looking up. "After things fell apart for me, I got Lyla. I thought having another dog, one that is so beautiful she takes your breath away every time she walks in the room, would take away some of the hurt," Asha slid down in her chair and cocked her head to look at Lyla under the table. Lyla caught her eye and thumped her tail against the floor a few times. "Good dog," she murmured. She sat back up and looked at Charlie, with his thin veiny old man arms folded across his clean white undershirt. "It didn't work. I'm just as lonely. Just as hurt."

"Lonely." Charlie unfolded his arms and banged both palms onto the tabletop, knocking over his empty bottle. "Lonely." He lowered his voice. It was definitely scarier than his yelling. "Listen Smokey, mebbe you think you know what lonely is, seein' as how you've been missin' your man for what? Mebbe a whole month now?" Asha shrank visibly. "Lonely." Charlie belched like a fifth grade boy. "I'll tell ya what lonely is. Lonely is headin' up Lone Mountain from the Neversink in November. Cold, gray, short day with no goddamn snow to make it pretty, no goddamn tracks to follow, no one waiting at home to hear your story, no one to know or care if you live or die out there. Jes' you on that hill, all alone out there, in the goddamned middle of nowhere. No roads fer miles. You make a mistake," Charlie was on a roll. He paused to open another beer and take a swig. "- ya make a mistake out there with yer compass or somethin', yer done. That's it. Yer sleepin' in the woods, findin' yer way out the next day. If ya can."

Asha had heard of this Lone Mountain. It was on her list. Charlie peered at her, frowning, thinking.

"Lone's different. She ain't like Bearpen here. She ain't got the friendliness, the berries an' the ol' ski slopes to make ya think yer not so far from help. Lone's out there, half a day's walk from nowhere but more mountains." He took another swig. "Lone'll show you what yer made of. An' she'll teach ya a thing er two about loneliness." He stopped, set the bottle down and took a long breath. The fact that this girl in front of him didn't know shit about loneliness wasn't worth getting all riled up about. She was just young and strange, out hiking for no damn reason but to finish a list. He relented. She didn't mean no harm. She couldn't touch what he held inside, but that didn't make her a fool and it didn't make her wrong for trying. "You don't know what the hell I'm talkin' about, do you, Smokey-girl?" His tone gentled, like he was speaking to a young child. The storm had passed. "You ain't lonely. Yer jes' waitin'. I bin lonely, an' I done my share o' waitin'." He looked old, tired, sad, relieved, a lifetime's worth of emotions crossed his face in a chaotic parade. "Yer gonna git what yer waitin' fer, Smokey, an' so will I. So will I."

The phone was ringing as Walter walked in the door. He checked the caller id and let the machine get it. Just not in the mood to chat.

The machine beeped and Walter ignored his work buddy's invitation to join the guys from his local at a charity bowling event. Not in the mood to go bowling either.

He emptied his lunch box, putting dirty containers in the dishwasher, banana peel in the compost bin, reading material (a Woodworker's Journal this week) back on the magazine stack.

Walter considered working out. He glanced at the clock and reviewed his exercise so far this week. Last night he'd run his mile and a half and done a set of push-ups and pull-ups. He could get away with taking a night off. He stretched his arms out in front of him, lacing his fingers, palms turned out. Nice and sore, he admitted; pecs and triceps felt nicely worked. But it was an abs day. A twenty minute video or a set of Pilates exercises and crunches, that was the routine. Walter sighed, ignoring the answering machine's blinking light, ignoring the pile of junk mail competing with condiments for space on the huge kitchen table, and failing in his efforts to ignore the bad mood settling in for the evening.

"A workout will make me feel better," Walter argued out loud, but to no avail. He just didn't feel like it.

"Oh, all right," Walter pulled a Grolsch bottle out of the fridge and poured himself a glass of homemade brown ale. Then he clicked on his laptop, also vying for horizontal space on the kitchen table, and forced himself to check what was going on in the online dating world.

"I'm down to only checking once a month," Walter realized, looking at his last log in date. "Wow." He sipped the brown ale and smiled. Whatever else happened, at least he could brew beer. This batch was the best yet, medium body, plenty of roasted grain flavor, not too bitter. He allowed himself to wonder if Charlie had even tasted it before declaring it unpalatable. Who cares? His smile broadened. At least I know that next time I'm at Charlie's there's a beer there for me. Not that nasty pisswater Charlie drinks.

Walter scrolled and sipped, laptop on the kitchen table, not yet out of his work clothes. Five to a page and five pages later, Walter admitted to himself that he wasn't really seeing what he was scrolling past. He was just pretending to look, pretending to be realistic, pretending to give up on The Customer with The Dog, and move on. Whether or not Charlie's hiker-woman with the dogs was actually Her, Walter was in the throes of trying to force himself to admit defeat. There was nothing left to do. It was a moment, but it was just that. Sure, she was beautiful in that gypsy princess way, but she was impossible. Even if he could find a way to make contact, and that there was a chance that she was indeed open to even meeting him socially, she lived too far away for any kind of dating to make sense. The whole thing was just past far-fetched. It was impossible.

And to claim that she was the love of his life was, Walter finally admitted, self-defeating. It was a set up, preventing him from finding someone real, local and available. Sure she is beautiful, but so is, he searched his mind for an appropriate comparison, Halle Berry. As soon as he made the connection, his heart sank and his train of thought derailed. The purpose of the famous person comparison was to point out just how ridiculous he was being and just how impossible the whole fantasy relationship was. But no. She does look like Halle Berry, he thought to himself, and he was undone anew. Sip, click, and a fresh screenful glided past his unseeing eyes.

Match.com offered Walter the option to expand his search, maybe change the criteria to a larger geographic area? Forget it, he decided. Enough of this. He logged off the site and considered checking his email. Nah, he decided, and clicked through the shut down sequence. Not in the mood for that either. He took his time finishing his beer, enjoying the way the flavors changed as it warmed to room temperature. Good cold, but even better cool. Walter smiled. It was a particularly good batch.

I'll call Jonathan. Maybe he'll feel like doing something tonight. A movie would be okay, some brain candy, a little two-hour vacation. Or maybe Jonathan will want to take the kayaks out. Walter looked out the window. Seems like a nice enough evening.

Walter pushed back from the kitchen table and sat up straight. He looked around the room, mentally ticking off projects completed and those that remained on the list. Well, lists, plural. There was the nagging, immediate future list, containing items like: 1) buy mousetraps, 2) replace the under-the-sink filters, 3) wage the next battle against cobwebs above the cabinets, etc. But there was also the longer term, larger project list: 1) choose, design, and install the backsplash for behind the stove. Copper? Tile? Stone? 2) finish the trim under the cabinets, 3) choose colors and paint.

Everything was still builder's white and Walter had lived in the house long enough to start making decisions that would mark it as his own. In the face of these chores, he procrastinated. It was easier, in some ways, to just go help Charlie.

Walter had bought the land years ago, right after Annie left. He loved the solitude, the quiet, the pond at the end of the road, and the total absence of visible neighbors. He had just enough cash to put up a modest cape, a vinyl sided modular, and put in the time finishing it himself. As the years passed and the hurt and anger morphed into loneliness and boredom, Walter lost enthusiasm for the finishing. "I guess I thought I'd be making these decisions with someone else's input. Bouncing ideas around. Getting a partner's preferences." Walter spoke to the white walls as he made his way to the bathroom, deciding to shower first, then call Jonathan. "Hell, even arguing with someone would get the creative juices flowing." He pulled off the orange Verizon t-shirt and tossed it into the hamper.

After Annie, Walter had tried to date. He tried to be open minded, to adopt a nothing ventured, nothing gained attitude, and, he admitted to himself as he turned on the hot water and examined his face in the mirror before it steamed up, he had met some nice women. There was that one, Linda, a few years ago, that he actually saw for a few months. It was nice, he remembered, adjusting the water temperature and stepping into the shower, to have someone to do things with. It was nice, Walter smiled ruefully as he soaped up, to feel wanted. Annie had been a real sexual playmate: adventurous, creative, passionate – a little wacky, perhaps, but she was fun, and she made sex fun. He learned to laugh at himself and let anything happen.

With Annie, being intimate was, well, intimate. He missed that terribly when he embarked upon a sexual relationship with Linda. She was just not like Annie. I know it's not fair to compare, Walter thought and hung his head and then had to snort to blow the shampoo out of his nose. Not long after they started sleeping together, Linda had initiated the "Us Talk" with Walter, asking all the questions she had a right to ask. All the questions

Walter would have paid money to hear Annie utter. Coming from Linda, Walter knew there was only one answer that preserved everyone's dignity. Walter held himself to his father's standards; he had to be a good man and do the right thing. He broke up with Linda on the spot. He knew he didn't feel for her the way she needed him to feel, and he realized that he never would, so he was honest, clear and final. He'd been alone since then.

Asha checked the weather online. "Damn," she muttered. The weekend threatened the triple H again with thunderstorms predicted. No hiking with Pearl. "Shit." Asha frowned at the screen as if her glare could change the forecast. "Shit, shit, shit." Friday looked perfect. Clear, sunny, temps in the low seventies, low humidity: it was going to be a perfect day in the woods. But school starts for Pearl on Thursday, Asha whined silently. I can't take her out to go hiking on the second day of school.

"Hey Pearl," Asha yelled from her seat at the computer. "Wanna take a day off from school?"

"Can't hear ya, Peach!" Pearl yelled back, quoting from *Finding Nemo*. She was in her room, door shut, music on.

Asha bounced out of the chair, leaving the weather forecast on the screen and bounded into Pearl's room. Both dogs accompanied her. "Wanna go hiking on Friday? Take the day off from school?" She had barged in and made the offer, surprising Pearl who was trying on outfits for the first day of school. The current selection involved khaki Bermuda shorts with a crisp button-up short sleeved shirt. "Looks good," she added, indicating the clothes.

"Sure. And thanks."

She plunked herself down on Pearl's bed to watch the fashion show.

"Out." Pearl sure could be blunt. Asha took a deep breath, not wanting to take it personally, but taking it personally. She hesitated for a moment, then left. Both dogs accompanied her.

"If I ever write my memoir," she informed them, "I'm naming it Ten Legs."

The summer routine continued. Coffee and internet classified ads every morning, chores and entertaining Pearl during the day, worrying, watching the weather, and feeling sorry for herself after dinner. Only a few more days of summer remained. Pearl's first day of eighth grade was on Wednesday. "What am I gonna do," Asha asked herself, "when Pearl is back at school?"

Get creative, she admonished. Get excited about something (other than hiking? Do I have to?). Follow your passion, she chided. But nothing seemed to present itself as a candidate for passion. Nothing on the internet and nothing in her imagination. Nothing, nothing, nothing. She felt like throwing a full blown tantrum, as if that would somehow convince the job hunting gods to toss something inspiring her way.

The days were good. She and Pearl rode bikes on the rail trail and took the dogs swimming in the Housatonic. They ate ice cream for lunch, a huge splurge to go out to Fudgy's for ice cream, but she figured it was okay this one final week of summer. And there was laughter when Lyla first tried to swim and splashed around spastically, when Asha fell off her bike standing still in the parking lot, when Pearl got ice cream up her nose. She felt a bit like her financial state had been declared terminal, so she was living her last few days soaking up every nuance of all that was good. These days with Pearl were pure good.

So when Thursday night rolled around, she set her misgivings about stealing her child away from the public school system aside and pulled out her daypack. "Extra clothes, extra food, extra water. Carrying all that should slow me down enough to keep the pace pleasant for Pearl," she murmured to herself as she selected the child's favorite flavor Clif bar from the cupboard. Pearl was watching TV, uninterested in the preparations. I guess she is a fairly normal preteen, Asha acknowledged, listening to the Disney

channel blast from the other room. A few more items in the pack
and then she joined Pearl on the couch.

The next morning, on the way to the trailhead, she had an
idea. "Hey Pearl -"

"Yah?" Pearl affected an indistinguishable European accent.
Asha grinned.

"Behind you, on the floor, there's a pair of binoculars." Pearl
began feeling around behind her seat. "I bet it would be kind of
cool to look through them while I'm driving."

"Isn't that dangerous?" Pearl located them, but did not hand
them over.

"Not me, you turkey-nose!" Asha was laughing, the idea
much funnier to her mother than Pearl thought it should be. "You!
Try it. Tell me what it's like."

"Oh." Pearl exhaled, sheepish, but intrigued. She put the
binoculars to her eyes and looked out the windshield. Almost instantly, she started screaming. "Look out! Watch out for that tree!
Omigod, there's a car coming!" She snatched the field glasses
away from her face then burst out laughing and flung them back
into place. She panted and tried not to scream as they went around
a few curves, and then gave in and resumed screeching. "Look
out for those mailboxes!"

Minutes of this elapsed, Asha laughing at Pearl's condition.
Finally exhausted, Pearl laid the binoculars in her lap. "That was
cool, mom."

"Thought you'd like it."

"You ever try it?" Pearl wanted to know.

"Nah. It just popped into my head, just now."

"Well, maybe next time you and Rob go," Pearl remembered
two words too late. "Sorry, mom." Pearl watched Asha chew the
insides of her mouth and study the road through the windshield.
"I'm really sorry."

"It's okay, Pearl." Asha sighed, breath escaping between
clenched teeth. "I do it too. It's okay." Asha tried to smile at
Pearl, but it didn't work. Pearl looked out the window and they
rode on in silence for a while.

"When things ended with Dad were you upset like this?" Pearl wanted to know.

"No." Asha was scrupulously honest. "Not like this. Your dad didn't behave badly. We didn't break up because of some dramatic, disgraceful act that was unforgiveable. We had tried everything, for a long time, but we really weren't able to be a married couple together. When we finally decided to end things, it was more of a relief, for both of us, than a surprise that hurt either one of us." Asha checked to see how Pearl was receiving this information. She looked okay. She continued. "When I left, it was out of hope and the desire to be married, to be in a real marriage and to have you see what that looks like and feels like so that one day you'll be able to figure it out for yourself."

"You and Daddy never fought." It was a statement, but it was also a question.

"That's true, honey. We almost never fought; we almost never even argued," she smiled a small nostalgic smile, remembering. "We liked each other. We respected each other. We had been good friends for a long time." She turned to Pearl for emphasis. "I thought that was enough for a good marriage."

"Eyes on the road." Pearl gestured with her finger turning in a circle. Asha turned back to the road.

"We really were like brother and sister. And I still love him and care about him like a brother. And," Asha's smile finally reached her eyes, "like your father."

Pearl was quiet, the binoculars in her lap, her face unreadable.

The dogs lay in curled tight circles on the back seat, quiet and happy.

Asha's mind wandered around events of the recent and distant past. She thought about the past month or so from Pearl's perspective. How stupid I've been, she marveled silently, to think that I was hiding all that hurt from her. She knew. Asha held in a sigh, catching herself and letting the breath escape slowly, silently. She knew. How does it feel, Asha wondered, to watch your mom go through something like this? And to know she hurts more over

some random asshole than over your father? Asha tried to imagine what it was like for Pearl and stole glances at her a couple of
times before letting it go. Pearl wasn't stoic. She wouldn't suffer
silently. She wouldn't bear some private pain to spare her mother.
No way. Asha felt certain she could trust her daughter to communicate. Asha knew communication was Pearl's blessing and
burden being the only daughter of a psychotherapist.

She slowed down and hit the turn signal, aiming for a spot at
the pull-off for Giant Ledge. The moment the tires crunched on
gravel, the dogs sprang to life, wagging, pacing and panting in the
small backseat. Despite the exchange with Pearl, Asha felt good.
Anticipation of hours on the trail filled her with something close
to jubilance. The day was all it had promised to be, high skies
and clear. The views would be postcard perfect, a three fire tower
view, if they could pick them out.

Pearl popped out, stretching her long limbs and looking
around. "Can I let them out?" She indicated the dogs.

"Yeah. Keep an eye on them, though." Asha busied herself
with getting her pack, finding all the leashes, and stowing the
keys. "All good?" she asked Pearl once she was finished.

"Sure." Pearl pushed her bangs out of her eyes. "How long
'til ice cream?"

"Soon, oh Hike-Hating Patient One. Soon."

Walter helped himself to a hearty serving of Ben and Jerry's.
Phish Phood this week. He ate it in front of the TV, watching the
sci-fi channel. Mindless entertainment and dark chocolate phish-
es: life was good.

He sighed deeply and set the bowl down on the end table
while he stretched and shifted around to get more comfortable.
He ached the pleasant ache of having earned sore muscles. Work
was for real today, one of those great days on the job where he
truly felt useful and tapped. An intermittent trouble, static, but

only after it rains, and Walter had been able to find the bad spot and fix it. He loved those tricky ones. The sunlight hits the box, evaporates the condensation, hence trouble disappears at a certain time of day mysteries. Or the mouse-nibbled lines that haven't been chewed all the way through yet; they have their own particular sound.

Today one of those was followed by a tough physical one, climbing poles, dragging cable through the woods, carrying ladders back and forth because it was just a little too far for the bucket to reach. Yeah, it was a hot day, but out by Big Indian where he was working through the hottest part of the day, it was breezy and a swimming hole lay in wait just three poles down the road. After getting thoroughly sweaty and getting a family of five back in service, cooling off in a frigid Catskill stream was in order.

Walter had slipped into the woods quickly, not really able to linger and enjoy much more than a quick dip. Relax, he had told himself, I worked through lunch and fixed that dog of a trouble that had been turned back three times. A quick rinse on my lunch hour shouldn't bother anyone. Perhaps not, but, Walter pointed out to himself, the phone guy probably shouldn't take all his clothes off while at least technically at work. There is probably some rule against that somewhere, he acknowledged, pulling his shirt over his head. Fuck the rules, he grinned, unbuckling his tool belt and slipping out of workpants and underpants all in one movement.

Walter leapt into the creek, and boom, he was out, standing on the grassy bank, shivering. That water must be about forty degrees, he decided. It felt amazing; all neurons firing at once, all trace of hot sticky discomfort gone. Just for sheer pleasure, Walter tossed himself in a second time, into the deepest part of the swimming hole. Head fully submerged for a split second, Walter felt his core temperature drop and his brain shrink its awareness to one thing and one thing only: COLD. Walter exploded out of the water, splashing, leaping and whooping a spontaneous cry, one part lung spasm and two parts delight.

To round out the work day, Walter's last trouble took him to Charlie's neighborhood. After taking care of it, a simple service order, he stopped in at Charlie's. Charlie was in fine spirits, awake, relatively sober, and reliably cranky. He had been reading his dog book, which gave Walter the opening he sought.

"Did that woman with the dog come back?" Walter asked.

"Smokey?" Charlie asked, as if Walter should know her name.

"Smokey?" Walter repeated.

"Her damn name is Ashes or something like that. I ain't calling her no stupid Ash name." Charlie enjoyed yelling at Walter about how insufferable Asha's name was. "Smokey. And she gave her dog some damn fool frog name."

"Frog name?" Walter wondered, his heart starting to pound.

"Yeah. Goddamned French frog fools. Dog's name means burnt. Goes with Smokey, don't it?"

Walter smiled. Charlie had just confirmed it for him. "Asha and Brulee," he strove to keep his voice even. "You call her Smokey?"

"Yeah," Charlie angled to book a little to let the light from the open window hit the page. "Lemme read you this part, Walt. Listen to what the book says about them Belgian mallinwah dogs."

Charlie read a paragraph about the breed's temperament, but Walter didn't really hear it. He stood in the doorway, feeling one thing after another: delight, frustration, hope, and worry. When Charlie finished, he asked, "Is she coming back any time soon?"

"Nah. Well, mebbe," Charlie looked up from the book and grasped the import of the question. "She ain't the one, is she, Walt?"

"Yeah." He heard his voice as if from far away. "Yessir, Charlie, she is the one."

Charlie shut the book. He walked across the room and set it down on the table. "Goddammit, Walt," he said. "I'da asked her fer her number er somethin' if I'd known."

"That's okay," Walter managed to say. "So, y'think maybe she might come back here again sometime?" He couldn't help but ask again.

"Yeah, Walt. I think she jes' might," Charlie said, hoping it was at least part-way true. "She didn't say nothin' 'bout comin' back this way, but I guess I got a little bit of a feelin' about it. But I'll promise ya this, if she does, I'll tell her she needs to call ya."

Walter was both elated and worried. "How are you going to have that make sense? I'm gonna sound like some kind of stalker."

"Don't you worry, Walt," Charlie smiled, his sprinkling of teeth looking artfully arranged, "I got decades worth o' lies and exaggerations to cull from. You jes' might need some sort o' information 'bout her damn list of mountains. Er mebbe yer tryin' ta find out about mallinwah dogs. Don't you worry, Walt," Charlie's voice softened and he laid a hand on Walter's arm, "I'll say something that'll make her want to call you."

Walter smiled, his head still buzzing with the realization that she had been there, right there, in Charlie's cabin. And now Charlie was offering to play matchmaker. "Thank you," he said.

He started out, and then turned back to look at Charlie. He looked at the old man, who stood there in the cabin looking back at Walter. "I really mean it, Charlie. Thank you."

And so here he was, pleasantly tired, having earned his ice cream calories by honest hard physical labor. He sat back, letting it sink in that Asha, "Smokey," was over on his side of the Hudson, hiking her way through a list of mountains. That, it seemed to Walter in his sugar and fat-induced euphoria, was a giant step closer to meeting her. Charlie knew her well enough to complain about her. Hell, he even offered to make the connection. That seemed beyond promising.

What with Pearl back at school, Asha's daily rhythm took on that school day beat. Pearl was out of the house by seven, back home at two thirty. Asha was amazed and dismayed by how little time it really was. She rearranged her early morning to have breakfast with Pearl, and then after Pearl got on the bus took her coffee with her up to the computer. This morning, after zipping through the social work jobs again without seeing anything new, she gave up and headed back down to the kitchen.

She reached for the phone and dialed her mom's number while putting the kettle on for a second cup of coffee.

"Hello?" Mom's voice was blurred by sleep.

"Hi Mom." Asha realized from her mother's hello that it was a little earlier than people without middle schoolers normally function. Oops.

"Hi honey. Are you okay?"

"Yeah, I'm fine, Mom. Sorry, I didn't look at the clock before I dialed. You want me to call you back?"

"No, no, that's okay." Asha heard the scrunching sound of sheets being moved around. Mom is still in bed, Asha groaned to herself. "What's up, honey?"

"Nothing much. I guess that's kind of what's up," Asha trailed off. The kettle whistled and she focused on measuring grounds and pouring water.

"No job interviews coming up?" Mom asked.

"No."

Mom was silent for a moment, then asked, "What comes next, Asha? What are you going to do?"

"I'm planning to talk to Carl. It's in our divorce papers that if I lose my job, my child support increases. I just haven't asked him for money because I know he doesn't have it." Mom made a disapproving sound. Asha continued. "Look, I know what he earns and I know what his expenses are. There is no extra money; he's not saving, and he's definitely not living large. He and his sister bought Pearl all her back to school clothes and supplies. He does stuff like that without my even asking. But I think I'm gonna have to bring up the child support issue. I just don't see another way."

"How dire are things?"

"I can cover my expenses for this month..."

"September?"

"Yeah, I have September covered. And I have enough to cover October's mortgage." Asha felt nauseous, saying these words aloud, making it all so clear and concrete. "I don't have enough liquid now to cover any more after that."

Asha's mom was quiet. Asha heard her long exhale.

"I can take another few thousand from my IRA, but it just seems like such a bad idea, I can't quite stomach it." Asha then voiced the thought she'd been batting around for the past few days. "I'm thinking about going back to school and taking out big student loans to cover my living expenses."

"Oh?" Asha's mom, remembering how relieved Asha had been to finish her master's and be done with school, was surprised.

"Yeah. It's a possibility. It's just hard to get comfortable with the idea of getting into major debt now when I still owe a ton on the master's degree I'm not currently using." Asha paused, taking a sip of coffee and switching the phone to her other ear. "There are degrees I'd love to pursue... " She didn't dare elaborate. Her mom could only stand so much. "But I have to think about getting a job afterward. I'd just have another degree to add to the already bloated education section of my resume and another forty thousand dollars worth of debt." She trailed off, thinking about it again. "As a stopgap measure, it might work, and who knows what might happen in the meantime."

"Honey, I've thought about a few options too." Asha's mother sounded a little rehearsed. Asha tensed. "I've been to a lawyer. I can give you some of your inheritance now. I worked out the details."

"Mom, are you sure?" Asha's voice raised, her grip on the phone tightened.

"Yes, I'm sure. Once you have a job, you can make the payments. It's a home equity line of credit." Asha's mom pre-empted the next interruption. "It's fine. I wouldn't do anything that would put my own retirement at risk."

It was a godsend. There was nothing more to say. "Thank you, Mom." No longer edged in panic and guilt, Asha's voice resumed its gentle cadence.

"You're welcome, honey. It's going to be okay, Ashie. It's a tough time, but you'll get through it." Ashie. God. She hasn't called me that in about twenty years, Asha thought. Not since I didn't have a date for the prom. Mom continued, "Are you dating anyone?"

"No."

"What are you doing with yourself? I know you; you're not sitting around. Are you repainting the kitchen? Or have you taken up the lute?" Her mom was only half-joking.

"I'm hiking the Catskill 35."

"Really?"

"Yup."

"How many have you done so far?"

"Table, Hunter, Balsam Lake, Southwest Hunter, and Bearpen. Five."

"Cool. Nice job honey. Who knows? Maybe you'll meet someone out hiking. At least you'll have similar interests." Mom sure was determined to be cheerful. Asha made a mental note not to wake her mother up again without first finishing a cup or two of coffee herself.

She provided updates regarding Pearl's new school year: teachers and classes and after school activities. Mom filled Asha in on the latest gossip from the laboratory where she still worked. Asha gave her mom her bank information, and they agreed to check in about the transfer later in the week. She hung up, shoved her hands into the deep front pockets of her cut-off Levi's, and went outside.

She walked around her garden alone. No dogs right now. They watched her from their perch on the living room couch and made nose prints on the window. She meandered around the perennial beds, visiting the spot where she had begun digging beds for vegetables, the place she'd dragged all the trees she'd cut down. She wandered over to the shady beds under the hemlocks, the lilac area she'd created over by the mailbox, and the front walkway, which until recently had been lined with dead roses. She made her way to her favorite spot, a sunny patch with the best view of it all, and sat down on the grass.

I almost sold this. She was silent, thinking the words she'd never let herself say out loud. I almost left. Now maybe I can stay, but I don't know if I want to. She looked at all the evidence of her two years of living there; every plant she'd planted, every idea for renovation of the house or garden, every wish, every pipe dream. They were shot through with Rob. Rob the landscaper, Rob the plant-artist, Rob the partner. Part of me wants to walk away from all of this – from Rob, from losing my job, maybe even from Carl too. I want to start over. I want a geographic cure. Asha scratched a mosquito bite on her calf. She looked away from the garden and squinted hard at the house.

Three months ago she "knew" she was moving, and had begun the emotional as well as the literal packing up. This second chance, the opportunity to stay, at first it seemed so natural. Of course she would leap at the chance to stay, to keep Pearl with her friends and near her father. But as Asha sat looking at her house, it dawned on her that she had already left. She looked at her house more closely than she had in months; just looked at the cedar shakes and the old-fashioned windows made from wood and glass and ropes and weights, the patched and cracked foundation that gets hit with the sun and is home to the big black snake. I love this house. But I don't know how long I can live here, being "the one who..." The one who lost her job at the school – whisper whisper. The one who dated that landscaper who screws around with rich housewives up on Quaker Hill – whisper whisper. She sighed, plucked a blade of grass and twirled it between her forefinger and thumb, crushing it. She realized that she was frowning at the stain it was making on her finger. "I don't want to stay," she admitted out loud. "But I don't want to leave either. No," she corrected herself, "I do want to leave, but I'm not ready. Like that old guy said: I'm waiting for something. I don't know what's coming next for me and Pearl. I don't have a plan." She sighed more deeply than before. "I don't have a plan because I don't want one. I'm not ready." And then the light bulb clicked on. This is grief.

This immobilized, apathetic, go hiking while Rome burns attitude is a reaction to loss. Asha laughed at herself, laughed at the relief she felt at switching from feeling it, being in it, to analyzing it. "Okay, grief." She attempted to turn on the therapist part of her brain. "What's the treatment for that?" But she knew, before she had even formed the question. The treatment was time, and the more of it spent hiking the better.

Charlie took his time pulling the card table over by the window where the light was better. It wasn't hot out yet, but looked like it might get there. Charlie had gotten up early, even by old man standards. Today, he decided, was the day, and he wanted to get at least the bulk of the work done before it got too hot. He dragged a chair across the room then headed off to the bedroom closet. He returned moments later with the Winchester in one hand. Charlie paused for a moment and laid the gun on the table, his left hand on the back of the chair. He caught his breath, and then shuffled off in search of sandpaper and his screwdriver.

"I know I got 'em somewhere," Charlie spoke aloud, coaching himself through the project, task by task.

The back room was the mud room, supply closet, and tool shed all in one. Charlie kept the shelves along the back wall organized the way he always had – the way his father set things up a half a century or so ago. He paused, leaning against the doorway, thinking. "Gotta make her look pretty for Walter. He's the kind of man who'd appreciate seein' that gun all cleaned up." He scanned the shelves and selected the turpentine, wood stain, and boiled linseed oil. The jars were small enough and sufficiently well-sealed to carry back to the table, all three at once. Charlie took his time, walking slowly, patient with himself.

The three hand-labeled glass jars set down next to the Winchester, Charlie set off for the kitchen. "Think I got some steel wool under the sink," he grunted as he bent over. Getting back up, he exhaled a long groan, but returned to upright without incident or injury.

Back at the table the cast of characters awaited his direction. Charlie took inventory: gun, screwdriver, fine-grained sandpaper, turpentine, wood stain, the oil, and steel wool. "What else?" He asked, resting his left hand on the back of the chair again. He turned the gun over, examining it as if he were thinking about buying it for a family member. He considered the shiny scratches on the barrel critically. "Butcher's wax and lamp black," he growled, and set off for the back room again. Moments later he returned, an old kerosene lantern in his right hand, the tin of butcher's wax in his left.

He sat down, and arranged his supplies before taking up the gun. He examined it again, this time with warmth. It was a good gun, reliable, accurate even without a scope, at least in the range these woods offer, nice simple reload (none of that bolt action nonsense), good balance between power and kick. He sighed. That damn Walter and his health food ideas. Venison is good food. He grinned. "Hell, there've been winters, back 'fore Walter started gettin' in my way, when venison, beer and coffee were all I needed. Stringy ol' bobcats don't eat no vegetables, and I didn't neither." Charlie smiled down at the Winchester and the memories, and enjoyed giving Walter a hard time, albeit in his imagination.

And so he got to work. He removed the stock and forearm and sanded them. With them off, he waxed all the dings and scratches on the barrel and reached for the lantern. "Need a rag," he mumbled and set off for the back room one more time in search of the right rag. Standing there, scanning the shelves much the same way you might recite the alphabet even though you know O is going to come right next to P, Charlie's hand twitched. He looked down, and realized that he was reaching for the dog. "That dog would be damn good company, day like today," he acknowledged. "Wish she was here." He grabbed a few rags and made his way back to the table.

"Might be a quick fix, but I ain't got bluing." Charlie inspected his work, squinting a little, frowning a lot. The lamp black worked fine; the barrel was now uniformly as black as night in the western Catskills.

With a clean rag, Charlie wiped away any dust and grit from the wooden parts. He ran his fingers over them, reading the wood with his old calluses, remembering and projecting. Would Walter like the feel of the stock, extra smooth like this? Would he appreciate the deep rich color the wood had darkened to after years of applying the holy trinity of stain, oil and turpentine? Charlie also probed for imperfections, missed spots. The eyes worked great, but sometimes the old hands didn't follow suit.

Once he was satisfied that the wood was ready, he mixed the strong smelling liquids, pouring stain and turpentine into the linseed oil jar. He grimaced, the smell stronger than he remembered. "Okay, outside with this mess," he grumbled, and carried the steel wool and gun parts out first. Banging the screen door open and shut, he made the second trip for the liquid. "Spillin' this would be a nasty mess. It'd stink in here for months." He brightened at the thought of Walter trying to clean up and deal with the ugly stain and stink.

He settled himself down on the porch steps, by now mid-morning sun warming the wood beneath him as well as the siding his shoulder rested against. Nice day, he acknowledged. Damn nice day for fall. He considered his dark blue work pants and boots. "Hell, if I sit here long enough, I'm gonna git too hot." He though about it for one more second, then shrugged it off and refocused on his work. It'll be okay, he decided. I've been hot and I've been cold. What the hell difference does it make?

Charlie dipped a corner of the steel wool into the mixture and began to rub it on. The forearm didn't take long; wipe on, dip in, wipe some more. Straightforward. The stock took a little more time, "what with all them curves." Charlie took his time, enjoying the sun, enjoying the task, and enjoying his thoughts for a change. The thought of dying used to bother him, the feeling of it being too close, pressing in on him, hassling him, hurrying him, and him just not being ready yet. Unprepared. But now, after that lawyer visit, things felt better. He could go soon and rest easy knowing that Virginia's wishes would guide what happened with the place once he was gone. It was a good feeling, almost eased some of the aches and stiffness, just knowing that his affairs were in order. "Well, almost in order," Charlie corrected himself. "Gotta git back to that lawyer's office and sign them papers he's writing up. And," he shifted his weight and eyed his work on the wooden components of the Winchester critically, "gotta finish this gun for Walter."

Asha was ready, having stalked this day for the better part of two weeks. The route had been committed to memory, her pack packed. Grace had been informed, the weather forecast was finally beneficent, and Pearl had plans for the after school part of her day. Today was the day to head out to Lone Mountain, as soon as Pearl got on the school bus.

Ever since that conversation with the old man, Asha had wondered about Lone. That trailhead felt like the end of the earth, the last stop, the end of the line. To strike out from there, to head up a trailless mountain named Lone; she just couldn't shake the sense that it was somehow important for her to meet this mountain and conquer it. She was beginning to assign it symbolic meaning and mystical power, as if some of the answers she sought about her life's crossroads may be accessed in all the hours she'd have to herself, driving, hiking, driving. It would be a long day.

With a kiss and a wave, Pearl was gone. Asha was happy to head out alone with the dogs. This would not be a Pearl-friendly hike. Bushwhacking was not Pearl's thing. Truth be told, it was not exactly Asha's thing either. Southwest Hunter had come with explicit instructions, and boy had she botched Bearpen that first time. This time, Asha scolded and threatened, a navigational error could easily mean an unexpected night in the woods. Besides all the obvious risks and discomforts, the idea of Pearl being that scared for her mother's safety was unacceptable. Armed with a GPS unit, borrowed from Grace, a lesson in its use provided by her husband, Eddie, as well as a map and compass, Asha was confident that even if distracted by dogs or depression, she would climb the right peak and make it out safely.

The mid-October date meant a fair amount of daylight. The first and last miles were on woods roads, easy walking. And Asha packed a headlamp, just in case, so that doing that last mile in the dark wouldn't be a problem. She offered up a silent prayer to the Catskill powers-that-be that there would be no need.

She hit the trail at 9:00 a.m. Both dogs exploded out of the Jetta at the empty trailhead, needing to pee as desperately as she did. Weekday, early start; no cars at the Denning parking area. Asha kept her eyes peeled for the good-looking man with the Belgian dog, but there was no sign of him. The place was beautifully deserted.

Well-fueled by coffee and excitement, she set a quick pace. "Make time," she muttered to herself, enjoying the abstract notion. Make time while I can, don't know when or where I could get slowed up bad. Best to move fast while I can. She strode along the woods road, mentally reviewing her preparedness: long pants instead of shorts, in case of prickers or nettles, extra shirts and a windbreaker in the pack, matches and a lighter for emergency fire starting. Oh yeah, she grinned to herself, and the GPS thingy. She didn't stop to get it out and fire it up. Later, she told herself. I just don't want to slow down yet.

The October morning air was cool and brisk. Charlie woke up feeling hungry; more alive than dead today, he told himself, and groaned less than usual as he insisted his stiff old limbs organize into a cohesive and functioning whole.

He put on brand new boxers and socks and the accompanying grunt was appreciative; the new undergarments felt good. He inspected his clothing options and thought about what he might do for the day. It came to him as if someone else suggested it: Why not head up Bearpen today? Last week's frost killed back a lot of the annoying vegetation. No more nettles in the lowlands. He could scout, look for signs, get ready for the hunting season. The old man smiled. Bullshit. He was curious about the girl and her list and the idea of hiking, just to do it. Something about Smokey and her dogs made Charlie want to head up Bearpen one more time. One last time. I ain't sentimental, Charlie growled at the thought, but I probably should say goodbye. It ain't right to go without saying goodbye.

Charlie enjoyed a strange awareness of himself as he finished dressing and ate some breakfast. Coffee this morning, not beer, and a bowl of instant oatmeal to fuel the long walk. "That should do just fine," he told himself out loud as he shuffled around the kitchen. He just couldn't quite shake the sense that he was watching himself; that some part of him was separate, external, and watching. The outside part was young, or maybe just without age. Anyway, it wasn't old, and Charlie enjoyed having any part of him feel something other than old. Feeling strange and kind of detached? Hell, I've felt all kinds of strange over the past eighty-six years, Charlie thought as he pulled on his boots. Add this one to the end of a long, long list.

A stick. That girl didn't carry no stick, but when Charlie tried to conjure up the notion of hiker in his mind's eye, a beard and a stick were essential. Ain't gonna be no beard, but I can walk with a stick, he decided. In fact, it sounded kinda good. Pride and denial prevented the use of a cane under normal circumstances, but going hiking meant a stick would be allowable. "I'll pick me up one in the woods," he mumbled aloud.

I ain't got a pack like she had, he realized and started back toward the utility shelves to inventory his options. What the hell do I need to carry anyway? A little water, maybe. Not much else. I ain't carryin' the Winchester. She's almost too pretty to use now.

By the time Asha hit the trail junction where she turned off the Phoenicia East Branch trail and onto the Peekamoose-Table trail, she had already promised herself that she would not spend this hike obsessing about her lack of a job nor her lack of moving on past Rob. She had to make and remake that promise; the emotional hand-wringing was proving to be depressingly addictive. She used all the tricks she taught her obsessive clients to use: focus on the here and now, pay attention to your breath, forgive yourself each time you slip up and start obsessing again, and lovingly choose to refocus. And then, heave a sigh, take a deep breath, and run through the whole goddamned process again.

She reached the bridge over the Deer Shanty Brook and hesitated, looking upstream. The bridge was impressively overbuilt such that Asha decided this area must flood pretty bad every spring. Someone, she figured, must have gotten totally sick of replacing bridges that got destroyed in the spring floods year after year. This bridge, she had to concede, looked pretty damn kick-ass; she had to climb up to massive rock-filled support structures to get to the deck. This thing wasn't going anywhere.

She pulled the camera out of her pack and snapped a few photos of the brook and the fall foliage. She checked her watch; it was 9:25. She was doing fine. She pulled the GPS unit out next, and fired it up. It was a fairly simple older model, and didn't have any maps loaded. Still, between the compass and the coordinates, she knew at the very least in which direction to head. She had scrawled the coordinates for Lone's summit on a scrap of paper that was folded up in her back pocket. There's probably a more streamlined way to use this thing, she acknowledged, but bare bones was good enough. Remembering Eddie's instructions, she created a waypoint at the bridge. Just in case I get off course on the way back down, now I have this spot to aim for.

It had been hours since her whole wheat bagel and soy margarine breakfast with Pearl. Although she wasn't feeling terribly hungry, seeing the Clif bar in her pack triggered the notion and her taste buds wanted the chocolate. When moving, Asha moved, but when still, it was time to take care of everything. She sat down on the grass at the far side of the brook with her pack open. Both dogs took to sniffing, chasing, swimming and overall raising a ruckus. She ate her Clif bar, fighting to stay in the moment and losing that battle. Still chewing the last bite, she organized her gear and began zipping up.

What's the big hurry, she asked herself. Indeed, she had hurried out of the house, driven to the trailhead as if she were in danger of being late to a job interview, and had covered 1.3 miles of trail in twenty-five minutes. By any standard, Asha was rushing.

She sighed, slinging the pack back up onto her back, walking forward as she adjusted straps and buckled up. The dogs danced around her, just as eager. "I made sure I got impatient dogs," she murmured, ruffling the damp fur on Lyla's pretty head. Just in case I relax, they push me to speed things up. She smiled at the black dog and enjoyed the thought of living life at dog speed. At Belgian dog speed. We're a nice match, she decided.

At the edge of the woods, where Charlie had said "see ya later" to Asha, he paused. He looked around for a stick and, not seeing one, ran though a litany of second thoughts. It was true that he hadn't been up in a long time, ten years maybe, but he knew the way like the back of his hand. Nah, Charlie smiled a little at the womanish thought. I ain't gonna git lost. So what is it, he wondered, that's makin' me hang back to rethink it one more time? The ol' legs not strong enough? Mebbe not, Charlie admitted. So what? What's the worst that can happen?

"Aaaaaahh, hell." The words were drawn out, long then sharp. "I guess I'm having a conversation with myself," Charlie acknowledged. "May as well git comfy and have it out with myself so's not to waste energy standin' here." Charlie spotted a fallen tree that looked about right for sitting on and made his way over to it. "Fine," he sighed audibly. "What the hell."

The worst case scenario might be dyin' out there. Might be that the ol' ticker will give out headin' up that hill. Would that really be so bad? Charlie sat still and listened hard. He heard a whole lot of nothing. That's it, ain't it? Afraid to die out there, all alone? Charlie waited but no answer came to mind right away. He sat and waited and listened and considered. And then he reconsidered. That wasn't it. Dyin' out on Bearpen: hell, that'd be perfect. It'd be a goddamned honor, not a tragedy. Naaah. I ain't afraid to die out on that mountain today. It's somethin' else. Charlie thought about being out on Bearpen and all the hunting he'd done out there over the past thirty years or so. Way back when the ski area was still open, it was a little trickier to hunt all winter long, but I managed all right. Mostly, back in them days, I kept to my own land, stayin' off the upper parts of the mountain. Back in them days, I was too busy to go off gallivantin' around the whole damn mountain. That came later. After Virginia was gone, an' both boys buried. Then I could go wanderin' around out there as much as I felt like it. Blackberries an' huntin'; those were both as good reasons as any to head on out. Shit, workin' for the town, an' comin' home to an empty house… this here mountain was big enough to catch up all them empty hours and hold 'em up tight for me.

Charlie rubbed his hands together; enough leaves remained on the trees to make for a chill in the shade. He ran a hand over his face, feeling the stubble, the sideburns, the deep lateral creases on his forehead. Virginia. That was it. He wasn't done with that lawyer, and if he died out on Bearpen today, he'd have let her down. After all this time he'd be damned if he was gonna let that happen. Gotta stick around a while longer an' finish the job. Charlie grunted softly as he regained his feet and started heading up the path. Gotta see it through.

The next mile required a different kind of attention as Asha followed the now-you-see-it, now-you-don't fisherman's trail along the Neversink River. She was "on," every sense organ on alert for important information. Listening to the river on her left, looking for signs of the fading trail, she watched for the cue to turn right and head up Lone. The longer she traveled upstream, the more intense her focus, until she stopped to rest in a campsite. She noticed a little stone bench assembled by some enthusiastic campers. She sat down, opened her pack, and checked the GPS. It was time. She could start heading up.

Leaving the river and plunging into the trailless wilderness really gave her the willies. The dogs helped; they stayed close but emanated pure joy. "This is good," Asha panted as she slogged up the steep slope. "Clearly they love it. It must be good." The off trail navigation focused her such that she hadn't thought about anything since the bridge. No thoughts of Rob, no worries, no fretting about anything beyond her immediate position and goal. The tension and excitement around finding the canister and then getting down safely completely replaced all other worries. In its own way, it was a blessing and a vacation.

She was heating up, the climb continuing long after her strong leg muscles complained about fatigue and abrasions. No nettles, but plenty of brush, saplings, weeds and what-have-you to snag feet, grab at laces, and scratch through pant legs. She could feel the back of her pack getting wet with sweat through her clothes. She knew she'd need to remove all her wet clothing at the top. "It'll be cold and windy up there," she predicted. "Gotta stay warm enough."

Warm enough. Somehow the simple notion of adequate warmth broke through all else, and Asha felt tears prick her eyes. "When have I ever been warm enough?" It all came crashing in, a torrent of memories, a flood of emotion: her father's death, her mother's depression, the years of being so afraid that her mother would die too, and how her body had reacted with shivering, long before she understood. She thought about her years of marriage to Carl and how the emotional Siberia developed and deepened over time. She remembered the joy and relief she felt thinking that Rob was her soul mate. A true match and a reliable source of heat. With losing Rob came a new chill, the profound cold of abandonment wrapped in betrayal and lodged under a chink in the armor. Rage failed to heat the deep cold of this loss. These thoughts came thick and fast, and Asha hesitated for a moment, a touch disoriented by the suddenness of the emotion.

It all hurt. Every memory lowered her core temperature and sank her deeper into chilled ache. She blew her nose, a farmer's blow, snot flying first left then right, and kept going. Movement and effort were the only antidotes she knew for this condition.

She couldn't stop thinking, though. Movement helped, but Lone was big enough, and this damn ascent from the river was long enough and simple enough (Asha checked the compass and GPS several times before giving up and acknowledging that "up," at this point, was the only instruction) that she was able to flounder her way up without any navigational subtlety. Just up. Gain elevation. It made space in her brain, enough space to think.

Rob was a mistake. Asha broke off a low-hanging dead tree branch and whacked the trunk with it. The impact hurt her hand a little. Both dogs leapt at the stick, wagging. She let it go, and Brulee took off with the stick, Lyla in hot pursuit. Rob was a stupid mistake. I'm a therapist, for crissakes. I couldn't spot a liar and a cheat? Shit, if he was cheating on Halia or Grace, I'd have been warning and lecturing after the first ill-timed "headache." I forgave, excused, joined in all the lying. I made it easy for him; so easy, it probably wasn't even fun for him. Probably took all the joy out of it for him.

She picked up speed as she indulged in her silent rant, the anger pushing her up the mountain. Rob was stepping in shit, she raged. It stank, but for all those months, I tried to tell myself that I liked that smell. I really did try to like it. Truth be told, I also really believed it would change. I thought it would get better, it wouldn't smell so bad, after we moved in together or if we got married. But now I'm left with shit on my shoe and it stinks and somehow I'm the one that feels the shame. Like the poor innocent kid back in second grade who got dog shit on her shoe, and then stank up whole classroom, somehow the bad luck mistake turns into shame. I smell it, but he is it. And I carry the shame. It's just not fair.

I didn't do anything wrong. I didn't misrepresent who I was or what I wanted. I was honest and clear. It wasn't my fault that everything changed midstream. I tried to face losing my job with dignity and poise. Asha was storming uphill, lips parted and breath coming in loud, furious pants. That wasn't my fault either.

Or was it? Was it all my fault? Was there, or is there, something I'm doing that's fucking it all up? Asha wracked her brains for the millionth time, asking herself yet again: What am I supposed to see about myself here? What lesson am I getting handed? What is it that I did or didn't do that cost me my relationship and my job?

Search farther back, Asha counseled herself. Whatever it was, it was there in my marriage to Carl, and it was there when I held the job, not just that last year, but the first year too, and all the years in between. "Shit," Asha chucked the swearword at the birch trees and the rocks and the Neversink now far behind her. "History," she muttered. "Emotional archeology. Fuck that."

"Yep," Charlie spoke to the layered rock formations, nodding in recognition. "Yep. This way takes ya 'round the steepest parts." Charlie patted the rock as he passed it and continued up, slowly.

Virginia didn't do much wanderin' 'round these woods. Always somethin' inside to keep her busy, what with two little boys, and the dog, laundry, cookin', what have you. These here woods were my own place, my solitude, my escape when I wanted some peace an' quiet. He trudged steadily, watching carefully for signs that the faint trail jogged right or left. He also stayed alert for signs that he wasn't feeling safe to go on, but so far, he felt fine. "Fine," he mumbled to the trees. "Jes' slow." He paused, then hollered out, "You got a problem with that?"

The silence pressed in close, and Charlie chuckled, then cleared his throat and spat. He smiled, pleased with himself.

This here is my mountain. He drank it in with his eyes, willing himself to remember the past, the good times and the bad. This was where he came to weep when Virginia left him. The boys were back in town, in Halcottsville, with Granddaddy. Charlie took the Winchester and came out here to shoot whatever he could find, in season or out of season. Charlie didn't know and didn't care. Blind, deafened, and near senseless with grief, he had left the gun locked up in the cabin and just plain walked. He walked miles that day, his fury and his hoarse sobs scaring away any game within miles. He hadn't wanted to be alone in the woods with a gun that day, and he had hidden his vulnerability in the safe, comforting wildness of the mountain's broad flank.

Yep. I remember that day. Charlie looked at the summit hump, just another half mile or so to the east, and remembered. That there was a day I didn't know if I'd get through. He shook himself all over, like waking up or shaking off a chill, not surprised to find the tears welling up. What, Virginia? What do you want with me now?

Forgiveness. Asha sighed deeply, stopping the uphill slog to catch her breath, drink some water and rest her rubbery legs. What did that old guy have to say about forgiveness? She leaned against a sizable birch tree, facing downhill, and took a long drink of water. After re-catching her breath, panting child-style from her long chug, she decided to make it a full-blown refueling stop. She shrugged off her pack and located an apple and some nuts. Both dogs located Asha and nuzzled her insistently. "Good thing I remembered cookies for you," she teased, taunting Brulee with her singsong voice. The dog yapped and she handed each a biscuit.

Forgiveness. The notion had nagged at her, tugged on her sleeve and lurked in the darkened corners of the back rooms of her mind for years. But Charlie's words were different. It wasn't that same old you-must-forgive-in-order-to-move-on lecture. Thank god, she grinned. I've delivered that trite and platitude-filled speech enough, without some old redneck making it sound like homespun wisdom. So refusing to forgive isn't a spiritual crime after all: well, hallelujah! And it isn't a prerequisite for moving on. Huh. But this anger and hurt, Asha argued, is stuck like a bitter pill, lodged in my throat. It feels like nothing else can go up or down. There has to be more to it.

Okay: Mom. Asha started the list. I forgave mom. That was part of growing up. Part 1: blame mom for everything. Part 2: forgive mom for everything. I guess one day it will be Pearl's job to forgive me.

She sat down on the ground, and leaned back against the big old birch. She drew her knees up, feet flat upon the ground, and took stock. She was sweaty, but not cold. Not terribly hungry and staying hydrated. She was, she checked the GPS again, on track to hit Lone's summit, maybe about a half a mile or so away. The dogs finished their biscuits and lay down nearby. All was well.

Forgiveness had haunted her; it stalked her in her quiet moments. She had responded by running. Forgive mom: check. Forgive dad for dying? Check. Forgive Carl for being incapable of taking on the role of husband? Loaded question. She grinned. She tried again. Forgive Carl? Long story, but okay, to sum it up – check. Forgive yourself for whatever part of the failed marriage is your fault? She squirmed. Yes or no, she badgered herself. No disclaimers, no explanations. Okay, she relented. For the most part – check. Forgive Rob? No. That was easy. No way. Rob did wrong. No forgiveness and none on the horizon. It stuck in her throat and left a nasty taste in her mouth, but any effort at forgiveness was false. "Shit, I want 'liar' tattooed across his forehead. I want his actions published in the local paper. I want everyone who comes in contact with him to know our history, to know what he did. I want him shunned. I want him punished." Asha had spoken aloud, and her voice rose louder with each wish. She half-shouted, half-sobbed the last sentence, admitting to herself what she hadn't allowed herself to know before. Justice. Fuck forgiveness. And if justice proves elusive, revenge seems an adequate consolation prize.

And yet she knew even before the thoughts formed into the words, that underneath all that rage lay forgiveness. Not him. Herself. She had to forgive herself for loving him, for trusting him, for letting him into her life, and into Pearl's life.

"I need to forgive myself for being stupid and blind," she explained to the dogs. Both wagged enthusiastically. "Maybe if I can find the canister by noon, I'll consider it." Way to go, Smokey, she teased herself. Way to avoid a serious conversation with yourself and escape into an athletic competition. Nice job.

The challenge issued, she pushed off the tree trunk and re-gained her feet. Twenty-seven minutes before noon. She looked up at the summit hump, rising up sharply in front of her. A good half a mile or so, she judged. This is gonna be close…

There weren't any berries left, the best patches having fin-ished producing a solid month ago. Smokey hit 'em good; the berries she brought back were damn good. Sweet, but not tame-tasting. They had the wildness in 'em, but they'd sweetened up during that long hot summer. All that heat might not be so good for old people, but it was good for the fruit. It was the kind of summer you could grow melons in, long and hot. Melons need a long hot summer to find their sweetness. Charlie remembered Virginia fussin' with muskmelons year after year, telling him over and over again, "Melons need a long hot summer to grow," she used to say. Well blackberries too, Virginia. Blackberries too.

Something was still nagging at Charlie. He made it to the old woods road that led straight to the top, to the abandoned ski lift equipment. "Ain't too tired," he told the No Standing Any Time sign, still nailed to the tree where the woods road had been the ski area's entranceway – a comic reminder of the days when Bearpen was still in operation as a ski mountain. "Nope, actually I feel pretty good," he observed, noticing that he was walking pretty well. Nice and slow and easy. No, it wasn't physical concerns that bothered him. It was something else.

Virginia had died a young woman. He stopped walking, knowing that he had to leave the relative safety of the woods road to push through the brush and prickers to get to the true summit. He rested, leaning against a big maple and let his eyes fall closed for a moment. Virginia wasn't fancy-lookin,' just pretty in a normal, Delaware County farm-girl way. She was pretty, and the more he got to know her and see what she could do, the prettier she looked to Charlie. She could butcher a deer by herself, then cook up a stew that'd make the fussiest man alive happy. She could write letters to the newspapers in Kingston and Delhi, pointing out what folks might need to know about school budgets or national elections. She was special, Virginia was, and maybe that's why she didn't last here long. Charlie's eyes squeezed closed tighter. Or maybe it was just shit luck that she caught the infection and died like that.

Lone's summit was relatively open compared to its neighbors, Rocky and Table. Several hundred feet higher than Rocky, the lack of dense balsams was almost odd. Or would have been considered so if Asha knew enough to realize how different Lone really was. All she knew was that now she was playing a game with herself, a race against time, and that she was determined to triumph.

She crashed through the underbrush, GPS unit out and frequently consulted. She scanned for higher ground and pressed on, dogs picking up the urgency and charging around the woods chasing with renewed abandon anything that moved. Up, check GPS, adjust, scan. Repeat. All at a half jog, pack contents bouncing and jingling.

And then she saw it. Panting, she honed in, a herd path leading her the last fifteen yards or so. She shoved the GPS back in an elasticized side pocket and checked her watch. 11:58 a.m. "I won," she breathed, reaching up for the canister's lid.

She tossed her pack to the ground and pulled the Ziploc bag out of the can. The spiral memo book made her smile: the triumph of getting here alone, deep in the wilderness. The mountain that seemed to hold real mystique for that old guy; it felt good. She read through other entries, composing something of her own to say. She racked her brain for a quote and came up dry.

Water. She got out her water and drank deeply again, pleased to lighten up the pack for the hike down. Guess I was thirsty, she acknowledged. She rummaged around for more food in her pack and found her bagel sandwich. Now is the time for this, she thought. This is a summit bagel. A bagel of completion. A perfect circle, to remind me that all ends are beginnings. Shut up and eat, she giggled at her internal conversation. The dogs paced and sniffed until she snarled at them "Enough! Go lie down!" They slunk off.

She sat down and took a bite. That old guy, Charlie – his words about loneliness belong in the book. She frowned, concentrating, chewing. "Loneliness is …" that's how it should start. She balanced the book on her thigh and wrote what the old guy said, the words that made her curious about this mountain. "I'll tell you what lonely is. Lonely is heading up Lone Mountain from the Neversink in November. Cold, gray, short day with no damn snow to make it pretty, no goddamn tracks to follow, no one waiting at home to hear your story, no one to know or care if you live or die out there. Just you on that hill, all alone out there in the goddamn middle of nowhere." She wrote "Charlie, the old guy from over on Bearpen" underneath his quote, then signed her name and the date.

The sun was shining, creating hard shadows and contrast. Asha thought about Charlie's words and thought about loneliness.

I have Pearl, she thought. I can't ever be lonely the way someone who isn't a parent can. She wondered about Charlie, about his being so alone in the world. She wondered how it happened and to what degree he had wanted it and helped create it. He certainly wasn't warm and welcoming at this point in his life, and he chose to live in that cabin, out at the ass end of nowhere.

Am I doing that? Am I pushing people away, working on a self-fulfilling prophecy here? Naah. Asha discounted that pretty thoroughly. But the profile I wrote for Match.com was bad. She smiled in between bites of bagel. It was bad. It was awful. But it was a direct result of being lied to, cheated on, and dumped. Nothing deeper.

What is deeper? Asha asked herself. What kind of archeological dig do I have to go on? Yeah, I have a past, I have a history. I guess I have baggage. She interrupted this train of thought to check the time and re-pack the few items she'd pulled out of her pack when searching for her bagel. And I have a present tense situation that needs life support at this point. What's the past got to do with that?

She sighed, shrugged, and settled back down. She blew out a long slow exhale between pursed lips. Everything and nothing. Yeah, my dad died before he hit forty; that leaves an indelible mark. I've carried that around for a few decades, taking it personally, as if his death was proof that I wasn't worth living for. Carried it with me up this mountain. As if one day I'll have done enough to somehow prove my worth. She ran her hand through her twig infested curls. This shit is old. And probably irrelevant. So my dad is the reason I push myself so hard. Trying to earn Daddy's love. No, even worse, trying to earn the right to be lovable. So what? So I bust my ass on projects big and small daily and by the decade, to try to prove that I'm worth loving, as if that will one day make up for the fact that I'll never believe it. It'll never be enough for me because his death proves my lack of value. Five cents, please. She yawned. That's not news.

What about mom? She was there; he wasn't. Shouldn't she be more important? Isn't the whole cup half full versus half empty at play here? Why should the guy who wasn't there be more influential than the woman who was? Asha mentally wagged a professional finger at herself: false dichotomy. One isn't more important than the other – just different. Different influences, different legacies. Besides, it wasn't the distant past that was haunting her anyway.

Rob. Goddamn him. What would it mean to let this episode end, to borrow the old guy's metaphor. To be done, to let it be over. I am letting it be over, she defended herself silently. I don't know what I could be doing differently: I don't call him, I don't email him, I don't drive past his house (anymore), I don't visit places we went together, I don't Google him, I don't try to find out her name, I don't call his friends "just to say hi," I don't friend his friends on Facebook.

But you suffer, Asha pointed out. You suffer every time you see a green Jeep. You suffer every time you think you might see a green Jeep. You suffer every time you think about fireworks. You suffer when you go to The Eft, even though you know it's safe there; the shields are up and Larry is on security detail. You suffer every time Pearl gives you that look and then cracks a dumb joke. And you suffer more when she takes the phone into her bedroom and closes the door to discuss your mental state with her father. You suffer as if you're living in the center of ten square miles of emotional land mines, avoiding people, places, thoughts, conversation topics, movies, art. A maze of safe passages has been constructed to get through the day without detonation, but the anticipation has become a way of life.

I just wanted so badly for it to work, Asha sighed. I just wanted all the normal things anyone would want – love, commitment, affection, security, some semblance of family, a sense of us. I wanted to move from singular to plural. Her sigh deepened into a groan. Boy did that fail.

She looked at the dogs sprawled on the forest floor. She craned her neck to look up at the sky, framed by branches. She looked at the trees atop Lone Mountain, and she knew that she was in the presence of truly ancient beings. Although they were not all that big, they had that look: that wizened, toughened appearance of trees that had lasted through centuries of exposure to all that the highest elevations of the Catskills' seasons could dish out. She thought of Charlie and remembered a book from her childhood, a book about a man in Prospect Park who could turn into a tree. An old man who befriended pigeons and squirrels, she remembered dragging her grandfather all over Prospect Park, looking for the tree, believing they could find it. Willing it to be real...

Asha listened to the relative quiet; it was hot and little was stirring. The dogs panted. No traffic sounds penetrated Lone's wildness. It really was miles from any road. No airplanes either, Asha noticed. It was far from everything.

So shouldn't I be thanking god that this episode is over? Asha challenged herself. What if forgiving him, forgiving myself, what if all that's irrelevant? What if it is just over? No processing the loss, no analysis, no rumination. Just The End. Next.

Charlie was right. She knew it; she also knew that she didn't quite believe it. Asha pleaded with the sky, the trees, her own heart; I'll do anything to get unstuck. Anything to move on, she offered.

No answer came to mind. The magic of Lone fell flat. I thought coming here, making this pilgrimage would somehow lead to answers, to revelations, to absolutions, Asha complained. She sat, perched on top of Lone, all alone, and felt nothing. "It's just another mountain," she said aloud. "And now I've checked it off my list."

The view from the top was pretty. Charlie had picked a good day to say goodbye to Bearpen. Colors were damn near peak. Charlie found his favorite spot to gaze out over Schoharie County. He squinted at Utsayantha and Huntersfield Mountains to the north, and beyond. Nice and clear. Charlie got done with all the usual looking and checking off the things he'd always looked for from this spot: Can I see Mount Greylock? Yep. Southern Greens, in Vermont? Mebbe. Buildings in Albany? Yep.

He stood still, finishing the looking ritual but not moving on. He let the moment go melodramatic, feeling damn near eighty years of runnin' around this old mountain culminate in this one last look. Eyes moist, he coughed hard and spat. And he made his decisions.

Smokey.

And Bearpen.

It was because of her dog. That was one damn fine dog. As good a reason as any.

Charlie turned his back on the view. He was ready to go.

Sometimes you just can't know what to do. All there is left is to wait and trust that it will come to you.

Asha had wracked her brains, searched diligently, followed advice, soul-searched, and hiked. She still hadn't purged Rob from her soul and she still didn't know what to do when her unemployment ran out. She hadn't come to any conclusions in either area. The stuckness was balanced; no insights, no movement, no revelations in either area. While Charlie was right that suffering would point her down the wrong road, if she didn't fix her career gridlock quick, she wouldn't have the luxury of living to be old and alone.

She headed back down the mountain the way she had come up, minus the spring eagerness had placed in her step. There was nothing left to do but go home and do all that home entails. Cook dinner. Clean up. Check emails. Call Pearl. Go to bed. Get up tomorrow and give it all another shot, waiting for the planetary shift that will render some possibility to pop up. She was certain that something from outside herself was going to have to change. The one result Lone Mountain could claim responsibility for was that Asha felt a sense of peace and certainty that she had done all she could. She felt relief that if nothing else, at least she could claim that she had given it her all. This wasn't avoidance. She just had to wait. It was a matter of trust and an act of faith.

Asha continued down Lone Mountain, one foot in front of the other.

"What are you going to do for Thanksgiving? Are you planning to run in any of the local turkey trots? There's a five mile race over in Arlington; oh, you probably already know it," Grace trailed off, realizing that Asha was pretty well connected in local running circles.

"Naah," Asha didn't consider long. "Not really in the mood to race these days. It's the woods that seem to call my name." She grinned self-consciously. "I was thinking about trying to do another thirty-five hundred peak." Asha propped her elbows on the table at The Eft and rested her chin on her fists. Thanksgiving. Ugh. Grace's question had caught Asha off guard, although it shouldn't have. Once Halloween has been hurdled, Thanksgiving is on every kids' lips; every kid, that is, that counts the days until the next day off from school. Halloween had been done up in style at the Jackson homestead with Pearl and cohorts finally settling on a Flintstone theme. Asha had been parent on duty that night, first hosting the party then supervising the trick-or-treating on Nellie Hill Road. She hadn't recovered sufficiently to begin planning the next holiday event despite the intervening weeks. This time she wouldn't have Pearl to entertain; Carl had Thanksgiving and Asha would get Christmas with her daughter. On Thanksgiving, she would be on her own.

"You wanna join us?"

"Thanks." Her response was polite, grateful, noncommittal. Realizing Grace was waiting for an answer, Asha hastened to add, "No. Thanks." It wasn't the Swamp River Porter that was numbing her brain and slowing her tongue. It was just the requirement that she deal with another event and with the decisions to make, the costs to be encountered; the stress mounted. Her brain had shut down sometime last week and all she really seemed to do these days was sit on the couch with Pearl, giggling at SpongeBob, or hike.

Halia planned to volunteer at a soup kitchen in Poughkeepsie for Thanksgiving. Asha listened to her describe her plan for the holiday and felt tempted. Maybe, she thought. Giving back appealed to her. Making a deposit in the karma account, she joked. But her consideration was serious; it would require showing up and little else. Tempting, she thought. Very tempting.

"Maybe I'll join you," she said to Halia. "I'm just trying to figure out how I can also sneak a hike in that day."

Halia frowned. "Why don't you just bring dinner over to that old guy that lives on Bearpen? I'm sure you can find a mountain on your list in between here and there."

Walter flipped the blinker on and waited for an opening in the eastbound lane on Route 28. The shopping expedition at Wadler Brothers had been fruitful, brief, and accomplished on company time. Walter was sufficiently well pleased to refrain from cursing at the traffic (citiots, no doubt).

He inched out a little and allowed the line of cars to pass into and out of his field of vision without paying any attention. "I wonder if the sliding doors would be a better place to set this up," he mused, arching his back against the seat. He'd been thrown hard a couple of nights ago at jiu jitsu, and his left hip was still unhappy about it. He shifted his weight in the seat, seeking comfort. "More bang for the buck," he mumbled as he saw his opening and pulled out.

The truck lumbered up the rise out of Fleischmanns. Walter's thoughts rock-hopped from his low-tech solar heating project to a solar hot water arrangement he'd seen at a customer's house a few months ago, to the notion of an outdoor shower set up on the deck, right by the hot tub, to... Smokey. Outdoor showers and hot tubs: it was inevitable. Walter grinned to himself: I can start the most unromantic thought process and within six simple steps be undressed with her. Six degrees of Smokey-lust. He chuckled.

He had purchased the makings of a passive solar assist for Charlie's home in Halcottsville. The old Victorian was a bear to heat and Walter actually worried more, in some ways, about Charlie when he was there, than when he was up at the cabin. Isolation and remoteness bothered other people; they didn't concern Charlie at all. That big stove in the small cabin – as long as he's got wood, he'll be warm. And Walter had made sure there was plenty of wood, what with all that foolish tree work last summer when Charlie was fishing for his company. No, the cabin had its own issues, but the house down in the village was worrisome to Walter. For a few years now it had needed more attention than Walter could give it. And it was big – big to heat, big to clean, big to fill with life. It dwarfed Charlie. The ghosts were more firmly in charge than he was. The cabin fit him better; probably always had.

Walter rumbled along, windows open halfway and the public radio station out of Albany blaring. At the crest of the hill in Highmount, he pulled over and checked voicemail messages. A blessing and an inconvenience, on the west side of the hill cell service was not available. Junk voicemail from headquarters, junk text messages from Verizon Central, Walter waded through them, his mind on the project for Charlie's house. The last message was Kip; Walter roused himself and listened.

"Hey brother," Kip sang out, crackling and distorted. "Stop in on your way home today. Got something I want to ask you."

Cool, Walter grinned. He stayed put at the side of the road and did his closeout and took care of checking the home voicemail, too, while he had a signal. No messages meant jiu jitsu wasn't canceled: good. Walter was eager to work out, to see if he could undo the damage last week's sparring had inflicted. Or if not, perhaps put a hurtin' on someone else to share it around a little.

With his back to Belleayre, headed for Phoenicia, Walter rolled down Route 28 in fine spirits. His creative problem-solving skills were tapped, and that made him happy, or at least satisfied. Design and construction to solve a problem. It was a beautiful thing.

"Hey buddy!" Kip's voice carried across the restaurant when Walter walked in.

The afternoon regulars were scattered around the café. Kip was behind the counter, scooping ice cream into a bowl. Walter felt himself relax, as if it were the weekend. "Hey Kip," he answered.

"Fiona was cooperative with Wennie all afternoon," Kip gestured toward the ice cream, "so she earned a treat." Kip dropped the scooper into the sink and slid the stainless steel freezer door shut, hiding the five gallon tubs of Jane's ice cream from view. "I'll be right back." Kip moved like a man who had many irons in the fire, out from behind the counter and through the door marked "private." He was back moments later, the door to his apartment banging shut behind him. "How was your day, dear?" he joked.

Walter gave a brief recounting of the day. "How are things here?"

"Good," Kip answered, looking around. "Maybe in a few months, if everything works out ok, I can actually take a day off while the restaurant is open. Y'know, start to have a life again."

Walter had known Kip only in his café owner incarnation. He wasn't sure what having a life would look like for Kip.

"So listen," Kip began. "Wennie and I decided to close the café on Thanksgiving and make a meal here. My brother's coming, and Wennie's family is planning to be here too. We just wondered, do you have plans? You want to join us?"

Thanksgiving. Walter groaned silently. Love the concept, hate the hassle. "I'm not traveling this year," he told Kip. "Already informed the folks." He considered Kip's offer, noting that his first impulse was to say no. He had no idea why; the meal was guaranteed to be excellent, and Walter usually sought out Kip and Wennie's company. And he had no other plans. But that initial intuitive impulse won out. "I'm sorry, but no thanks. You guys are so sweet to offer, but I can't take you up on it."

"Got plans?"

"No." Walter wouldn't have tried to lie to Kip. "But I might go to the beach."

Kip raised his eyebrows. "The beach?" He arranged his face into an expectant look, awaiting the punch line.

"Yeah. Jones beach on Long Island can be really great on Thanksgiving: quiet, lonely, peaceful. You get to see the beach as a park, totally deserted. It's pretty powerful."

Kip looked at Walter for an extra moment digesting his words, then shook his head slightly. "Listen, buddy, I gotta go prep for dinner. You think about it. We'd love to have you."

Kip came out from behind the counter and gave Walter a hard, pounding hug.

"Thanks, man." Walter smiled, and watched his friend disappear behind the swinging kitchen door.

"Mom, why don't you come to Dad's with me for Thanksgiving?" Pearl opened the door to her mother's room at 6:47 a.m. on the Saturday before Thanksgiving to ask this question.

"Huh?" Asha asked, stretching and reaching across the bed for clothing to walk the dogs in. A pea green fleece sweatshirt and snoopy-print fleece pajama pants were the only garments within reach (because, of course, they were the last garments to have been removed). Okay, Asha shrugged to herself, they'll do. "Now, Pearl? You need to discuss this with me right now?"

Pearl tittered and sprawled on the bed. Asha tugged a snoopy-pant leg out from under her. "Why not now?"

Both dogs had entered with Pearl and paced around the small room, wagging and panting.

"Because now I have to deal with the dogs. And because I won't make any sense until after I've had my coffee."

"I put the water on for you."

"Wow. Thanks." Asha rolled over and sat up. She pulled the hooded fleece on over the tee shirt she had slept in. Pearl bounced off the bed and began playing with Asha's bronze Hindu figurines on her dresser top. Asha shoved a foot into a pant leg, and scrounged around on the floor for socks. Pearl's play escalated to include Durga's swords slicing away at Ganesh's head and lots of grunting and squealing. "Okay, enough! Out!" Asha raised her voice just enough to send both dogs skittering across the old hardwood floor and out the bedroom door. Pearl followed. Asha found a couple of purple Smartwool socks – not quite a pair, but close enough. Boots were down by the front door. Asha shot the clock a look as if she expected sympathy from the plastic appliance. "Oy vey."

Dogs attended to and coffee in hand, Asha reconsidered Pearl's questions. "You want me to have Thanksgiving with you and Daddy?"

"Yeah, and Aunt Bridget and all my cousins too. Don't you miss them? Well, maybe not the boys that much, but don't you miss Shana and Laurel and baby-Chloe?" The words tumbled out in one breath. Asha wondered how she did it.

Asha took a long sip of coffee and wrapped both hands around the mug. "They're growing up," she acknowledged.

"Yeah, and they miss you."

"I miss them too, sweetheart." Asha picked her way carefully through the next few sentences. "For me, missing them is part of understanding that it's over. In leaving your dad, there were losses – things I had to let go of, even though I might not have wanted to. It's partly out of real respect and caring about your dad that I accept my losses and move on."

Pearl frowned and shoved her bangs out of her eyes roughly. "That makes no sense."

"Well, almost none," Asha half-joked, half-admitted. "Your dad needs me out of his life. It wouldn't be fair to him for me to lurk around, staying partly connected. Trust me on this one."

"But it's one stupid dinner," Pearl countered, shifting gears, hiding defeat in humor. "Come on over, eat some stupid turkey, go back to your stupid house, all stupid and alone."

"And cry my stupid lonely self to sleep?" she teased. "I don't think so. I plan to cook a stupid meal for a stupid old man who lives way the heck at the end of a stupid road halfway up a stupid mountain and go for a stupid hike on the way home."

"Really?" Pearl was mildly interested.

"Yeah. The guy I met up on Bearpen Mountain." Asha watched Pearl's face soften a little. "He talked about being lonely for real. I think he doesn't have any family left. I thought I could spend a little time with him. Maybe I could learn something from him. You know, you're supposed to learn from your elders." She grinned and aimed a poke at Pearl's ribs. Pearl evaded her easily.

"I'll help you cook." Pearl's blessing given, she disappeared.

Asha looked at the clock and marveled at how she could feel such love and anger simultaneously. She settled into coffee-at-7:00-a.m.-on-a-weekend mode, and started menu planning for Thanksgiving with Charlie.

The beach. It did beckon in an offbeat, quirky sort of way. Where the hell did I pull that out of? Walter lounged in bed early Saturday morning and enjoyed not going to work. Jones Beach on Thanksgiving... Walter shook his head. That was pure Annie.

Walter got up and hit the bathroom. For the many hundredth time, he congratulated himself on the brilliant idea to design a bathroom with a urinal and the good fortune to have scored the fixture for free from a grateful customer who was liquidating the inventory from his commercial plumbing supply business.

Cleaning the bathroom was quicker and easier now, and, Walter decided looking around, on the list of chores for the day.

What else? Walter asked himself as he prepared breakfast. Eggs with mushrooms and roasted red peppers, goat cheese, a little salsa, in a wrap: Walter liked having enough time to cook a nice breakfast. What else to do today? Clean the house and split wood. Laundry could wait 'til tomorrow. Thanksgiving. "I'm gonna have to do something for myself, at least," Walter told his egg wrap. "The porter I brewed last month should be ready to bottle." Walter started to think about combinations of foods and beverages. A cranberry sauce made with port. Porter and port. Walter grinned to himself, the beginnings of a menu in his head. I guess I'll bring food up to Charlie, he decided. He usually calls to set up a trumped up reason why I need to swing out there on Thanksgiving Day. This time I'll call him. Thanksgiving with Charlie sounds just fine. Who knows, maybe Charlie will have more information about Smokey.

Late November in Ulster County is cold, hard, and gray. Just like Charlie had said about hiking in the Neversink basin, no leaves on the trees, no snow on the ground. Just gray earth, gray trees, gray sky. Like being in limbo, in between seasons, late November offered none of the showy colors of fall nor any of the stark contrasts of winter. A time of transition, winter being held in abeyance, fall already completed, it was a good time to throw a shindig, to do something to make the sullen gray emptiness claim meaning or at least identity. It always struck Asha that it was a tough time of year for a parade in New York City, but a perfectly fitting time of year for a nice hot meal.

She and Pearl put in many hours both Sunday and Wednesday prepping the meal Asha planned. She thought that most Thanksgiving dinners were so over-the-top in terms of quantity that they were hard to enjoy. She wasn't sure what Charlie would like, given that all she'd seen him eat were sardines and saltines. Okay, she thought as she considered the herbs and spices, probably shouldn't skimp on the salt.

On Wednesday night, Pearl seemed torn when it was finally time to get in the car with her father. She found sixteen different things she needed to show Carl, first in her room, then in the kitchen. Both Asha and Carl were patient with her, indulgent with her sudden need to linger and watch her parents interact. Carl even showed polite interest in the project of bringing Charlie a meal. Finally, Pearl seemed satisfied and they left. Asha waved from the front porch, watching the taillights disappear.

Lyla leaned against Asha's leg as she waved goodbye. She thought about sharing her daughter, holidays, and giving thanks. She stood there getting cold, long after it made sense to stop waving and go back inside. Brulee nosed the front door open and joined them on the front porch. Asha folded her arms and sighed. "Now who's torn?" she asked herself. Another moment and then she turned and headed back inside, slippers scuffing the cement floor on the way in.

The sink was piled high with Thanksgiving meal preparation detritus. She grimaced. God, I hate washing dishes, she thought and set her jaw. Must be done; I won't like it any better tomorrow morning. As the water heated up, Asha took off her rings: first the silver one she bought herself when she finished graduate school, then the tag sale one Rob gave her eight months ago. She pocketed the silver band she had purchased all those years ago and paused for a moment. She grasped the purple glass bead and wire ring she had considered her "engagement ring" from Rob between her thumb and forefinger, the water starting to steam up the window behind the sink. She walked across the kitchen and dropped the Rob-ring into the garbage can. Both dogs now lying on the kitchen floor lifted their heads to watch the can lid open. Both dogs started when the can lid banged closed and looked at Asha. She walked back to the sink, rinsed out the scrubby sponge, and reloaded it with dish detergent. Pressing her lips together, she turned the water off and began soaping and stacking dishes to be rinsed.

She packed up the car in the morning, aiming to be at Charlie's by noon. Just for exercise, she figured she'd run up Overlook Mountain on her way out to his place. Well, maybe not "run." Probably won't feel like doing a whole lot of anything after a meal, but it will feel good to earn it up front, she told herself. She packed the big red cooler with items to be heated up at Charlie's. She noticed that he did have an oven. It had looked clean and unused. She hoped it worked.

Rock Cornish game hen, rice pilaf with dried cranberries and walnuts, green bean fassoulia, all neatly packed into containers and loaded into the cooler. A smaller cooler, six pack size, held a green salad and a split of champagne. A blackberry pie, made from Bearpen blackberries, balanced carefully on top of everything.

"You guys can't jump around in the car. Anyone messes with my pie, they're dead." Both dogs wagged at Asha's threats, but once the door was opened managed to contain themselves in the Jetta's back seat.

To turkey or not to turkey, Walter joked with himself as he strolled the supermarket aisles on Wednesday afternoon. It's too much food, he argued, on the one hand. But I really like turkey, came the response. Walter pictured an angel and a devil on each shoulder egging him on. Waste of energy, all those hours of having the oven on. Lots of leftovers: cook once, eat many meals. Finally it was the idea of making a big pot of soup stock that swayed him to the pro turkey side. Homemade stock separated the men from the boys, he reminded himself.

The idea of making a meal and bringing it up to Charlie had grown on him over the past few days. As he simmered cranberries in port and mashed potatoes with roasted garlic, he imagined all the years Charlie had managed alone. Decades, Walter realized, first with two young sons and then abandoned by two wild teen-age boys. One by one, burying everyone in his family, mother, father, wife, and both his boys, and facing those first holidays without them. Walter stirred the sticky red sauce and thought about how easy he'd had it in comparison. Parents both still alive, fairly healthy, even happy in their Georgia retirement lifestyle. Maybe Annie messed him up bad, but he was lucky to have met her and tickled her fancy. He had the honor of having been her adventure into something more conventional for a while. As bad as it hurt to be discarded, he knew then and held firm to it now that it was A Good Thing to have been her lover. She cut a window into his thinking, injecting her beatnik ease with the world into his second generation Polish immigrant values. He was better for having known her. He knew that.

I'm in a rut now, he told himself as he scooped the seeds out of an acorn squash, but that won't last forever. If I keep doing what I enjoy, staying fit, staying active, staying positive, something good is bound to happen. Walter grinned to himself and took a sip of porter. Good things come to those who wait? Maybe. Walter sa-vored the sip. Maybe something like that.

Asha glanced at the clock on the dashboard and her stom-ach grumbled. Overlook had been surprisingly crowded for Thanksgiving Day, and she had been slowed down by repeatedly needing to corral the dogs and prevent unpleasant interactions with strangers. It was that nip in the air that weekenders love and Overlook was a little too accessible. Note to self, Asha silently vowed, no more popular hikes on holidays. That was a pain in the ass.

When they rolled up Charlie's driveway, she failed to see Walter's white Toyota pick-up parked just uphill from Charlie's ancient Ford. Focused on managing the food and the dogs, she didn't see the white on white and came to a halt just downhill from both vehicles. She hopped out and Lyla followed suit, jumping into the driver's seat and then out behind Asha's back. "Hey!" she whirled around as the dog scooted away. "Fine," she muttered, opened the back door, and released Brulee.

The explosion of Lyla's booming barks startled Asha. She looked up from the open hatch-back door to see Lyla backpedaling out of the cabin, barking. Brulee joined in, barking and leaping around, snapping at Lyla and shouldering her away from the cabin. Asha strode toward them, yelling "enough!" above the din.

Walter emerged from the cabin next. He surveyed the scene – Asha's hatch stood open, and he could see the coolers and pie nestled carefully in the way back. She was yelling at the dogs, who were circling her, still barking, but looking a bit sheepish. Charlie was shuffling across the cabin floor, cursing and coughing. Walter sighed deeply, smiled, and plunged in.

"Can I help you carry something? I'm Walter. You must be …"

"Smokey!" Charlie hollered from the top step, then spat. "What the hell are you doing here?"

"Hey Charlie!" Asha waved, then petted her dogs, finally quiet. "Happy Thanksgiving."

"Smokey! Well I'll be. Get them dogs inside. Walt, help that girl carry what she's got in." Charlie, beaming, looked twenty years younger, barking orders at Walter.

"May I help you with something?" Walter approached Asha, wondering if she recognized him. So far, it seemed like she didn't. Asha handed him the pie then wrestled the big cooler out of the trunk. She waddled under its weight. He studied her but for the moment said nothing. With Walter off the porch and down by the car, both dogs greeted Charlie, wagging, licking, and leaning against him. He looked up at Walter and Asha approaching, laden with food, and his face shone.

"Lemme give you a hand," he grunted at Walter, taking the pie. "This here's made from the blackberries up on Bearpen, ain't it, Smokey?" he asked, as he carried it on in. "You shoot a turkey up there too?" he teased, eyeing the cooler.

Walter took the other side of the cooler and carried it in with Smokey, sharing the load. He could feel his face muscles refusing to relax, the beaming grin plastered front and center. Only Smokey looked normal, happy without the manic dream-come-true quality both Walter and Charlie emanated.

Asha focused on getting the food in and getting set up. She headed back out after setting the cooler down in Charlie's rapidly shrinking kitchen. Walter was at her heels.

"Got more to bring in? Can I give you a hand?"

She stopped and turned around to look at him. His voice was familiar. She studied his face, trying to place it, trying to work quickly before both of them caught the awkwardness of her stare.

"I'm sorry," she admitted defeat to herself and began offering an explanation. "Your voice was familiar for a second. Have we met?"

"Yes. I work for Verizon. I fixed your phone a few months ago." Oh my god. I remember and she doesn't. Walter cringed. I sound like Stalker Phone Guy.

"Oh yes. I remember. You left me a message a few weeks after that." Asha flashed a smile. "That's why I remembered your voice." She turned to head out the door, then stopped and turned back to him. "Thanks for calling to do a follow up. I thought that was really nice of you." She skipped down the porch steps. Walter felt his cheeks ache from the wideness of his smile.

Oh god, that day when he fixed my phone, Asha silently groaned. She remembered the state she had been in: unshowered, nasty, sharp-tongued. She shuddered, realizing that he remembered her too. Shit, she cursed freely in her head, he's cute, too. Fuck. I blew it by being a miserable bitch three months ago. Goddamn it.

She looked around as she collected the smaller cooler and closed the hatch. No dogs. They had chosen to stay inside with Walter and Charlie. Crazy coincidence that Walter knew Charlie. Crazy, and kind of nice, she decided, if she could somehow undo that first impression she made. Without the hard hat, tool belt and bucket truck, she decided that he really was pretty cute, in a Middle America, beefy man way. There was an honesty and solidity to his good looks, no bohemian edginess that so often drew her in, only to then make her feel inadequate. Around him and Charlie, she suddenly felt safe, as if she had wandered into a bullshit-free zone. It was refreshing, she decided.

She came back in with the cooler; both dogs greeted her enthusiastically, as if she'd been away for days. Walter offered her a homebrewed brown ale but when he went looking for it in Charlie's fridge, discovered that she had already enjoyed it, two months ago. "It was absolutely delicious," Asha assured Walter. Charlie snorted. She ended up with a glass of the recent batch of porter and complimented Walter on it more than once.

They agreed to eat her game hens as an appetizer while Walter's turkey finished cooking. Charlie tried to help, got in the way, argued unnecessarily with Walter, and fussed with chairs, glasses, plates and bowls. He finally gave up, got himself another beer, and sat somewhat out of the way with both dog muzzles in his lap.

"So you met Charlie hiking?" Walter invited the story's telling.

"Yeah, well, sort of," Asha answered self-consciously. "I mean, I was hiking, but Brulee ran off, so I ended up chasing her all the way here from the old jeep road on the other side of Bearpen."

"Wow," Walter looked at Asha's build as clinically as he could and decided that she probably could run the whole way. "So you're hiking the thirty-five?"

"You heard o' that dang list?" Charlie interrupted.

Walter nodded.

"I thought it was something," Charlie caught himself before he said the word citiots, "out of town people thought up."

"Y'know, wherever there's mountains, there will be people making up lists about them," Walter offered. He listened to himself, decided that sounded dumb, and tried again. "I guess any sport, right? You have your ways of measuring yourself, levels of achievement to master. Maybe a little like working towards different belts in martial arts." Walter stopped there and took a sip of porter. He was trying too hard, he knew, but his face just kept on aching, and his stomach was doing cartwheels, and he couldn't help himself. He looked at his hands, then checked the time, then checked Asha's glass. "Can I pour you another porter? Or something else?"

"Thanks, I'm fine for now." Asha was thinking about lists and the idea of striving towards something. "I think some people just naturally seek to compete with themselves or against nature. Like, I do a fair amount of road racing," her voice rose in question "y'know? Like 5k's, or five mile races, little stuff like that?" Walter nodded. "I run for so many reasons, and I push to do more for all different reasons too." Her eyes rested on her finger's naked spot where she used to wear that ring. "I think it's not always competition. Like for me, the list turns the mountains into a game. There are rules and an objective, but I can play it any way I want."

Walter nodded again. Smokey has a deep voice, his awareness of its gentle cadence distracting him from her words. He blushed, realizing the way he was listening was akin to staring at her breasts. He focused his gaze on her face and refocused his thoughts.

"I don't need the list to hike the mountains, and I'm sure I'll finish the list and keep hiking." She smiled broadly and looked up from her hands to meet Walter's gaze. "It is so great to be out there. It is just so worth it – the long drive, the bug bites and the scratches and the sore muscles."

"Did you git up Lone?" Charlie interrupted.

"Yes." Asha swung her head around to meet Charlie's challenging bark. "A few weeks ago."

"Ye git up to the top?" He asked. "Sign in an' everything?"

"Yeah."

"Alone?"

"Yeah."

Charlie whistled low. Both dogs leapt to their feet. He laughed, yelled something unintelligible at them, and then headed for the front door. Walter and Asha exchanged a brief grin. He returned after his phlegm expulsion expedition and eyed Asha. "Smokey-girl, you got more goin' on than meets the eye. That there is a big one, Lone is." He paused, scratching Brulee's ears. "Ya like it?"

"It's not like Bearpen," Smokey began. "It has a different feel to it. Wilder. More remote." Smokey's halting answer made Walter wonder if she had thought about whether or not she liked it at any point prior. His appreciation of Asha grew again: she didn't evaluate the mountains, it seemed. She seemed to just experience them. "Yeah, I liked it. I guess. The huge birch trees were really special."

"There ain't nothin' like it," Charlie agreed, although Asha and Walter weren't quite sure what he was referring to. "You might climb all your thirty-five. That's fine for you. Git to know 'em, Smokey-girl. You do that." Charlie spoke softly, his voice gentled by the beer, oven-warmth, and nostalgia. "I think I've climbed ol' Bearpen more than thirty-five times. Prob'ly more than seventy times. Winter, summer, I've been all over that mountain. Found every special spot, hunted everything ya can hunt up there – blackberries, deer, bear, turkeys. I've hunted her plenty and I don't doubt that I've been hunted up there too." Asha cocked her head, not getting it. "Catamounts. Mountain lions to you out-of-towners." She grinned at Charlie's dig at her.

"I ain't local," she conceded to Charlie, teasing him with her imitation of his Delaware County twang. "An' I don't doubt that even if I stayed here forever, which I have half a mind to do, I'd never be local. I'd be that out-of-town girl with the crazy name from downstate that ol' Charlie up top o' the Vega valley took under his wing. That's who I'd be 'til the day I die. An' not even my gran'kids could really claim to be local. That's just how it is around here."

Charlie laughed. "Yeah, Smokey, I guess that's true enough." He leaned back in his chair, still petting Brulee, and surveyed the scene. He looked like he was going to say something more, but changed his mind and reached for his beer.

Walter had been laughing too. He nodded in agreement and added, "I've been living in Ulster County for twenty years. I'm still a newcomer."

"How did you meet Charlie?"

"Same way I meet everyone," Walter made the universal telephone gesture, thumb up, pinky down. "Out here, there are miles and miles of bad cable. I meet everybody."

"Walt's been damn good to me all these years," Charlie put in. "He's livin' proof that there's still some good men out there in that mess."

Asha smiled a small serious smile, remembering. Walter had been kind to her, within the bounds of his professional duty, that day he fixed her phones. She could see him "bein' good" to Charlie. It fit with everything else she was learning about him.

She backtracked to the previous topic. "I've lived in Dover Plains for seventeen years. My daughter was born and raised there. But the real local folk? The old timers? They've been the same families since the original patent was granted in the 1700's. I got nuthin' on that!"

"Your daughter?" Charlie asked. "You got a kid, Smokey?" Charlie tried to picture Smokey as a mother. It didn't work for him. Mothers were different from Smokey, not so independent and crazy-lookin.' Charlie sighed. Smokey just kept catching him off guard.

Walter kept the food coming. He set out a piece of Harpersfield cheese with homemade crostini and placed a bowl of spiced nuts in front of Charlie. Side dishes got unwrapped and reheated. Asha sampled Walter's culinary efforts and tried to hide her surprise at how delicious everything was.

Walter asked her about the mountains she'd already knocked off her list, and Charlie offered his two cents about most of them.

"You ain't tried Halcott yet?" Charlie pronounced it Hawk-itt; he guffawed as Walter and Asha exchanged quizzical looks. "Jes' you wait. You gonna do it in the summertime?" Asha shrugged, clearly not getting the joke. "There's nettles in there so bad folks call 'em 'Screamin' Fields.' There, an' up on North Dome an' Sherrill, screamin' fields to make you wish you'd never left the house. Make you go roll in a patch of jewel weed jes' to knock the stingin' back some. That's what helps, y'know. Jewel weed. You know that stuff?"

Asha nodded, her mouth full. She held a hand in front of her mouth as she mumbled "Do you hike?" to Walter.

Yes! Yes! Walter was emotionally leaping in the air, high-fiving himself, and strutting around the endzone while he gave up trying to look nonchalant. "Yeah," he answered as calmly as he could manage. "We should go some time."

"Hey!" Charlie yelled, sensing the opportunity. "Walter! Git Smokey's name and address and what-have-you written down for me, will ya?"

Walter assumed Charlie was just helping him out, one man to another, picking up on the vibe. He was way too delighted to stop and wonder why Charlie wanted her contact information too. He wasted no time in getting a scrap of paper and a pen from Charlie's junk drawer. Asha complied, writing her information in large print for Charlie's old eyes. Walter gazed at her pretty letters. Inwardly, he rolled his eyes at his mooning over her handwriting: Am I really going to think everything she does or says is just beautiful? Yes. The answer floated back to him from the deepest parts of his psyche. Yes. For the time being, that is how it is going to be. Okay, Walter smiled graciously at the answer. Fine with me.

Asha straightened up and handed Walter back the pen. "Can I have your number too? So that we can plan a hike?" she asked politely, as if she anticipated being refused. "Is it okay with you?"

"Sure." Walter accepted the pen from her and tore the bottom off her sheet of scrap paper. "May I call you sometime?" he asked, hoping Charlie wouldn't get involved.

Charlie cleared his throat and hauled himself to his feet. "Don't mind me," he grumbled. "Jes' gittin' myself another beer." He shuffled past them at the table, heading for the cooler on the porch. The dogs flanked him.

Asha watched Charlie and the dogs. She thought about how she had set up a couple of dates on Match.com, with essentially total strangers, men she knew less well than Walter. Hell, she and Walter were old friends in comparison. She considered – this is a man my dogs approve of, one who would cook a fine Thanksgiving meal for a cranky old redneck. He can brew damn good beer, fix phones, and at least pretends to like hiking. And definitely cute, with that spiky thing going on with his hair. Not my usual type, but the last time I got enamored with a ponytail and art snobbery, look where it got me. "Yeah," she answered, pulling her gaze back into the room. "Yeah," she repeated, searching Walter's face. "I'd like that."

"No way!" Kip bellowed.

Walter nodded, trying to downplay his own amazement and delight. The café was closed, but Kip was cooking breakfast for the family. Walter had noticed both cars were parked out front and the café's lights were on, so he decided to stop in.

"No way!" Kip shouted again, laughing and clapping Walter on the back.

"What? What's going on? Why are you yelling in here?" Wennie appeared with the baby monitor from behind the door marked "private." Her voice had that inimitable snarling, whining quality of an exhausted mother of a physically ill toddler.

Kip immediately covered his mouth with his hand and stage whispered, "I'm sorry honey, but Walter got a date. With that woman. The hiker chick."

"No way!" Wennie hollered. A wail erupted over the baby monitor. "Shit," she added, then disappeared back into the living quarters.

"So where are you taking her? What's the plan?" Kip asked, turning back to the grill where eggs and home fries sizzled. "Shit goddamn! This calls for a celebration – lemme crack open the good stuff." With that, Kip opened the walk-in door and disappeared inside. He returned with an odd shaped package wrapped in butcher's paper and a bottle of Martinelli's. He deftly unwrapped the bacon and arranged slices on the grill while Walter opened the Martinelli's and found glasses. He poured for all of them, anticipating Wennie's return with Fiona on her hip at any moment.

Wennie carried a cranky, feverish and damp version of Fiona into the café as Walter set the bottle down. "There," Wennie crooned. "There's Daddy. He's making breakfast. Walter's here too."

Fiona peeked out from her curled position on Wennie's shoulder and whimpered "Wa-wa has fizzy jew."

Walter offered her a cup.

Kip got down plates and Walter set a table for them. Fiona, satisfied that she now had a visual to go along with her mother's report of where her father was and what he was doing, moaned and struggled in her mother's arms until Wennie took her back to bed. She reappeared with the baby monitor and said in a soft but stern voice, "Okay, let's try this again." Kip and Walter nodded and pressed their index fingers to their lips.

Kip served up breakfast: scrambled eggs topped with snipped fresh herbs, bacon from the farm down the road, onion-pepper home fries, and sparkling apple juice.

"I think breakfast might be my favorite meal of the day," Walter admitted, tossing a napkin onto his lap and slurping his coffee.

"So tell us," Kip took his first forkful of egg and reached for the black pepper. "When? Where? What?"

Walter hesitated. He had certainly concocted a wide range of ways to meet and woo her back when she was frozen in memory as somehow wronged. Not that he needed or wanted to see her as a victim, but it sure helped with the testosterone-fueled fantasies. At Charlie's place, she seemed happy. All the way happy. No traces of a hurt or trauma. She was a different woman, still beautiful with her cocoa puff hair and fertile crescent skin tone and still intimidating with her athletic body and sharp glance, but without that air of recent injury. Seeing her in this new light, on a holiday, in good spirits, being generous and playful was really different.

"I don't know," he answered Kip, still trying to sort out all he thought and felt. "Y'know she lives all the way out in Dutchess, almost in Connecticut. In all my thinking about meeting her, I kind of glossed over what it might be like if we did actually start dating." Walter paused to take another bite.

"Well, to start with, maybe you should suggest something over where she lives. Show her you're ready to accommodate her." Wennie made the suggestion.

"But she comes over here to hike," Kip pointed out. "Maybe you should pick a mountain she needs for her list and plan a date around that. Y'know there's that new brew pub up in Windham; maybe a hike and a meal? You said she likes good beer." Kip talked quickly and ate even faster. He finished and got up to get himself more coffee. "More coffee?" he offered Wennie and Walter. Both nodded.

"Well then maybe you should ask her. Maybe she wants company for her list mountains, but maybe she wants to be able to say that she did them all alone. And maybe she wants a break from driving over here every weekend. I think you should ask her."

"But," Kip's voice rose naturally. Wennie gave him the Mom Look, and he grinned sheepishly in response. "You don't want her to feel pressured to make all the decisions." He took it down a few notches, knowing that he would get louder without meaning to. Wennie covered his hand with hers. He continued to hiss, "She'll feel like you have nothing to offer if you don't participate in the planning. It's really important to have suggestions for what to do. If you let her make all the decisions, she'll resent that."

"And she won't get to know you," Wennie put in.

"But on the other hand," Kip gave Wennie's hand a quick squeeze, then released it to lean back and lace his fingers over his stomach.

"Enough," Walter cut in laughing quietly. "I got it." He shook his head. "No, I don't really have it, but I got enough of it to run with it on my own for a while." He finished his breakfast and cleared the table for Kip and Wennie. The dishes clattered into the sink. He returned to the table still shaking his head, a self-conscious grin plastered across his face. "I feel like a teenager," he admitted.

"The phone guy? Really?" Grace didn't know whether to congratulate Asha or attempt to talk some sense into her. This week it was Halia's call to meet at The Blue Eft for breakfast on Saturday, instead of on their usual Friday night. Grace had just enough time to stop in for a spicy hot chocolate before heading over to the animal hospital.

"Walter-the-phone-guy," Asha corrected. Her smooth brow and relaxed composure revealed little. While Grace failed to glean meaning or import, Halia would have been able to wax eloquent. Unfortunately, Halia had not yet arrived.

"What's he like?"

"Nice." Asha tortured Grace with the one word answer. She shrugged at her friend's narrowed eyes. "Well, he is nice." She thought about where to begin. "He's not super tall, maybe 5'10"? Kind of beefy, not overweight, but not thin. Looks solid and strong. Crew cut blondish hair, blue eyes. I know, I know," Asha laughed in response to Grace's ever widening eyes. "Not typically my type."

"Blond, beefy, blue collar utility worker. Asha, have you lost your mind?" Grace teased. She took a sip of her Loup Garou and checked her watch. The hot chocolate was only tepid, and it was time to go. She swore on both accounts. Asha giggled.

That laugh. Grace gathered her purse, keys, and gloves and put her coat on. Asha sounded genuinely happy and relaxed. Grace hadn't heard a laugh containing those qualities escape Asha in a while. Tense laughter, self-deprecating laughter, a few times the laugh had been sharp, almost angry-sounding. This happy laughter? This was a return to the Asha Grace had met over a year ago. "Hey," Grace realized that she hadn't asked about Asha's job search in a while. "Have you found any jobs to apply for lately?"

Asha looked up at Grace and smiled. "No, no jobs, but I do keep looking." Her smile didn't fade. "I'm thinking pretty seriously about going back to school. Right now I'm still in the middle of crunching the numbers to see if it can work. But I'm trying to be realistic about job prospects and honest with myself about what I really want. I just keep coming back to the same thing. I don't really want to find a social work job." There it was: no misery, no tears, no apologies, and no guilt. Grace was floored.

"What will you study?" Grace checked her watch again and gave it the finger. Asha chuckled. "I haven't decided yet." She waved Grace away. "Go! You're late. I'll wait for Halia."

Grace leaned over and embraced Asha, then headed for the door. She looked back over her shoulder as she paused to yank on the old, sticky door. Asha looked okay. It wasn't an act, Grace decided. It was real. Unless she was currently in the eye of Hurricane Asha, the worst was finally over. Well halla-fucking-lujah, Grace thought. Finally. She sailed out the door.

Charlie nodded at the piece of paper sitting on his kitchen table. "Them two hit it off," he said out loud. "Good." He took out the leftover turkey Walter had packaged up for him and grabbed a fork. Turkey is good for breakfast, Charlie decided. That Walter, for all his damn fussing, was a fine cook. The turkey was delicious, even days old and unheated. Charlie thought about having a beer with his turkey and decided against it. "Not yet," he grumbled. "Gotta make that call first."

Charlie's gaze rested on Asha's handwriting. He thought about her out in the woods all alone with the dogs. He tried to get mad at her and her foolish ideas, "climbin' a bunch o' mountain jes' cause they're on some damn fool list," but deep down he felt proud of her. That girl has spunk, he realized. And heart. She came all the way the hell out here to bring a holiday dinner to an old man she hardly knows. Just because she thought I might be alone. Not bad, Charlie decided. Not bad at all.

That lawyer down in Margaretville had told Charlie that he needed to name a beneficiary for his life insurance policy and someone to inherit the land. Someone who would consider the conservation easement a gift, not a burden. Charlie'd wrestled with the idea some, especially after he found out that Smokey had a kid. Ain't right to uproot a kid, he thought. But he kept circling back to the fundamental rightness of leaving it all to Smokey. Virginia would have liked Smokey. Maybe would have tried to talk some sense into her, but not with any rancor. Virginia would approve.

Armed with a bellyful of cold turkey and the lawyer's business card in hand, Charlie picked up the telephone.

"Stissing House, eh?" I hear it's really nice," Halia said. "Joann and Henry go there from time to time." Joann and Henry, Halia's only extended relatives, and only related to Halia by ex-marriage, were the most romantic couple Asha knew. If Joann and Henry frequented the Stissing House, that was a clear indication of the type of place Walter had chosen.

The women walked quickly along Nellie Hill Road, headed for the Valley View cemetery, Brulee, Lyla, and Halia's Bezef creating a traffic hazard along the way. Their panting puffed steam into the cold morning air, and the women folded their arms against December. No snow yet; the frozen grass crunched underfoot, and the warmth of the dogs' feet left barely melted paw prints haphazardly criss-crossing the graves.

"Tonight?" Halia asked.

"Yeah." Asha answered.

Halia strode on ahead, trying to catch up with the dogs. Asha hustled after her, hearing the train a moment or two after Halia did. The women called and all three dogs came running. Asha continued, "Y'know, this date feels kind of different because I don't need anything. I'm not exactly even hoping for anything."

Halia narrowed her eyes a little and nodded. "No?"

"No." Asha said simply. She spread her mittened hands out in an unarmed gesture. "No. Whatever happens, happens. I'm not interested in trying to push the river."

Halia rolled her eyes. Bezef brought her a stick and Halia hurled it. All three dogs took off, claws scarring the frozen earth.

"Really." Asha paused, then added, "So what do you think I should wear?"

The truck glided across the crowded parking lot, Walter's touch light upon the wheel. He scanned for Asha's Jetta. He willed his heart to stop pounding, afraid that he'd made a bad choice with the slate blue silk shirt he'd chosen. Yeah, nice color, brings out my eyes, he had decided after trying on about six other shirt-pant combinations, but the silk will show sweat. Damn. He coached himself to relax and took a few deep breaths. I'll calm down once we get in there and start talking, he told himself. It's just the anticipation that's got me all tangled up.

There she is. Her car, anyway. No spot next to her. Okay, Walter felt the adrenaline course through his veins. Okay. Park. Deep breath. Approach. Oh shit, forgot the gift. No, leave it there; get it later if it feels right. Lock the truck. Fix the hair. Check the teeth. No light – can't see the teeth. Well, hell – I just brushed 'em. Oh go on.

"Hi Walter." Asha got out of her car as Walter walked up. She greeted him by lifting up onto her toes, kissing his cheek, then offering her arm as they turned to enter the restaurant. Okay, Walter sighed a silent and grateful sigh. The goodnight kiss is officially acceptable. She had just erased his question mark next to that item.

Inside, he indulged in all the trappings of a man on a date. He opened the door, pulled out her chair and hung up her coat. He was about to mention that Stissing House often had something different and worth trying on tap when she asked, "Would you consider ordering a beer to share? I don't want to drink a whole one myself." She grinned impishly. "The lampshades won't be safe and I'll end up with 'No second date' in LED lights across my forehead if I drink a whole one by myself."

"Really? That much of a lightweight?"

"No." Walter laughed as she explained, "I just don't like to drink that much. I get too full and then I don't enjoy my meal."

Their orders placed, they began to talk. They had covered the menu options, the political and economic implications of vegetarianism versus the local food movement, the USDA standards for organics, and were just starting to share personal food-related anecdotes ("When I was pregnant, parsnips made me sick" "Oh yeah? I used to make a mean parsnip cheddar soup before I cut back on super cheesy dishes") by the time the appetizers had arrived.

Asha didn't notice that the conversation struck a balance between personal and fairly intimate sharing and more light and safe
topics. She just noticed that she didn't feel like she had to "steer."
Walter found himself repeatedly impressed by how well-rounded
Asha seemed to be. She might be a school social worker, but she
had an incredible familiarity with local history, natural history,
politics, and art. She didn't seem to know much about hot rods or
telecommunications, but other than those two topics, she was able
to hold court.

Over salads, they traded off-color jokes. Asha was at grave
risk of having seltzer come out of her nose when Walter told her
about the Jewish gentlemen who wanted new black coats. Walter,
in turn, needed to cover his face with his napkin when Asha told
him about the costume party where attendees needed to dress up
as emotions. The date was progressing well.

Walter excused himself with a muttered, "I'll be right back."
He left the room, and as far as Asha could tell, left the restaurant.
She glanced at his coat on the rack and shrugged. She looked
around and rubbed her cheeks, sore from first-date-face. This
place is gorgeous, Asha noticed, appreciating the colors and archi-
tectural details still in place despite two hundred years of use as a
tavern. This place is romantic.

Asha thought about getting involved again. Am I really ready
for this, she asked herself, and then rolled her eyes at the timing of
the question. I am flirting with him. I am definitely being flirty.
What was that kiss hello all about? It was totally spontaneous,
she realized. Impulsive even. But it smacked of interest. A little
too late to start wondering, you dipshit, she berated herself. She
was about to get rolling on the look-before-you-leap internal tirade when Walter reappeared. He set a small square box upon the
table next to her and re-took his seat.

She looked down at the neatly wrapped gift. Purple bows,
indigo wrapping paper. Big points there. "For me?" she joked.

"It's nothing." Walter flicked his hand as if shooing flies.
"Well, not totally nothing. I mean, the box isn't empty." He looked

at her as reassuringly as possible and said "It's okay. I promise. Nothing that could cause an awkward moment. Really."

Asha unwrapped the present and looked questioningly up at Walter once the N&S plumbing supply logo was exposed. She opened the box, now thoroughly curious and found two cans of pepper spray nestled side by side. She laughed.

"You hike alone." Walter offered the unnecessary explanation. "That stuff could come in handy." Asha nodded. "Actually, I get it for free. Verizon supplies us: y'know, dogs, bears, angry customers."

Asha offered a perfunctory grin. "Was it really free?" She wasn't sure if he was kidding or not.

"Yeah." Walter shrugged. "I figured you probably don't carry a gun."

"Correct." Asha nodded confirmation.

"Nor a knife?"

"Right again."

"I wanted to offer you some tools of the trade for being out there." Walter looked at the cans of pepper spray and chewed his lower lip for a second. "You always have your dogs with you?"

"Yes." Asha caught the meaning behind his question and the gift. It was nice of him to give her something kind of empowering, something that made it safer to do what she was going to do anyway. She decided to appreciate the gesture at that level. The quirkiness of deciding to wrap stolen work-related freebies up as a date gift was a little wacky. She liked it.

She ate sea bass; he ate lamb. She ordered a glass of wine. The conversation simplified down to groans of delight and exchanged bites. Plates gradually were cleaned. Asha felt incredibly aware of Walter's hands, not realizing that her gaze kept flicking down to the table and back up to Walter's face. Walter, figuring out that she was considering holding hands, kept trying to leave his right hand lying around, available. Asha couldn't quite summon the nerve to take the step and Walter didn't want to push things.

Dessert, coffee, more conversation; the waiter brought a nearly full bottle of mineral water to the table for them. "Otherwise it'll just go to waste," he explained. They accepted it graciously.

Asha finally called it. "The dogs will get me up early tomorrow," she apologized.

Walter helped her with her coat. She turned to him too fast, surprising him by leaning in for the kiss. He recovered quickly and kissed her back, laughing at his awkwardness.

"First kiss on first date…" Asha giggled.

"Real smooth, huh?" His face was red, but he had wrapped his arms around Asha and made no move to release her.

She nodded. "Slick, even. You must be a real player." She tilted her chin up and let her eyes close. Walter let this kiss hint at all he'd felt for the past few months. Asha responded in kind.

Driving home, Walter stole glances at the stars through the windshield. "Thank you," he whispered, a touch self-consciously. "Thank you."

Charlie made the move down to the house in Halcottsville on the Saturday after The Date. It went pretty smoothly, Walter mused, as he finished up his last job of the day in Fleischmanns. He checked his watch, squinted at the sky, and decided to check on Charlie tomorrow. It's Friday, it's getting dark, it looks like snow, and I want to go home and call Asha. He listed his reasons silently. I'll head up there tomorrow.

The truck swayed a little in the stiff breeze that picked up. Those're some strong gusts, Walter acknowledged, gripping the wheel and steering out of the oncoming lane. A front was blowing in. The sun offered pale yellowish-gray light. Definitely snow coming.

Hmmm, Walter returned to a previous train of thought. Will snow mean that Asha won't hike? Does she have snowshoes? Does she like winter hiking? He wondered about his new "real" version of her, and guided the truck towards the Shokan central office with a fat happy grin on his face.

What a great first date, he reminisced, a little self congratulatory. She is so beautiful, and she looked so good all dressed up. And she kissed ... Walter felt his body remember. He and Asha had spoken on the phone a few times since last weekend; she had made it clear that she wanted to "go slow" and that, at least for now, she would not be introducing him to Pearl, nor would she consider including him in her plans during weekends with Pearl. On the one hand, he totally understood and agreed. On the other hand, he felt a bit like a kid at a make-your-own-sundae shop. He wanted to pile it all on now without regard to the potential bellyache.

Pulling in at Shokan, he decided to call Charlie. Perhaps a phone conversation could eliminate the need to drive all the way out there over the weekend. But Charlie didn't pick up. Walter rolled his eyes: "Goddamn cranky old man," he swore gently, even admiringly at Charlie. That man never did anything he wasn't in the mood to do. Charlie did seem to have a special hatred of the phone. Walter sighed. Hopefully the snow won't be too bad, he grumbled silently. Looks like I'm headed to Halcottsville tomorrow.

Walter kept busy that evening, cooking, cleaning up, reading, taking his shower a little earlier than usual, and checking the machine as soon as he was out, waiting for her call. At nine-thirty the phone rang; Walter felt the smile grow from somewhere deep inside as he reached for the cheap plastic cordless. "Hello?"

Her voice gave him chills. He settled in for a great conversation. They chatted for a while about Pearl and parenting. The snow began to fall, softly, gently, thoroughly. And then Asha told Walter about the other reason why she wanted to take it slow, why she wanted to be careful.

Walter drove out to Halcottsville thinking black thoughts about Rob. She had cried a little when she told him about the scene in the parking lot and the feeling of having all her trust demolished in a moment. Walter remembered when he first met her. That sense of having been wronged just pervaded the house. It clung to her, but even then Walter thought he detected something else too. Something stronger than her past, something core and clear. She was rocked back on her heels perhaps, but not fundamentally changed by what had happened to her. She described it as having cut him out of her heart like cancer; she talked about having dead spots remain. Walter believed he saw a whole lot more life than death in her heart. Part of him wanted to track Rob down, take him to a lonely spot deep in the Catskills and break every bone in his body, with his bare hands, jiu jitsu style. But no, Walter sighed heavily, knowing he wouldn't do that. He focused on the fantasy that he could be the antithesis of that prior experience, that he could help her see how much of her heart was still alive.

The snow lay like a thin layer of frosting, about an inch, maybe two, covering everything. Judging by tire tracks and footprints visible at 10 a.m. as Walter ran a few errands in Boiceville on the way, it looked like it had stopped snowing sometime last night. Walter jumped back in the truck, tapping the snow off his boots. Sure is pretty, he thought, zipping up his jacket, but damn, it's cold.

The house in Halcottsville was empty and the truck was gone. By the look of it, Charlie had left before the snow started. No tire tracks in the driveway. Goddamn Charlie, Walter slammed his palm against the steering wheel. Why? Why head up to the cabin in a snowstorm? Goddamn stubborn old fool. Walter was pissed at himself; he should have known. Getting Charlie to move down to the village this year had gone way too smoothly. Walter should have known Charlie was cooking up something like this.

The road up to the cabin was still snow-covered. The last mile, after the neighbor's place, Walter followed faint truck tracks up the hill. So he drove up here in the snow last night after all. I'm gonna hafta yell at him, Walter decided.

At the cabin, Charlie's truck sat snow-covered where Charlie always parked it. Sun-dazzled and muffled by the white blanketing, Walter hesitated for a moment in the driveway, taking it all in. He squinted, even with his sunglasses on. Down in the valley, it hadn't warmed up much, but up at the cabin on the slopes of Bearpen, it was still bitterly cold. Walter guessed with the wind and the snow, it had been right around zero degrees overnight. And there was no smoke coming from Charlie's chimney.

That's not good, Walter thought, and simultaneously his heart started to pound and he tasted sharp metal. The cabin steps were snow covered. The door was unlocked. Walter blasted in, yelling.

The silence pounded along with his pulse. He crossed the living room in what seemed like a step or two and flung open the bedroom door. The bed was neatly made, an ancient-looking quilt covering the bed instead of the usual 1970's bedspread and a handmade doll sitting atop it, staring back at Walter.

"Charlie!" Walter yelled again. His nose was getting cold. The cabin was freezing.

He strode back into the kitchen. The papers on the table; they weren't there when he moved Charlie down to Halcottsville last week. He snatched up the envelope, saw the return address and swallowed hard. Haynes, Rusk and Halcott's Margaretville office, postmarked this past week. Walter pulled the documents out and unfolded them. And then he began to cry.

"Charlie!" His yell was broken, choked.

Where is he? Walter crashed through the tiny cabin, looking. Where is he? Walter ended up in the mud room, and then he saw the tracks.

Out the back door and across the field, heading for the trail up Bearpen, bare footprints half-filled with snow led away from the house. Walter yanked open the door and followed them at a dead run.

Charlie lay curled up on the log, that fallen tree where he'd stopped to rest and think things through on his last trip up Bearpen. He was barefoot, in thin cotton pajamas, covered in a couple of inches of fresh snow. He lay on his side, hands under his head, knees tucked up towards his chest, eyes blessedly closed. He looked as if he were just sleeping, expect for the macabre coating of snow.

Walter crumpled to the ground next to him and sobbed.

Fudge – or Making It Up As You Go Along

"Blue is the color of death." Asha caught only the last sentence of whatever it was Grace was explaining to Halia. They both rose to hug her and make room at their small table in the back corner of The Eft. She thought for a moment about blue being the color of death. She made a face and shuddered.

"How was your week?" Halia asked Asha, changing the subject. Asha smiled and looked at each of her friends, really looked at them, before answering the question. "It's still a roller coaster," she admitted. "I'm happy, I'm relieved, I'm scared, I'm sad, I'm guilty. I'm a mess!" She laughed, teared up, and blew her nose.

"Things have been completely crazy for you for - what? A year now?" Grace patted Asha's arm as she spoke. "I don't know how you do it – how you stay sane and keep taking care of your house and Pearl, and the dogs… I think I would have given up and taken to my bed months ago."

Halia made a dismissive "pffft" sound. Both women looked at her. "Please." She added an eye roll.

Grace grinned and agreed, "Okay, maybe I was exaggerating. But still…"

"So we get to see you two Friday nights in a row, huh?" Halia asked Asha. "How did that happen?"

"Yup." Asha took a deep breath and blew her nose again. "Last weekend was a 'Pearl' weekend and she was out with friends on Friday night. This weekend, Walter and I are meeting up with some people from an internet hiking forum ..."

"Views From The Top?" Halia asked.

"No, ADK High Peaks. But how did you even know about ..." Asha caught the "Don't bother, she knows everything" hand gesture across the throat Grace was making and stopped herself. "Where was I?"

"You and the phone guy are meeting some internet hikers." Halia, who looked rather pleased with herself for referring to Walter as "the phone guy," prompted her.

"Yeah," Asha jumped on board. "The phone guy and I are meeting to go hiking during the day tomorrow, then heading over to Saugerties in the evening for the John Street Jam."

"That bass player you like so much," Halia turned to Grace. "What's his name? Somebody Levine? He plays there sometimes."

"Too bad Saugerties is such a long drive." Grace sighed, looking rather starstruck and moony.

"Pearl hasn't met him yet," Asha didn't hear Grace's comment and continued on her own track. "I really mean it about taking my time with this. Pearl knows about him." Asha's smile broadened. "She calls him 'the phone guy' too."

"How's he dealing with losing his friend? How is he feeling?" Grace asked the questions tenderly.

"He's sad, confused, overwhelmed at times. I guess he has good days and bad days." She shrugged. "It's so crazy, y'know? I mean, I just met Charlie a couple of months ago. He'd known Walter for years. Decades, actually," Asha realized as she spoke. "He left Walter his hunting rifle. I guess in a way that's like really symbolic; that gun helped Charlie survive. It's like he passed on to Walter the thing he saw Walter needing, or deserving maybe. The single most important thing he owned." Asha shook her head, her eyes open wide, searching her friends' faces. "Why did he leave me everything else?" Asha spoke almost plaintively. "Why me?"

With neither work nor worry to structure her time, Asha started sleeping. She slept late, she took naps, she fell asleep after Pearl left for school and after she came home from school. She slept the sleep of the dead, deep sleep, dreamless sleep. She slept each night for many hours without stirring. She slept each day, the afternoon nap beckoning her like a new lover. She dove into bed with the enthusiasm of one seeking the thrill of new flesh, and she slept lustily. She slept as one overcoming sleep deprivation. She slept, and she dreamed of sleeping when she was not actually asleep. She slept happily, delighting in her unconsciousness, her escape from thought and action. She slept thoroughly and often, feeding her half-starved nervous system. She slept hungrily, biting off huge juicy chunks of sleep, devouring them. She took deep draughts of sleep, drinking it in, replenishing the reserves that had run dry. She slept as one who had not enjoyed a good night's sleep in about a year or so. She slept as one finally released from the prison of anxiety, released from the tensed crouch, no longer awaiting the next onslaught.

"Hey mom," Pearl had that 'I'm getting revved up to ask a million questions' tone. Asha inwardly groaned. She tried to sneak a peek at the clock, but Pearl caught her and filled her in. "It's seven o'clock, and I fed the dogs and let them out already." She climbed onto Asha's bed, and then, with a truly wicked smile, patted the bed next to her. Both dogs lost no time joining in, and once again Asha was forced to start her day breathing hot dog breath and answering a thirteen year old's questions. Asha dove headfirst into her pillow and pulled the covers over her head.

"So mom," Pearl started again. "Are we rich?"

Wow. Asha pulled the covers back and sat up. She shooed the dogs off the bed and reached for a fleece sweatshirt to throw over her tee shirt. Wow. She hadn't anticipated the question being formed quite like that. "Um, ... define rich."

"Well, that guy, Charlie. He left you his house and his hunting cabin and all his land," Pearl made a comical gesture, stretching her arms wide. "And all his money." Pearl looked at her mother, all innocence and enthusiasm. "So, are we rich?"

"There are some things that I really had to worry about before that I don't need to worry about now."

"Like getting a job?"

"Yeah, at least for now, like getting a job."

"Can I have a horse?"

"Maybe. Are you ready to talk about that?"

Pearl stiffened. "Talk about what?"

Asha took a breath. "Are you ready to start talking about concrete plans? About what will happen next?"

"I don't know," Pearl hedged. "Do those plans include me getting a horse?"

"Possibly," Asha answered honestly. "But look out the window, kiddo. Do you see room for a horse?"

Pearl didn't answer. She leaned back against Asha's headboard and examined her fingernails. Her brow went from creased to furrowed and then cleared. "You want to move."

"Maybe. There are pros and cons to moving."

"Do you want to live with that guy? The phone guy?" Pearl looked over at her mother.

Asha bit her lip to keep from asking who told Pearl to call him "the phone guy." "Not now honey. We're just dating now." She wondered how much to say next.

"You want to live in the old guy's house?" Pearl wrinkled her nose. "Isn't it going to smell like Grandma's house? I hear you can't get that old person smell out of a house no matter what you do."

"Very funny." She rolled out of bed and began the project of finding suitable clothing for her next set of tasks. Snoopy pants were in the laundry, she remembered, and searched for her pineapple print flannel pajamas. "I'm thinking about it, kiddo. The cabin is in an incredible spot, with enough room for a horse, chickens, a huge garden, sheep, and a llama."

"How far away from here?"

It was the question Asha dreaded. Two hours. It was her turn to examine her fingernails.

Snow fell steadily all day Tuesday. Late February snow, to be precise; the kind of snow that is at once soft and gentle and emotionally exhausting. To the populace of the Hudson Valley hungrily searching for signs of spring, these late season heavy snows bring denial and a bad case of the Fuck-Its. Asha didn't bother shoveling the front walkway, and completely forgot about the possibility of a propane delivery, so that pathway remained unshoveled too. The trail to the compost bin filled in as the inches piled up. Nellie Hill Road lay pristine, the town's plow guy apparently also just not in the mood.

Pearl's visit with her father was nixed for the time being, as no one was about to take on driving up or down Plymouth Hill. Shaking off the sleepiness of having done nothing all day, Asha pulled her pink waterproof boots on and bundled up to walk the dogs. Pearl curled up on the couch with a book and basked in the warmth of the propane fireplace. She grunted in response to her mother's announcement that she was taking the dogs out.

Forty minutes later, Pearl heard the stamping of snow removal and voices on the porch. She got up, unlocked the door and turned on the outside light to see her mother, Halia, and Grace on the doorstep.

"We decided to come over here to hang out with you," Asha explained to Pearl. "Louise closed The Eft early so that her staff could get home."

"I took my car to work today." Grace shook the snow off her hat and coat, standing inside and reaching backwards out the door. "Don't ask – I have no idea what I was thinking." She rolled her eyes at her failure to select the four wheel drive truck on a day when she would so obviously need it. Wingdale Mountain Road, a windy steep switch-backed affair, was the sole route home for Grace. She was clearly not going home tonight.

"I'll get a towel for the dogs," Pearl offered, sizing up Lyla, Brulee, and Bezef.

"Thanks honey," Ash tracked snow into the house, then slipped her feet out of her boots and promptly stepped into a puddle of melting snow. She hurried upstairs to get slippers and to ease the congestion at the front door.

She returned in time to overhear Grace talking on the phone to Eddie. "Yeah, I'm gonna stay at Asha's tonight. Halia's here too." A pause and then: "No! Pearl's here too." Another pause. "Well, maybe after Pearl goes to bed."

Pearl giggled at Grace's wink and finished toweling off the dogs. She returned to her perch on the couch and turned the TV on. The three women headed into the kitchen.

"So what are we waiting 'til Pearl goes to bed to do?" Asha wanted to know.

"Drinking," Halia suggested, setting off down the stairs to the basement to raid her stock.

She grinned, fussing around in the fridge, mentally crafting a meal. Sighing and pressing her lips together at the dearth of options, she checked the freezer.

"She's right," Grace stated the obvious, listening to Halia's light steps back up the basement stairs. Asha hip-checked the freezer door shut and brought an armload of vegetables over to the kitchen table, not responding to Grace.

Halia reappeared with a bottle in each hand. "Do you have anything open in the fridge?"

"No." Asha was in full swing, mincing garlic and rinsing kale.

Halia opened a bottle of chianti. Asha looked up, and recognition changed her features ever so slightly. Both Grace and Halia saw and grasped what had happened. Grace took the bottle from Halia and strode over to the sink. "Do you want me to dump it out?" Grace's half-joking tone didn't fool Asha. "You want to memorialize the asshole by dumping out the bottle you bought to drink with him? Or should we drink it and move on?"

Asha continued with food prep, eyes down, hands busy.

"I am totally sick of the way you manage to keep circling back to misery. Enough already!" Grace lit into Asha. "Could we please have an evening together that is not dominated by you and your problems? For crissakes, at this point they're manufactured problems!"

Pearl walked in. Grace hung onto the neck of the bottle, waiting Asha out. Asha hesitated, hoping an explanation would arrive, freshly showered and appropriately attired for Asha to offer Pearl. No such luck.

Pearl hesitated also, taking in the scene. "Can I have a glass of wine too?" she asked.

Asha sucked in a long breath, her eyes moving slowly from the bottle to Pearl and back again. "No, honey," Asha responded. Grace began to tip the bottle. "You can have a sip from my glass." With that, she laid down the knife and wiped her hands on a dishrag. She tossed it back over her shoulder and took the two steps over to the cabinet to get the glasses out. "You both having some too?" she asked Halia and Grace.

The snow fell steadily through the evening, piling up in the footprints on the front walkway, and erasing the fresh sets of prints Pearl and the dogs had made in the backyard. The girl had declared the wine "sour" and the kale "bitter." She disappeared briefly after dinner and returned with a box of dark chocolate bark sprinkled with dried blueberries and lavender blossoms. "Here," she plunked the box down on the cleared table. "My dad gave me this for Valentine's Day, but the flavors are just too weird for me. You guys might like it."

"Thanks, honey." Asha exchanged glances with Halia and Grace. "Port?" She asked, getting up.

"Mmmm," was the reply.

Armed with chocolate, port, and a snowstorm, they retired to the living room and settled in by the fireplace. Asha checked the clock, reconsidering what bedtime might be given the likelihood of a snow-related delay in the morning.

"Wanna stay up until ten?" She offered to Pearl, who lay sprawled on the floor with Bezef and Lyla. Brulee leaned against Asha's legs.

Pearl checked the clock too and shrugged. "I have some homework to finish and I want to take a shower. If I go now, will you braid my hair before I go to bed?"

"Sure. What homework do you have?"

"I need to finish a rough draft of an essay."

"On what?" Grace wanted to know.

"It had to be a persuasive essay. Like you have to convince someone of something, y'know?" Grace nodded. "I wrote it about being a vegetarian." Pearl turned to go upstairs.

Grace called her back, "Which side did you take?"

Pearl grinned a delighted grin, white teeth flashing in the fire-light. "Pro vegetarian." She turned to go again, then added, over her shoulder, "just as an intellectual exercise. Personally, I'm still undecided." With that she was gone. Lyla followed her.

"God, she just loves being provocative," Asha sighed, shaking her head. She took a nibble of chocolate and a sip of port and settled into the couch.

"She still likes you and she is thirteen years old. That's pretty amazing," Halia observed. Grace nodded, taking a piece of chocolate.

Halia tucked her feet up under her in the big white chair that had belonged to Asha's grandfather. She looked perfectly at home, framed by antiques and lit by firelight. Grace shared the couch with Asha, having kicked off her boots and stretched out her long legs. She reached for the light switch and flipped it off. The three women sat silently for a while, mesmerized and tipsy in the orangey glow.

"So what are you going to do?" Grace gave voice to the question that seemed to dog Asha.

Asha answered slowly, as if she were considering all the options and exigencies as she spoke. "I think I'll sell this place and the house in Halcottsville and use the money to build an addition onto the cabin. I think that's where I want to be." Asha's smile was a little fuzzy, her eyes focused on the fantasy of the cabin transformed.

"Does Pearl know that's what you're thinking?" Halia asked.

"Yeah," Asha's answer was a sigh.

"Does Carl know?" Grace verbally underlined Carl's name.

"Yeah." No sigh this time.

"You could sell all that land and stay here, and probably have enough money so that you wouldn't have to work." Grace thought out loud. Asha looked at her. "I'm just saying…"

"I know," Asha's tone was conciliatory. "I know. I've thought about a lot of different options." Asha tried to run her hands through her hair, but her fingers got stuck in snowstorm inspired tangles, and she had to give up and tug her fingers out, curl fragments getting stuck in her ring. "We could sell the cabin and live in the Victorian. Pearl used to say 'I want to live in a house where I can get lost on my way to breakfast.' The Halcottsville house is almost that big, and it does have a servant's staircase."

"Has she seen it?" Grace shifted to get more chocolate.

"No, not yet. I've been waiting for the weather to get a little better before dragging her all the way over there." Asha took another sip of port and savored it before continuing. "It's a little creepy too. I'm still figuring out how I feel about all of it. I mean," she turned to look at Grace for a moment, and then sought and held Halia's gaze, "can you imagine living in Charlie's cabin? It's just weird…" Asha trailed off, letting her gaze drop back down to the fire.

"What makes it creepy?" Halia challenged.

"Partly the way he died, I guess. That he planned it out and all. Y'know, Walter told me," Asha lowered her voice and listened for Pearl's footsteps before continuing, "Charlie left a quilt that Virginia made and a doll sitting on the bed, like he was leaving it ready for us. He knew I had a daughter. I remember telling him. I can just see him shuffling around in the cabin, taking his old flannels off the bed and putting the 'company' quilt out, and then thinking, 'Oh yeah, she has a little girl. Before I go kill myself, I'll get that doll Virginia made and put it on the bed for her to find.' That's creepy."

"I guess you could see it that way," Halia allowed. "You could also look at it as acceptance and dignity in the face of the end. He wasn't afraid and he wasn't ambivalent. He was passing the baton. Like leaving the keys or something, he's not only leaving you his place, he's also leaving you all his memories."

"That doesn't exactly make me feel better," Asha pointed out. "I don't know what to do with them. I don't know why I deserve them. God, what a load to be dropped in my lap. It's just so weird." Asha gave up trying to articulate the experience and used the word "weird" as a garbage can into which she tossed the creeped out fears of death itself, the guilt, the confusion, and the hope she felt. She finished her port and cocked her head. "I think I heard the shower turn off. Pearl will be down in a minute or two."

Grace and Halia watched Asha comb Pearl's long thick hair. Pearl sat on the floor, her back against the couch, her skinny sparobed shoulders between her mother's knees.

"Bangs braided or no?" Asha asked the girl.

"No. I'm gonna straighten them in the morning."

"One braid or two?"

"Two."

Asha's fingers parted and pulled through Pearl's hair, start-ing at the crown with the French braids, weaving tightly, tugging, smoothing. Pearl sat still, looking into the fire, enjoying the warmth on her damp skin.

"I'll miss nights like this," Pearl said.

"Yeah?" Asha asked, braiding the end of the second braid.

"The surprise visit, having these guys..." she jerked her thumbs in opposite directions, indicating Grace and Halia "... close by." Pearl handed her mother the hair tie. "Will you guys come visit us out in Charlie-ville?"

"Yeah!" Grace chirped, and then giggled at the sound of the staccato syllable.

"Sure," Halia confirmed. "Maybe we can help your mom with some of the projects she wants to do. We'll come up for weekends and help get stuff done."

Asha held up one hand. "Wait a minute." She looked around the room, from Halia to Pearl to Grace. "Nothing's decided yet. The plan isn't definite. I'm still trying to make sure it's the best idea."

"Mom." Pearl wore The Look. It was the look all single parents dread: the look that lays the parent bare and reverses roles in one precocious moment. "You know we're moving. I know we're moving. Sheesh. Why would you stay here? Your phone guy is two hours away, your stupid hiking list is two hours away, your huge tracts of land..." Pearl adopted the Monty Python ac-cent and gesture for this phrase "are two hours away. Let's face it: we're moving." Asha absorbed Pearl's words, thinking. "I've discussed it with dad. I'll be okay. I can still hang out with my friends online and when I visit him. It'll be fine."

After Pearl went up to bed, the three women shifted and stretched. Grace got up to pee, Halia got herself a glass of water, and Asha, knowing what she wanted to run by her friends next, poured herself another glass of port.

"I have to break things off with Walter." She avoided Grace's glance, her words from before still ringing rather insistently in Asha's ears. "Is it okay if we talk about me and my problems again if I don't get all miserable about it?"

"I guess so," Grace's voice was high and tight. She frowned at Asha for a long moment, then relented. "But only if you let me rearrange the furniture before work tomorrow. Maybe it's all this clutter and chaos that makes you so miserable." Both women grinned.

Asha started to protest, but Halia sighed impatiently and rolled her eyes at both of them. "What about you and the phone guy?" she asked.

"We both need some time... I mean, I need to figure this out by myself. So much has happened, and there's so much I need to do... I just don't want to dump too much on this relationship too soon. He's such a sweet guy, and I feel like I'm starting to really fall for him ... or at least, I was starting to... but now I feel like it's just not fair, it's too complicated. I need to step into this new role by myself and get used to it before bringing a partner into the picture." Halia was nodding support. Grace's mouth hung open, an expression of pure dismay dominating her pretty face. "I don't know what'll happen, but I know if I don't cut things off for a while, I'll pollute our connection with all the other garbage I'm finally sorting through and throwing out. I need to face these decisions and recreate a life for Pearl and me by myself."

She took a deep breath, and went on. "Last time I got involved with someone, I tried to weave him into my plans for the future. Hell, I tried to turn him into my plan for the future – our relationship was the plan. I have to do it differently this time. I need to prove to myself that I can. And I want to make sure I don't lean on a guy to get through all this." She swept her hands wide apart, indicating the grand everything, the emotional, physical, concrete, and abstract everything. "I think it's the only chance

I have of staying with Walter and having it end up really good one day."

"Have you told him yet?" Grace asked.

"No," Asha hung her head, "I haven't. I guess partly I'm dreading it because I'm not sure he'll understand. But also I'm dreading it because then it'll be real. And I'll miss him so much. I don't especially want to do this alone. I just know I have to."

"Well, shit," Grace complained. Asha and Halia looked at her. "I was hoping I could invite you guys to Easter dinner. It's become a tradition at my house over the years. I was looking forward to having another couple there."

"I'll still come," Asha offered. "I'll come with Halia." Halia nodded.

"It's not the same." Grace pouted.

"Thank God," Halia murmured. Asha looked at her sharply, then tittered. This time it was Grace who rolled her eyes.

Walter paced back and forth across the living room floor, shaking his head every few steps. She said they'd know when it was time to reconnect. She said she cared about him, cared about them as a couple, too much to be irresponsible. She said being together now while they each deal with Charlie's death and all that it meant to each of them individually, to them as a couple, to all of them as a potential family would be a mistake. She said, for her, time alone was key. She said she was afraid not to be alone for a while; afraid of what that might do to them.

With each discrete remembered sentence, Walter turned on his heel and changed direction. He disagreed with every single one of her assertions, and he knew they were all correct. He paced and argued silently, lining up and knocking down alternatives like cans at target practice. He wanted to hit something, to go to a bar, to get into a fight, to kick someone's ass but good just for the release. He knew he wouldn't. I'm a grown man now, he told himself. No danger of succumbing to adolescent foolishness.

But what to do with all this … Walter mentally thrashed around looking for the right word. Emotion. Pure raw multilayered emotion. He stopped pacing and looked around. "Fuck it," he said aloud. "I'm gonna finish this fucking house."

The Home Despot, as it was commonly known, became Walter's home away from home. He attacked the trim first; numerous trips back and forth to the millwork section. Not enough in stock to do the whole downstairs in the one he chose, he had to start over, re-making decisions: do just the kitchen in one style, the hallway in another, living room and dining room in yet another? At each choice, at every crossroads, he bit back the temptation to call Asha "just to get her opinion."

Trim. Lots of measuring, lots of cutting, lots of nailing. Evenings after work got even busier than back when Charlie was asserting himself into all the interstices of Walter's carefully organized social life. He still made it to jiu jitsu twice a week, but workouts in between got shorter and more haphazard. Trips to Kingston or out to Wadler Brothers for supplies killed evening hours, and weekends just evaporated under the heat of trim, trim, and more trim.

Colors were the hard part for Walter. He grew up with white, pale white, off white, antique white, and when mom went really wild, eggshell. It was as if mom wanted her home to look like a gallery. White was clean, bright, and required no decision-making. Walter wanted color. He wanted to impress Asha, to show her that he was not simply a "white" guy. He had noticed when he spent time at her home that Asha wielded color like a rapier; here brandishing, there jabbing. Walter had liked the result, the way it felt to be in her space. Her bedroom, he remembered, was painted in pastel shades of dove gray and sweet little girl pink. He missed those colors.

Meanwhile Asha hosted Friday nights with Halia and Grace as they cleaned, re-painted and packed up the house. It was hard work, between the sheer accumulation of one hundred years of grime in the corners and Asha's belief that a dirty house gave testimony to a rich and exciting life. That and two dogs. Lyla managed to get paint in her tail not once but twice due to Grace's indulgent attitude towards painting with a dog in the room. All the rooms required cleaning and tidying but only a few still needed painting. Ancient window sills with multiple layers of potentially toxic lead paint got covered with a nice new coat of white, and new sheetrock got slapped on top of peeling paint in the closets. Halia even attacked a few loose tiles in the bathroom with fresh glue and grout.

While Walter cleaned, repaired and finished to make the house his own, Asha took her task to be pulling up roots and removing the personal touches that had made the house so much an extension of herself. She put the house on the market at the beginning of March, figuring it would take a while to sell and also figuring that in the meantime she could get it ready. "Hell, if I get an offer, I can always sell it 'as is,'" she said to Grace and Halia over pizza and beer, the do-it-yourselfer's meal of choice. Grace belched prettily in agreement.

"No, not tonight. I have to get up early in the morning." Asha fielded the phone call from Halia as she tossed cassette tapes into a cardboard box. The clattering of plastic hadn't bothered her until she picked up the phone; this particular multi-tasking combination wasn't going to work.

Halia was home from school early, seeking Asha's company and interrupting her latest efforts at packing.

"Maybe," Asha responded to Halia's suggestion that they meet at The Eft instead. "I have Pearl tonight. I could bring her and we'll just get a table in the restaurant instead. She loves Louise's veggie burgers." Asha moved to the linen closet, kicking a new empty box along the floor in front of her, her free hand covering her exposed ear as protection from the "music" leaking out from around the edges of Pearl's closed door. Stacks of linen napkins, tea towels, hand towels and wash cloths awaited disposition.

"Grace and I will be there around six thirty," Halia informed her.

"Okay. We'll get there around then too." Asha hung up and deposited the cordless phone into the cardboard box along with all the tea towels she felt guilted into keeping because her mom had brought them back to Asha as gifts from all her travels. "Who the hell collects tea towels?" she muttered as she headed for Pearl's room, now carrying the box in her arms. "People who don't have a place to display thimbles or spoons, I guess."

"Pearl?" she dropped the box outside Pearl's door with a thunk.

"Yeah?" came the shout from inside. A moment passed and then the music got turned down and the door opened.

"Hey," Asha greeted her. She hadn't seen her in an hour or so; Pearl had entered the house and erected the acoustic barricade immediately upon arrival from school.

"Hey." Pearl's single syllable answer said it all: Hi mom. What the hell are you doing standing outside my door? Am I in trouble? No? Good. Go away.

"I just made plans to have dinner at The Eft with Halia and Grace. Six thirty, okay?" Keep it short and sweet and don't take anything personally, Asha coached herself.

"Okay." Pearl closed the door and resumed the blasting of god-awful crap.

Okay, Asha thought. That went well.

Back to sorting and packing. She went back into the computer room where she had been dealing with the cassette tapes. A yard sale staple, she chuckled, although fewer and fewer people actually bought any it seemed. Except me, she admitted ruefully, looking at the huge box full of dusty plastic boxes. She sorted into the yard sale, garbage, and keep boxes, the keep box intentionally a much smaller container than the other two. She picked up a tape and examined the handwriting on the label. A high school boy-friend bent on enriching Asha's musical education had made her a number of tapes. Her hand hovered over the yard sale box, then retreated. She read the song titles and thought about slow dancing to one of those songs with her cousin at a wedding when she was thirteen years old. Keep.

She dispensed with that task and took the overflowing keep box to her staging area in the living room. She planned to load Bessie up soon with the first load of non-essentials to get relocated out at the cabin. "There ain't a whole lot o' room out here, Smokey," Asha imagined Charlie barking at her. "Yer gonna hafta make some tough choices, girlie. That's jes' all there is to it." Not when I get done with your cabin, Chuck, Asha answered him. Not after I get through with it.

Pearl came down, dressed for dinner. Asha gave her the parental once over; she passed: nothing too tight, too short, too plunging, too high. She came in for a second glance. "I swear you got taller since you came home from school." Pearl laughed prettily. For a moment she was ageless and they were beyond the mother-daughter dyad. Asha just looked at her, as awed as the first day they met, on Pearl's birthday all those years ago. She grinned at her own crazy thoughts and at her daughter's loveliness. "Is it time to go already?"

"Yeah... well, a little early, but yeah."

"Okay." Asha ducked into the stairwell to check a mirror. "What do you think, Pearl? Do I need a shower, or just change?"

"Go jump in the shower," Pearl instructed. "I'll pick you out an outfit."

"Okay." Asha started moving up the stairs, two at a time. "Nothing too tight, please!" The dogs crowded into the small bathroom with Asha.

Pearl rolled her eyes and set off back up the stairs for her mother's closet, sighing heavily.

The May morning sunshine filled Walter's bedroom, warm and insistent, urging him to get up. Walter rolled over to check the clock. "Whoa!" He sat bolt upright, the 7:47 a.m. displayed on the clock's face shoving him hard into consciousness. He took a deep breath and then lay back down, stretching and allowing coherent thoughts to replace the panic of having slept late.

It is Saturday. No work. I didn't "oversleep" for anything. Okay, Walter sighed. But why did I sleep so late? He went over the previous day in his mind, putting the pieces back into order. Painting. I stayed up late, much later than what normal used to be back before I met Asha, before Charlie died, before I embarked upon this project.

That was the order it went in, wasn't it, he asked himself lying there. First it was finally meeting her, then Charlie took himself out, and then, it seemed like the next thing that happened was that he was ass-deep in home improvement. Asha broke up with you, he reminded himself. You're not admitting that part. Walter considered this. No she didn't, he argued back. Not exactly. She just set up a limit about being together right now. It's a temporary time out while we both do what we need to do to process and heal. Bullshit, dude, she broke up with you, came the voice from deep inside his reptile brain. Walter groaned in response, rolled onto his back, and closed his eyes. He called it checking in. He lay still, quiet, not listening to the sounds of life coming from outside. He listened internally; listened closely, trying to relax and let the message come to him. It was the best he could do, this internal magic eight-ball check: Did Asha break up with me? Is it really over? Am I in denial about being dumped?

The weeks had turned into months, and winter into spring, and still no word from her. He missed her terribly, mourned her absence from him just as much as he mourned for Charlie. But, digging deep and being as brave as he'd ever been, he couldn't find any real hurt or anger. He didn't feel dumped. He understood. He agreed. She had been right. He didn't hate her and he wasn't angry.

He opened his eyes. Last night's late hours had paid off: the painting was finished. Walter scrambled out of bed, a smile on his face. He couldn't wait to go downstairs and see how the colors he chose - a rich ruby-red for the trim, deep burnt orange (like butternut squash) for the walls – looked in the morning light. He pulled on the pair of Indian print pajama pants Asha had picked out for him at a yard sale (they had both giggled at how un-Walter-ish the pants were) and went downstairs.

Barefoot, with the pajama pant bottoms just a little too long, gently sweeping the floor as he moved, Walter made coffee and wandered around putting away all the stuff he'd left lying around while painting. Coffee ready, toast popped up, Walter sat down and looked, not at the smudges nor the touch ups needed. Not critically. He just looked at what he had done, how he had transformed the sterile utilitarian room into an incredibly vibrant imitation of an Indian brothel. He snickered and was pleased.

The idea came to him when he drove past a state forest parking area. Years ago, back in the pre-GPS days at the phone company, when lunch hour was a euphemism for the midday stretch from the completion of the third job to the time to go back to the garage, and exploring the Catskills forest was part of Walter's job description (his job description, not the phone company's), he discovered the stand of ironwood up in Halcottsville. Ironwood – that's a local name. Walter had also heard it called musclewood or muscle trees by little kids. When he looked it up, he was pretty sure the correct name was hornbeam. Whatever it was called, a stand of it transported him straight back to childhood, to imaginary play in the woods. Trunks reminiscent of giraffe legs or alien tentacles or anthropomorphically "strong" trees with their bulging muscles offered hours of play.

Every phone guy keeps a tree saw in his bucket truck, and every phone guy should. You never know when "fallen tree on wire" will require such a tool or when the perfect Christmas tree lurks in a wooded area near a nap spot or a swimming hole. Or, as in this case, when the four ironwood posts of a handmade neo-rustic four poster bed need to be liberated from their sleepy, albeit alive, existence in the forest.

Walter, a strong man, knew what he was up against. They don't call it ironwood for nothing. He selected four perfect specimens: tall enough to be cut down to size, straight enough (but not too straight) to be used as uprights, thick enough to lend strength, both visual and literal. His little bow saw was not the tool of choice, but a chainsaw was noisy, smelly, ecologically not PC, and would alert every landowner within earshot as to his tree rustling activities. Walter was pretty sure he was on state land (and thus stealing from the taxpayers of New York) but he preferred not to discuss his actions with anyone. He picked out another two lovely trunks as "alternates" in case anything went wrong with the other four and set to work.

His efforts to concoct a plausible phone-work-related excuse for his behavior kept his mind busy while he sawed. He enjoyed the first one, the breathless fresh sweat lubricating arms and shoulders. The second and third trees were just work, not unpleasant, but as the thrill of potential discovery faded, the rhythm of breath and muscles took over, a bit like zoning out listening to the dishwasher. By the fourth tree, Walter was tired. He played with other ways to approach the task, left-handed, engaging his abdominal muscles to turn it into a Pilates exercise, using smaller, quicker strokes. His mind wandered.

A bed. Walter had a bed, a bland platform affair he'd been sleeping on since he was about thirty. Purchased at a big box store, probably made by underpaid third world factory workers (as opposed to those overpaid factory workers, he snarked at himself),

it was an empty bed. Devoid of meaning, feeling, vision, and passion, it was made of MDF: essentially sawdust and glue. Plastic.
And veneer. Pretend wood. He had been lavishing attention on his
home, dragging it out of its mass-produced doldrums, transform-
ing it into a real expression of something. It got him thinking. It
got him looking around a little differently at all the stuff in his life.
He was critically and creatively reassessing everything.

Projects that had been abandoned in the basement for nearly
a decade awoke from their stupor, roused by the hope engendered
by Walter's seismic shift. The antique mahogany dining table that
needed a wheelchair finally got its hip replacement and bionic
legs. The gorgeous wing chair he had found on the side of the road
got dropped off at the re-upholstery shop. The painting downstairs was completed and a new bathroom, finished in bluestone
and a splurge on a stoneware sink handmade by a potter-friend of
Jonathan's, finally got finished upstairs. Walter had begun making statements – declaring himself – a little at a time, but now he
had waded in deeply enough that it was now time to start swimming. The bed, he grinned at the metaphor, was like a perfection
of his strokes.

Okay, and yes, it is a bed. Walter got through tree numbers
five and six by imagining Asha in it. It was like having her in the
forest, making love out in the woods. He didn't need to call her
and ask what she thought. He was confident on this one. As his
vision of the bed became more and more fully realized, his trust
in his own aesthetic also grew. The bed would be real, organic,
handmade, beautiful, lyrical, passionate, and, he promised himself, strong as hell, to withstand any and all acrobatics he could
envision. Eagerness fed his tired muscles, and finally the last tree
fell.

Walter crumpled up the eraser-thinned sheet of graph paper
and gave it a gentle toss toward the trash. It lay with its siblings

and cousins in a jolly jumble clustered around the wastebasket. The joinery of the bed, how to resolve edges and joints and corners while honoring his refusal to go rustic ("Adirondack" even) was proving difficult. He was completely, irrationally committed to organic joints, hiding all hardware, no visible seams. A bed that really nested in the trees. At the same time, he knew it needed to be engineered to work, to be functional. It was proving to be more difficult than he had originally pictured.

He leaned back, lacing his fingers behind his head and arching his back in a lusty stretch. When all else fails, take a break and drink a beer, right? Walter asked himself. The logs he cut last week were drying nicely, one benefit of this summer's dry spell. He checked on them, brushing away any ants or spiders on the bark and pressing his hands against the cut ends, feeling for moisture. Yeah, they need to dry out a little while longer. Good thing I can't figure out the design, he chuckled.

It was still early. He'd gotten home from work and headed straight to the drafting table where he'd wasted little time before adding another white paper ball to the arrangement growing on the floor around the basket. Like puffball mushrooms, Walter thought as he collected the fist-sized white balls and smoothed them all out, ready for the recycling. The crumpling and chucking was part of the creative process, but Walter was okay with the uncrumpling to do what's right.

A run, he decided. Change of scenery, fresh air, earn the inevitable ice cream calories: a run sounded good. He changed quickly, happy to shed the jeans and heavy tool belt for the antichafe spandex bike shorts he always ran in. A run will clear my head, he thought, and maybe open up the space for the design. Walter was ready to let that happen, to aid it where he could and to get out of the way when necessary. The bed was too full of hope, too full of good to become a source of struggle. Just like the design had to be organic and seamless, Walter realized, putting it into words for the first time as he laced his running shoes, so did the process. No pushing the river...

Last thought out the door, Walter had a moment of longing for Asha, Brulee, and Lyla. She had introduced Walter to running with dogs, and he liked it better than running alone. Oh well, he shrugged it off. Even that wasn't going to bring him down today.

Walter knew, when applied to his own activity the term running was a euphemism. Light jogging was another term he employed sometimes, although for a two hundred pound man such as he, there was nothing light about it. He didn't exactly enjoy the activity, but a mile and a half of it three or four times a week was tolerable. Evening was a fine time to get out, the sun slanting through the Catskill forest encouraging all manner of creatures to come on out and enjoy the evening's first sighing breezes.

Walter headed out the dirt road feeling fresh. The combined energy of hope and faith buoyed him up and pushed him along. He ran as easily as he ever did, as close to enjoying it (well, okay, not detesting every step and wishing it was over immediately) as ever. Turtles sliding off logs into the pond, plop, plop, plop. Frogsplash. Heron liftoff on the far side where it's shallow. He took it all in. Don't step in the goosepoop; don't step in the bear scat. Dead garter snake on the road – ooh, pretty iridescent blues on its back scales, too bad it got hit. Whoa, live black snake in the road, adrenaline making the legs even more wobbly than the end of the run.

Hot, sweaty, tired, and breathless, he decided to keep going past his house and up the private road. A quarter of a mile or so up the road there was a classic Catskills-style spring: a piece of galvanized pipe sticking out of a rock wall. The cold water would feel amazing after the run.

The metal pipe seemed to stick straight out of a rock, the water a steady trickle. He cupped his hands under the mouth of the pipe and caught the liquid ice. His heart pounded in anticipation, his palms numb before he held a cupful. He splashed his face and refilled, gasping. Again, he splashed, this time his neck. Once more he filled up and ran his wet hands through his close-cropped hair.

One more splash, he told himself, waving a mosquito away. He turned away from the pipe for a moment to whack a bug and scratch where it had landed. When he turned back, it was as if the pipe had just been placed there. Walter started, stared, and wondered why he hadn't seen it sooner. He grabbed his last splash, already mentally back home, back at the drafting table working on this new design before his feet even moved.

He decided to use the newly finished upstairs bathroom for his post-run shower. He peeled off the sweat-soaked clothes in the kitchen, leaving them by the washing machine in a heap on the floor. The kitchen table, handmade by Walter years ago when someone gave him the huge slab of granite, bore witness to Walter's nakedness. The dying daylight hit the table just right, illuminating its dire need for a thorough wipe down. Walter looked past that and saw stone. Stone top, iron pipe legs. A wedding of natural and manmade elements. He took note and kept moving, a nice hot shower beckoning.

Waiting for the shower water to heat up, Walter held onto the bluestone counter and stretched his legs. The iron pipe legs – the pedestal part of the pedestal sink – caught his eye. I keep doing that, he noticed. Stone and pipe, like the spring. Like the kitchen table. Like this whole bathroom, really, he admitted, making the connections. The bed would be no different. Male and female, yin and yang, wood and steel, fluid and rigid, Walter let the paired descriptors come to him and flow over him as he stood under the shower head. Yes. That was it. It had been right there, everywhere he looked all along.

He dodged any additional distractions, arriving at the drafting table naked and ready. The sketch was easy, the plans no less so. An hour or so later, the floor was still empty and the wastepaper basket was downright lonely. Walter was finished.

After sleeping late, letting Pearl take the dogs out, and lingering over coffee and the local paper, Asha dialed the architect's number. The solar consultants had referred her to Tess Audrey; Asha had giggled when she heard the name, thinking she sounded like a movie star. But Tess was the one the Sun Boys (not the company's real name, just Pearl and Asha's nickname for them) recommended. They claimed she would be able to design the addition Asha wanted within the constraints she was stuck with. Tess wasn't in. Asha left a message.

The connection was staticky. Asha took note, and thought about calling repair. She leaned back in her chair, noticing that her hair was now long enough to get stuck in the wooden joints of the kitchen chairs. Ow. She extricated the few strands and pulled all of it into a large, rather spherical ponytail atop her head. She settled back, looking out the window, feeling her flannel pajamas get too hot as the coffee warmed her from the inside and the nine a.m. sun blasted through the window. Yeah, she acknowledged the thought in its fullness. Gotta call repair.

She went outside to check the "interface" as Walter had called it. The feng shui cure was still in place, a little tattered from a year in the elements, but present. Gotta bust Grace's chops for this – her cure stopped working. She slapped a blackfly on her shin and moved on.

She had been wondering about moving the garden. She strolled down the perennial border, re-telling each plant's story in her head: this one was divided from Grace's stock, those were dug from up at Carl's house, a few stolen from the woods out by Bull's Bridge. Asha chuckled at her history of plant rustling forays. She looked dry-eyed at the donations from Rob. She touched some lemon balm leaves; the plant had been a gift from Louise last year for some trumped up occasion when the truth was that everyone just felt sorry for Asha and tried to feed her in any way they could.

She petted the plant, combed its leaves and flowers with her fingers, crunched it gently in her hands and then cupped her hands to her nose. "Mmmm," she groaned in delight.

All of it stays. It belongs here. All of it except I'll take a few pieces of bee balm so I can watch the hummingbirds there too. It will be someone else's to play with. She backed up away from the flowers until she was standing in the middle of the lawn looking at all of it. The house, the garden, the spot with Route 22 way too close, the ugly lights from the strip mall visible all night long, and all the drama of this life: the lost job, the will-I-stay-or-will-I-go conundrum.

And, of course, Rob: the hope, the crazy-in-love early days. That was two summers ago, Asha realized. Rob was the first time she'd opened her heart for business after the bankruptcy proceedings from her marriage. This house was where that happened. This house, this garden, this street bore witness.

It was such a rollercoaster. She grinned at the image of her life being a carnival ride. She was alternately excited, terrified, nauseous, and dizzy, hanging on for dear life to Halia and Grace when she could, gritting her teeth and white knuckling it when they weren't there. Was it time to get off and go home?

She sighed. Nice metaphor, she editorialized, but it doesn't exactly ring true. Totally renovating the cabin, building a solar-powered, green construction house-sized addition, selling two houses, resolving grief and guilt, and longing for her man... yep. Still at the amusement park.

And yet, she insisted, one day our lifestyle will be truly different. Living in the village versus living at the cabin at the end of civilization: it'll be different.

"Mom!" Pearl screamed out the window. "Phone!"

Asha headed for the back door. Pearl met her there and handed her the cordless, hand covering the mouthpiece. "It's the woman about the horse," she stage whispered.

"Hi, this is Asha Jackson," Asha answered the phone, inadvertently slipping into her professional voice. "Yes, I wanted to find out more about the horse you're selling: the dapple gray Arabian mix."

Full circle. Asha indulged in nostalgic recollecting as she stole a glance at Pearl, dozing in the passenger's seat. One year ago I took her out to Table Mountain for that first stupid hike. Asha smiled broadly, remembering the banter, that awesome bridge, the view and the losing and finding of Lyla. Back out again, this time to the Devil's Path, to do the loop on Sugar Loaf, Asha's heart swelled with pride and gratitude that Pearl could be convinced (well, okay, bribed, once again with ice cream) to come along, that the four of them could enjoy this adventure together... it felt great. Different from the way it felt great to conquer Lone that day last fall. That was great too, but this is different. Asha savored these thoughts, rolled them around in her mind as the miles rolled past the windows.

Pearl woke up as they pulled into the Roaring Kill parking area.

"Wanna check out the swimming hole?" Asha invited.

Pearl stretched, yawned, and shut her eyes again.

Asha and the dogs left her there, the swimming hole practically visible from the car. The dogs navigated the steep bank and were in the water before Asha had made it halfway down. It was pretty, with a closed in, intimate feeling, towering hemlocks and huge boulders closing in the creek and creating a room through which the creek flowed. Asha didn't hear Pearl until she was practically on top of her.

"You ditched me." An accusation? Playful? Asha listened hard but didn't know how to hear what she hard.

"You didn't respond."

"I was sleeping."

"I let you sleep more."

Pearl let it go. Asha unclenched her jaw.

The dogs leapt out of the water and shook on the pair's bare legs, cooling them off before they'd gotten the chance to get hot.

"Maybe after the hike we'll stick out feet in," Asha suggested as they headed for the trail." Pearl half-nodded, half-shrugged. Asha's delight in this family outing was under teenage siege. She hunkered down, defending herself by shutting up.

The silence lasted until they reached Dibble's Quarry, about an hour up the trail. The neatly stacked stone walls, chairs, patios, even lanterns made from leftover bluestone pieces so impressed Pearl that she became chatty. They took up seats, side by side, admiring the view and started to talk.

"I hate you because I can't be mad at you." Pearl opened with a doozy.

Asha let her blank expression stand in for an answer.

"It's not your fault. I mean," Pearl narrowed her eyes and swiveled around to look at her mother. "I don't think it's your fault."

"Could you be a little more vague? I still think I could guess what you're talking about." She risked the joke.

Pearl smiled. "Your life is a train wreck." Asha's stomach tightened. "Look at dad. Nothing bad ever happens to him." Pearl held up her hand, fending off the obvious response. "I know, I know. Nothing good ever happens to him either. Forget him," Pearl waved her example away. "Bad example. But normal people," Pearl whined the word 'normal,' long and nasal, to underline it. Asha bit her tongue. "Normal people don't have this much chaos and drama in their lives. Not even high school girls have this much insanity going on in their lives. It's annoying."

Asha didn't answer right away. She looked out, across the valley, to Kaaterskill High Peak and its neighbor, another Catskill mountain named Roundtop. Pearl was right: normal people worked normal jobs, lived in normal houses, ate normal food, and enjoyed normal pastimes.

Asha bit back the swell of pride that accompanied her utter lack of normality by those standards. Normal house? As of this moment, I own three houses, none of them remotely normal. She began to mentally list her crimes against normality. The house we live in is one hundred years old, with a half-pipe for a kitchen floor. The Halcottsville Victorian: sweet if you like that sort of thing. Pearl didn't. And Charlie's cabin: a two and a half room shoebox at the butt end of the last dead end road heading up a stupid mountain, currently receiving an addition the size of a house in and of itself, which will not make it any closer to normal at all. Nope, not even a hint of normal in the housing department.

Normal job? No. School social worker required way too much explanation and psychotherapist was just creepy. Besides, not currently employed due to having lost her job, then receiving an inheritance from a total stranger? Not normal. Normal food? Asha let herself off the hook on that account; Pearl actually likes the food we eat, when it isn't kale. Normal pastimes? She let the grin slip out from behind the mask of neutrality. She flicked a bug off Pearl's arm and held back from giggling.

"I hear you." She acknowledged Pearl's words. "Not normal. Not even close."

"Whatever." Pearl answered. 'It's not your fault. It's just…" She trailed off, searching for the right words. "It's not me. I am normal. And I feel a little lost in your world sometimes. Sometimes I just hate how interesting you make everything. Normal would be good enough, y'know?" Pearl looked at her mother in earnest. "Can we just go to the mall one day? Drive with the air conditioner on? Eat mall pizza and buy something that isn't on sale? And maybe go get pedicures when we're done?" She paused and Asha could have sworn she heard a catch in Pearl's voice. "And could you not act like you hate every minute of it?"

"Would that help?" Asha wanted to know. She'd do damn near anything for Pearl, but this was asking a lot. She needed the upfront guarantee before committing.

"Yeah." Pearl finally met her mother's gaze. "Yeah. Not for my birthday or anything," she included the new stipulation. "Just as something to do. As a visit to my world. Just to balance things out."

"Okay." Asha was unequivocal. "You got it. Want to set a date right now?"

Pearl sighed, but smiled. "No, you dork. Setting a date with your daughter is not normal. We have to just do it spontaneously. Idiot." She got up, having shed her too tight skin, ready to move on. "You gonna sit there all day?"

Walter called Jonathan on the way home from work. "How's your back, buddy?"

"Why?" Jonathan heard a favor involving heavy lifting, not solicitousness, behind Walter's question.

"I need some help. Gotta get some heavy pieces upstairs." Walter paused, then, pride getting the better of him, explained. "I made a bed. I'm thinking we carry it upstairs in pieces and assemble it upstairs."

"A bed?" Jonathan was revving up for some serious teasing. "First you finish the trim all Victorian and shit, and then you paint it shades of eggplant and butternut squash, and now a bed? What the fuck, Walt? Are you pregnant?"

"I guess I had to tell you eventually." Walter played along. "I was thinking we could name it Heath, since he was your favorite actor."

Jonathan made a retching sound.

"Okay, then, how about Dustin, honey?"

"What time?" Jonathan growled. Walter mimed chalking up his point.

"Come on over early. I'll grab a pizza on the way in. And bring some beer." Walter paused, then added, "Something good."

"Of course I'll bring something good, you moron. You drink all that brown ale you made? That was good."

"Yeah," Walter uttered the white lie and immediately regretted it. Jonathan would be hurt if he knew that Walter was saving it, the few bottles that were left, to drink with Asha. What with all this work on the house, he hadn't had time to brew another batch. And somehow the work on the house, which had begun as therapy, morphed into work on the bed. It felt important. It felt better than the obsession Walter easily admitted it had become. It felt like a lifeline, a trail map leading into the heart of the matter, up to the summit for some amazing views, and back out to the truck. The big, honkin' manly truck that would carry him home to where he wanted to be.

"I can't believe it! That was so fast!" Grace exclaimed as she hopped out of her truck into the damp, early morning humidity. She peered around the back at the empty horse trailer she was pulling and, satisfied that all was well, headed toward the crowd gathered a few feet away on Asha's driveway.

"Yeah! Who'da thunk it?" Lukey Jane replied.

"She must've priced it too low," AnneMarie commented to Lukey Jane, keeping her voice low.

"Who cares?" Lukey answered brightly, reaching for a doughnut from the open box on Bessie's tailgate. "It's moving day! It's a moving party! Lighten up, darlin'!" With that she bit into a Boston crème and offered AnneMarie a custardy bite.

Asha stood a little apart, hands buried deep in her hair with a faraway look on her face. She paced a few steps, then stopped, then started again. Halia watched her, frowned slightly, and slipped into the house. She emerged a moment later; wordlessly she handed Asha her coffee in a purple travel mug. Asha took a sip before speaking. "Okay, I have a plan."

Everyone shut up and held still. "I'm going to the Halcottsville house with Halia. We'll empty the house into Bessie and take stuff to the storage unit. Lukey Jane, AnneMarie, and Grace – you guys empty this house into the horse trailer, Lukey's truck, and AnneMarie's van. Go straight to the cabin. Halia and I will meet you there."

Having caught wind of the insanity moving day would entail, Pearl had taken off with her father for the weekend. The closings were next week: the Halcottsville house on Tuesday, the Dover homestead, staticky phone and all, sold on Thursday. Summer is a good time for selling real estate, Asha had to admit. But she'd be glad when this part was over.

The Halcottsville sale took her by surprise, and dealing with Charlie's furniture and possessions was just beyond what she'd had time to focus on, what with prepping her own home for sale and managing the construction of the addition at the cabin. The addition wasn't finished, but it was close. The old part of the building, the site of that Thanksgiving dinner they shared last year, was intact and fully functional. Asha and Pearl could make do for a week or two while the contractor finished up the punch list. And maybe the gang would stick around for the weekend and help with painting. Meanwhile, the most beautiful house Asha had ever owned, albeit briefly, and never had lived in, was to be sold within the week. She needed Halia with her for this.

Halia intuited as much as slid into Bessie's passenger seat without even asking if she should drive her own car. Asha needed her, her silence, her presence, her rationality. They were halfway there before either one of them spoke.

"What if he has a grand piano?" She asked straight-faced.

"I'll carry the piano, you get the bench," Halia didn't miss a beat.

"I've been thinking about calling Walter."

"Just in case there's a piano?"

Asha smiled and kept her eyes on the road. Bessie was behaving beautifully, but Asha hid behind driving for a few moments, trying to decide how much to say. "I'm almost ready."

Halia nodded.

"Today, I think, is the last piece I needed to do alone."

Again, Halia nodded.

"I miss him. Sometimes I start thinking he's moved on, washed his hands of this whole insane situation, and let it go."

Halia shrugged.

"I'm doing it again, aren't I?" Asha's voice was more than a little imploring. She hoped Halia didn't share Grace's impatience with her penchant for misery and addiction to psychological rumination.

"Yes." Prim Halia. After a moment they both smiled.

Asha took a deep breath and just said "I hope we can manage all of Charlie's stuff by ourselves."

"Mmmm," Halia agreed.

Walter grew tired of watching the rain. He turned and strode into the kitchen to put the kettle on. A cup of tea, he thought. That's the ticket. He smiled sadly: if that quaint phrase was the best ammunition he could muster up to combat the mood the rain fostered, well then he was destined to be depressed today.

Refusing to watch the water boil, Walter puttered around the kitchen. He got the tea bags down, got out a mug from the cabinet, got out the honey, unwrapped a tea bag and placed it in the cup... it was no good. In every move, in every decisive action, there was a memory. He saw his hands touch things they way a man's hands did, and he saw Charlie's hands some fifty years ago, deftly collaring a young boy to give him what for. He lifted the kettle to gauge the amount of water inside, his hands measuring weight and volume, and he knew years of instant coffee breakfasts had been prepared using that same gesture. He was a man alone, and he had come to live like one. He knew his place and the legacy he'd inherited from the family of men that came before him. He'd worked hard these past few months to bring this place to life and to place himself at the center of it all. He worked even harder these past eight years to be fully human all alone. Today the triumphs abandoned him and he felt it all, all over again: the despair, the rage, the threat of inevitability. Charlie's leaving left him in danger of taking up that baton. He saw the writing on the wall, heard it in the rain: he could be the next Charlie.

He sat down heavily upon a kitchen stool and sighed. The rain drummed against the deck roof, creating a loud staccato hush of white noise. The water inside the kettle began to join in, making its own pre-boiling hushing sound. Walter listened to the sounds of water against metal and tried to think about something. Thoughts of Charlie crept in from behind the sound, from behind the emptiness, under the front door with the gray dampness and through all the windows, open despite the late summer thunderstorm. Oh sure, it would take time. I could keep going like this for a few more years, Walter thought, keeping busy, staying fit, staying upbeat, working the job and not letting the job work me. In the end, all the alone time would catch up with me. I know it would. And I'd be the nasty, needy, angry old man Charlie became.

Walter stood up abruptly, pushing the stool away and storming out of the kitchen. He kept going, out the front door, and out into the rain. He moved thickly, feet not lifting high enough, and he fought his way through the tall weeds, tearing at them with his legs, his knees. The effort felt enraging; it felt good. He plunged into the woods and kept going, charging off into nowhere, running from, not running to. He roared pure sound into the sky, rain and treedrops pelting his upturned face. He seized a downed tree branch and golfed basketball-sized rocks off the old stone wall. The branch gave way and splintered, showering Walter with bark as it fell to pieces. Walter dropped it and grabbed a rock from the wall. It sailed deep into the woods. Several others followed, chased by sobs and roars.

But then Walter relented. A thought had finally entered his mind. A non-Charlie-infused thought. If I keep throwing these rocks, I'll end up needing to fix this stone wall, to put it back the way I like it. I'm making work for myself. That was the thought. An editorial thought, a message from the part of him that was omniscient, watching him emote. It was a start. It was enough.

Walter walked back into the house, soaking wet in spots, smelling like rain and dirt. He poured the water from the screeching kettle and turned off the gas with confident adult man hands.

He saw his hands, watched them do what they needed to do, and let it go at that.

After wiping them on a dishrag, he went for the phone and dialed Asha's number.

Epilogue
About two years later

July Fourth weekend, when the rest of the sane world planned bar-
beques and pool parties, Asha decided to go for a run. Earn those
beer calories, Asha joked with herself, knowing that she would sip
half a beer and be done for the evening, regardless of her intentions. Her running route was tough – downhill from the cabin,
down the dirt road, level for a while whether she chose right or
left, and back up that fucking hill all the way home. She groaned
thinking about it, but headed off into her bedroom to change her
clothes.

Pearl lay on her mother's bed – The Bed – reading. She looked
up, caught her mother's eye, and smirked.

"Hey!" Asha snapped. "No enjoying yourself. You're
grounded." She turned away from her to hide her own grin. Yes,
Pearl was grounded all right, but it was a bit of a toss up: ground
her or congratulate her. Asha was working hard at being the parent on this one, and keeping her back turned was key. Pearl and
her friends, knowing it was one of the biggest tag sale weekends of the year, had made off with paint and cardboard from the
basement. Keeping a straight face throughout, they had secretly

created gorgeous signs proclaiming "ENORMOUS YARD SALE: ANTIQUES, TOOLS, FURNITURE!" and other sexy offerings. They used neon paints; they hung the signs at central intersections in town. They used arrows and "FOLLOW SIGNS" signs, all red herrings, riding their bikes all over the eight mile circuit they covered. They might have gotten away with it and laughed right up to Labor Day about it, except that instead of snaring a citiot or a Jerseyite, they caught Asha and Walter. Two hours of wandering around the back streets of Roxbury before giving up and coming home thoroughly mystified and disappointed. Pearl laughed so hard at her mother the girl had damn near peed in her pants.

Asha had given her and the friends a choice: grounded for July Fourth weekend or set up a lemonade stand and sell to the tourists they had planned to torment. They chose the lemonade stand, but then she caught them on the computer, designing flyers for fictitious art shows at nonexistent galleries they planned to hand out to the lemonade customers. Grounded.

Pearl took in her mom's actions. "Going running?" she asked.

"Yeah."

Pearl reached into her hair and pulled on an elastic band. "Need a hair tie?" she offered.

"Thanks sweetie, but I like it loose when I run."

Pearl rolled her eyes and went back to her book.

Asha slipped out of her coveralls, the stiff woven khaki almost willing to stand up by itself. She grinned, thinking about her clothes standing around in the corner, waiting to be put back on, as if they were on a break. I'll come back from my run, and they'll be lounging on the porch, smoking, she imagined. Stripped down to the skin, she assembled the running requirements: cast iron bra, high tech t-shirt, running shorts, cool max socks, sneakers. I'll shower when I get back, she reminded herself, hesitating to put the clean clothes on her work-scented body. Walter might get here by then, she hoped checking the clock. She calculated the hours for his errands: pick up more supplies at Wadler's, grab the weekly produce pick-up from the farm, visit with his friends at that café

... yeah, he might be here by the time I get back. Asha located her jacket, then exchanged it for a windbreaker.

She stepped out onto the porch, testing the air, letting the dogs out first. They took off across the meadow, the dead bluestem a rich, luscious peach-pink in the late afternoon sun. Asha watched the dogs fly after a groundhog and then continue to run, gathering steam, seeking the next victim for their chase at top speed. Asha's breath caught in her throat. "Yeah," she murmured, smiling at the dogs, the meadow, the sun. "Yeah."

She sat down and laced her sneakers. Warm enough for no jacket at all, she decided and hung the windbreaker on the milk-can that decorated the porch and often held items some lazy-ass couldn't be bothered to bring back into the cabin. Asha grinned. She and Pearl seemed to be in competition these days for whose ass was laziest. Is going running being lazy 'cause I'm not staying home to cook dinner? she wondered. Depends on who's spinning it. She smiled again, the dogs anticipating her readiness and returning to the cabin as she straightened up.

Downhill was easy. She ran fast, not bothering with effort aimed at pacing herself. She mimicked the dogs, thinking of the joy and intoxication that came with their movement, the effortlessness of their speed, the relaxed flow of their muscles. She let herself fly down the mountain. She had grown her hair out; no longer curly, it streamed out behind her in dark waves. Long enough to graze the top of her bra strap when standing still, somehow its length and quantity seemed multiplied when she ran, and the impression was of a crazy mane.

At the intersection of the town road and the county road, she made the split second decision and turned left. Six of one, half a dozen of the other, she thought, and let the vague desire to see the alpacas at the farm up the road guide her choice. She pounded the asphalt, breath coming nicely despite the hot weather. She was feeling good.

I'll make pizza for dinner tonight, she thought as she noticed the sensation of hunger crowding out the pure joy of running. Mushroom and olive and maybe eggplant... do we have any eggplants left? … Watch out, don't step in the goose poop. Can I make a salad? she wondered. Do we have any of that nice white wine left? Oh shit, I'm getting hungrier, she realized. I'm gonna end up with a cramp.

The alpaca farm was the turn around spot; three miles was enough for today. Asha took the turn wide, but Lyla still crashed into her, failing to anticipate. "Good thing you're pretty," Asha huffed her standard joke at Lyla and began the uphill journey.

Flies from the farm dogged her, and as she continued, it seemed as though the greenheads came out of nowhere. She ran faster and swung at them, batting them away. She cursed at them and finally left them to swoop in circles in her dust. Then she ran through a cloud of gnats near the corner and laughed at how they hit her sweaty chest and got stuck there, like on a windshield. Gross, but funny. Laughing was even more gross. She swallowed a couple of the tiny bugs, coughed, spit, and heaved and then clamped her mouth shut and kept going, her eyes still laughing, up the hill. It was then that the mosquitoes found her. "Mother of God," she hollered as she slapped herself. Life in the country, she thought. She didn't dare smile. A few bug bites were chump change for that moment on the porch. No second thoughts. Asha heard buzzing in her hair, and whacked at the side of her head. Take that, she grinned, her breath coming in hard gasps. She shook her head a little, fluffing her hair. Anything that gets stuck in this mane will die there.

Almost there. The hill leveled out for a few tenths of a mile before hitting the driveway. Charlie's driveway? Asha asked herself. Nah, Smokey, it ain't mine no more, he'd have said. You went ahead an' made it your own, didn't cha? Looks okay, he would declare and then cough and spit and let it go at that. Asha slowed to walk, having crossed the imaginary line at the end of the drive. Her personal finish line. She walked, her chest heaving, her Achilles tendons sore and tender. One hamstring attachment felt injured, maybe a pull. Getting old sucks. She walked toward the cabin feeling all of it, breathing, and not much else.

Walter was there. She saw the truck, then saw him on the porch. He had flowers in his hand; sunflowers, a big bunch. He saw her and split the distance, greeting her at the bottom of the stairs.

"Sorry, I'm kind of bug infested," Asha apologized. "It was pretty intense out there for a while."

"Honey, you send me," Walter gushed. He wrapped his arms around her, and then flicked a couple of dead bugs off her neck before kissing it. She laughed. "You got some seriously gnatty dreds."

Asha laughed harder, hugging him. "Get everything done?" she asked. Walter nodded. "Did you have a good day?" Again he nodded. "Whatcha doin' with those flowers?" She asked.

"Happy anniversary," Walter extended the bouquet.

Asha raised her eyebrows. She took the gorgeous sunflowers and admired them and then looked up to search Walter's face.

"It's the anniversary of the first time I bought you sunflowers."

Asha still looked confused.

"When you lived at that house in Dover. That flat of dwarf sunflowers… that was the first day I met you. That was a really great day." Walter looked at her, sweat drying in her hair and on her skin. He knew her now, knew her well enough to know that he needed to let her go inside soon or she'd get cold.

"You bought those sunflowers?"

"Yeah," he admitted. "That was me. I just wanted to do something special, to make you remember me." He shook his head, laughing a little. "I guess that didn't exactly work out. You thought it was one of your friends?"

"Well, yeah," she nodded. "I figured it was Halia. She'd been stopping by, leaving me food or a little something like that all week." She wiped her forehead with the back of her hand and pulled her sticky hair off her back, twirling it into a loosely wrapped bun on the back of her head. "When I saw the feng shui cure, I just figured that Grace was with her." She looked up at

Walter, finally grasping what had happened that day, three years past. "That was you too?" She asked, now knowing the answer.

"Yup. I hit the library to brush up on feng shui cures on my lunch hour and then grabbed the flowers on the way back to your place." Walter wore a mixture of pride and sheepishness on his face, not confident that his efforts had been seen for what they were.

Asha let her kiss be the extent of her response. She lingered, leaning in for more when he stopped at the perfunctory stopping-before-things-go-too-far point. She kissed him as if the kiss were a work of art, a meal, a 3500 foot peak, with a beginning, middle and end. She let herself be kissed back by a man who knew what to do with kisses like that. And then she pulled away and smiled broadly. "I'm gonna go shower. Want homemade pizza tonight?"

Asha didn't hear Walter's answer clearly; the run and the kiss making her heart pound, her knees rubbery, and her hearing a touch underwater-ish. She went in, stuck the sunflowers in a big mason jar, and made a beeline for the bathroom.

"Mom!" Pearl was screaming from upstairs in the addition. "Mom! C'mere!"

Asha headed upstairs, pulling off clothing and untying sneakers along the way. The dogs got in the way, licked at her face, and got shooed away. "What?"

Pearl held her mother's cell phone between her thumb and forefinger. Her face was a cartoon of teenage disgust, as if she had just plucked the offensive item out of a porta-potty. "Rob called."

Asha took the phone from Pearl. Her breath hadn't fully recovered from the run and the surprise cranked her heart rate back to serious elevation increase levels. Rob. It had been three years since they'd seen each other. No, she corrected herself, standing still, calculating: almost four years. That's a long time.

She ducked into the big closet and grabbed one of Walter's oversized sweatshirts, forgetting about the jacket she'd left on the milkcan. Pearl watched her leave the room and said nothing. Asha did not meet Pearl's glance.

She slipped out the back door, not hearing it bang shut behind her. Rob. Why? She wanted to think this through, to decide how to respond. Respond, she told herself. Don't react. She hoped Walter didn't see her cross the field. She didn't want to discuss this with him just yet.

Post-run chill was setting in; her hi-tech clothes were soggy and cold. She pulled the sweatshirt over her head without slowing down, the apricot-hued bluestem tickling her shins. Instinctively she headed to the western corner of the meadow, far away from the trail up Bearpen. She sought a vantage point from which to survey her life, and up on the rise there would be good. She could see the whole house: both the old parts that Charlie and his father had built and the new addition. She could see the garden she had put in, cedar saplings cut from the meadow forming fence posts, and unruly wild grapevines impressed into duty as rails. She let her gaze meander, taking in the whole field as it swept up the gentle slope to meet the woods. She could see the spot where she and Lyla had emerged from the woods the day she met Charlie. And she could see the opening in the woods where Charlie had entered and not come back out.

She clambered up on a large boulder and sat down, elbows on knees, head in hands. The sun felt good, still offering warmth. Asha liked feeling warm enough. The world feels different, she thought, when you're warm enough. It's a little easier to take.

So he called. She let the fact stand and watched her feelings come and go. Curiosity flickered; anger waited in the wings. Who am I now? Where am I now? She thought about all she had done, all the changes she had gone through since that July Fourth, four years ago. Does he know I moved? she wondered. Does he know I moved on?

The sun baked the meadow and it buzzed with life. The house hugged the southern edge, humble and unassuming even with the addition, as if the human presence understood its place, dwarfed by the meadow, the forest, and the mountains. Lyla and Brulee chased chipmunks, hunting out of instinct, not hunger. Asha let her vision go blurry and saw them as wolves. She let go of time and place, seeing before the house was there, before she was there, before any of them were there. The grasses bent and waved, the canines raced and pounced, grasshoppers burst from the ground only to land a few feet away, forced to repeat the process over and over again.

This is what I did. This is where I chose to bring my child. This is what I made for myself. By myself. Asha closed her eyes and lifted her chin, letting the sun's last warm rays bathe her face.

The anger that remains, she slowly realized, is anger at the failure of life to hand me the expected, back then when I expected it. I fell in love with Rob, and it held promise. It had its moment, its day in the sun. Asha tried to grin; it ended up feeling more like a grimace. Okay, she corrected herself: more like an afternoon in the sun. He made mistakes; he did wrong. I did wrong too, she admitted. Turning a relationship into a rescue mission was a mistake. I guess I'll have to trust that we both paid. She scratched her leg, thinking that through. Is suffering some sort of payment?

She shook her hair out of the tangled bun she had constructed in an effort to shoo away the bugs. The sun continued to sink and day's end meant a brief but concentrated mosquito assault. Asha tucked her knees up a little more and pulled the sweatshirt over them, a stopgap measure. The sinking sun meant all the tasks of the evening awaited. Walter will look for me inside, and Pearl will tell him where I went and why. Asha sighed. He'll worry.

I'll need to tell him there's nothing to worry about and I'll need to mean it. Do I want to call Rob back? Do I want to see him? She ran through the reasons why she might, reasons why she might have tried to contact him – one, two or three years ago. To ream him out topped that list. To berate, accuse, abuse... to inflict pain, to try to make him feel what she felt. She smiled an easy, tired smile: those reasons lost their power about the same time Asha took a step back from Walter, back when she needed to focus on charting her own course.

What about to rediscover what was good between us? To re-kindle something? To go back to the way it was, when loving him was the intoxicant that got me through losing my job? Her smile didn't fade. She felt a surge of compassion for that version of her-self: the woman who got divorced, bought a house, took on a new lover, and then lost her job and her lover, all in the space of a year or so. Asha felt for her, something tender for the person she had been back then. This, she nodded to herself, this is forgiveness. This is it.

I don't want to talk to him. I don't want to see him. But I can. It doesn't really matter. I'm finished feeling all that. That chapter is finally fully over. Like Charlie said: The End. Next.

Blackberries on Bearpen by Mark Schaefer

Breinigsville, PA USA
07 April 2010
235696BV00001B/1/P